The
DARK
TRAIL

J.C. FIELDS

Publishing Coordinator – Sharon Kizziah-Holmes
Cover Design – Niki Fowler

Paperback-Press
an imprint of A & S Publishing
A & S Holmes, Inc.

ISBN -13: 978-1-951772-10-9

ACKNOWLEDGEMENTS

Once again it is time to thank all of the individuals who have helped get this manuscript polished and ready for others to read. Many of them have been with me since the beginning and several are new to the team.

Sharon Kizziah-Holmes, owner of Paperback Press, has been my publishing coordinator since *The Fugitive's Trail*. I cannot thank her enough. Over the course of these past five years she has continued to support and encouragement me. She is the one who deals with all the formatting for both my eBooks and paperbacks. If I had to deal with those concerns, I would have lost my sanity a long time ago.

Nick Weyland is a retired US Immigration and Customs Enforcement agent. He was instrumental in explaining the process and reasons a federal law enforcement officer must retire at the young age of fifty-seven.

To my developmental editor, Holly Atkinson. Thank you for your excellent job of correcting all the glaring inconsistencies in the original manuscript. You have helped prove the adage a writer should never edit their own work.

Shirley McCann and Tina Vyborny, the newest members of the team. Thank you both for smoothing out the final draft. It never hurts to have more than one final read-through before sending the manuscript off to the publisher.

Niki Fowler, a graphic artist extraordinaire. Thank you for producing a cover that conveys the theme of this new novel and continues to build upon *The Sean Kruger Series* motif. Everyone who previewed the image enthusiastically approved.

Paul J. McSorley, returns as the voice of Sean Kruger after his excellent production and performance on *A Lone Wolf* for Audible.com. The first question I am asked when I tell fans a new Kruger book ready is: When will it be on

Audible and will Paul be doing the narration? Once I tell them, yes and yes, the next question is: WHEN? You have a lot of fans out there, Paul. And, I am definitely one of them.

And again, last but not least, my wife Connie. She is, and always will be, the love of my life and my largest supporter. She has been instrumental in determining the next trail the Sean Kruger story will take. Stay tuned.

Other Publications
By J.C. Fields

The Sean Kruger Series:
The Fugitive's Trail
The Assassin's Trail
The Imposter's Trail
The Cold Trail
The Money Trail
The Dark Trail

The Michael Wolfe Saga:
A Lone Wolf

PART ONE

PRESENT DAY

Arlington, Virginia

The first glimpse of dawn lightened the eastern sky as Deputy Director of the FBI Alan Seltzer tied the shoelaces of a brand-new pair of New Balance athletic shoes. He rose on the balls of his feet to make sure the shoes were as comfortable as the day he'd bought them. They were.

Satisfied, he exited the kitchen into the garage, hit the button for the automatic door opener and retrieved his five-year-old Cannondale carbon-frame racing bike from its place of honor, a space-saving bike rack on the east wall. The bright yellow cycling jersey and padded biking shorts fit his slender frame snuggly, a reminder he was still in good shape even though his fiftieth birthday would occur in a few weeks. After fastening the straps of his boldly colored bike helmet under his chin, he guided the bike into the ebbing darkness and punched the code on the keypad to lower the door.

With it closing behind him, his eyes were immediately drawn to a dark-colored Ford Explorer sitting in front of the house across from his. A vehicle parked on the street in this neighborhood, while not illegal, remained a rare occurrence. He noted the unusual event, but it did not cause his sense of concern to heighten.

As he mounted the bike to start his daily routine, he remembered not kissing his wife before leaving the bedroom. Something he rarely missed. The thought of going back inside was quickly dismissed as he glanced at his watch. He was already behind his morning schedule.

Riding a bicycle ten miles a day and more on weekends helped him stay fit and gave him the solitude to contemplate problems connected to his high-pressure job. It was his favorite time of day.

Obtaining his current position had taken hard work and perseverance. As the first African American deputy director, he was responsible for keeping the various divisions working smoothly and overseeing high profile investigations. Notable predecessors of his position included men like Clyde Tolson and the infamous Mark Felt, who just before his death in 2008, confessed to being Deep Throat for the Washington Post reporters during the Watergate scandal.

The problem on his mind this morning was a particularly disturbing pattern he'd discovered within numerous FBI and municipal police investigations over the past five years. He'd told no one and was preparing to take his findings to the director the following day. If the director gave the go-ahead, he would assign a specific agent within the FBI to take over the case.

The special agent he had in mind was Sean Kruger. They had been classmates at the FBI Academy and had obtained agent status on the same day. Even though their career paths were different, they'd remained close friends throughout the years. Alan had become a rising star within the ranks of management and Kruger had established his reputation as the agency's top profiler. This being the reason he wanted Kruger to lead the investigation. If he was correct, there was a new serial killer on the loose and the FBI would need Kruger's skills to find him.

As he rode, and contemplated this problem, he noticed the dark SUV following him in the rearview mirror attached to his bike helmet. A note of concern crept into his consciousness as his morning ride entered a particularly beautiful park several miles from his home. Parts of the park were fairly isolated and his path would soon lead to one of those sections.

He heard the SUV rapidly approach on his left and pass too close for his liking. This caused him to slow his pace. As the vehicle raced ahead and skidded to a stop, it blocked the road ahead. Applying the brakes, he slowed his bike to a stop as his concern grew. No one emerged and he could not see the driver inside the vehicle due to the dark tint on the windows.

Wanting to avoid a confrontation, Seltzer prepared to turn the bike in the opposite direction and ride away.

At this same moment, the SUV's front driver side door opened and a man emerged with a suppressed pistol in his hand.

Seltzer did not have time to react as the pistol spat four times. The impact of each bullet forced him away from his bike as he fell to the pavement. Surprise and denial were the last emotions he felt as his head struck the asphalt. The last image he would ever see was his killer walking toward him. As blackness engulfed him, his body exhaled for the last time.

***

The assailant walked toward the fallen bike rider. A thin skin colored balaclava obscured his facial features as he approached his target. Standing over the prone man, he pointed the suppressed Glock at the individual's head. As he smiled underneath the balaclava, he pulled the trigger one more time, sending a bullet into the fallen man's temple.

Satisfied, he returned to the SUV and drove away.

Twenty minutes would pass before an early-morning jogger came across the body of FBI Deputy Director Alan Seltzer and called 911.

CHAPTER 2

Springfield, MO

The sound intruded into his dream. At first it was just an annoyance, then, as he swam toward the surface of consciousness, he realized it was his cell phone. Sean Kruger instinctively reached for the device on his nightstand. As he accepted the call, he glanced at the digital clock radio next to the phone: 5:32. Phone calls at this time of morning were rarely good news.

"Kruger," he croaked as he struggled toward alertness.

He listened, raised himself to sit on the side of the bed and cradled his forehead, his elbow on his knee. "When did it happen?"

He grew quiet as he listened.

Stephanie Kruger stirred beside him and rose to one elbow.

"Ah, geez."

She placed her hand on his back and he turned to her with an empty, distant stare.

After listening a few more moments, he said, "I think

that's a good idea, thank you. Call me when you know more details." The call ended and moisture welled in his eyes. "Alan Seltzer was executed this morning on his morning bike ride."

She sat up in bed, her eyes wide. "What do you mean, executed?"

"Someone shot him four times in the chest from a distance and then fired a round pointblank into his head. That is an execution."

"Oh, my gawd, Sean. When?"

"About an hour ago. That was Paul Stumpf. When the EMTs found his ID, they called the FBI Headquarters, who patched it through to Paul. He's on his way to the scene as we speak."

"What about his wife?"

"FBI agents are at the house now. Apparently, Alan was the only target."

She reached over, drew him into an embrace and whispered, "I'm sorry."

He returned the hug as a tear trickled down his cheek. "Paul wants me in DC to head up the investigation."

"I thought you were on a special team."

"Not anymore."

She closed her eyes and they embraced tighter.

***

By ten a.m. more details concerning the murder of Alan Seltzer emerged. Forensic evidence from the crime scene told FBI investigators a large vehicle had screeched to a halt, blocking the road. The bicycle and body had been found twenty-five feet from the skid marks. Four spent shells had been found in this area with one shell a few feet from the body. A security camera, positioned in the center of the park, captured the incident, although the distance caused the image to be grainy.

The video allowed the technicians to identify the vehicle as a dark five-year-old Ford Explorer. A similar truck was found abandoned in the parking lot of a Falls Church, Virginia Target store late the same morning. An Arlington police report identified the vehicle as stolen the night before. FBI forensic technicians pored over the SUV at their lab located at Marine Corps Base at Quantico, and by late evening, found no evidence as to the identity of the assailant.

At 5:14 p.m. central time, Kruger received an email outlining his new assignment as the lead investigator into Deputy Director Alan Seltzer's murder. He was to report directly to FBI Director Paul Stumpf at Headquarters the next day.

***

"How long will you be gone?" Stephanie sat on the bed as she watched Kruger pack his suitcase.

"At this point, I would say indefinitely. I just don't know, Steph."

She nodded. "We'll miss you."

He looked up and gave her a grim smile. "This is not what I want right now."

"I know." She paused for a moment. "When's your flight?"

With a glance at the digital clock on his nightstand, he said, "Bureau plane will be at the airport around seven, which will put me into DC by ten eastern time. I have a meeting with Paul at seven tomorrow morning."

"At least you don't have to fly commercial."

"No, the agency is making this a high-priority. I don't believe any requests for manpower will be denied either."

"What did JR say?"

"He fussed about it for about half a second and then agreed to accompany me to DC. He's meeting me at the airport. That way if he gets a chance to come back early, he'll have a car."

She took a deep breath. "I'll go over to Mia's after you leave."

***

JR Diminski, now an official member of the FBI Cyber Crimes Division, stared out the window next to his seat as the Gulfstream 550 slipped through the night sky. He turned to Kruger, who sat across the aisle. "I'm sorry about Alan."

Kruger nodded. "I'm thankful his kids are grown. They can help his wife get through the next few days, weeks and months."

"I've never met her."

With a smile, Kruger turned to his friend. "I really didn't know her either until we took a cruise with her and Alan the first year Steph and I were married. The two wives developed a close friendship during that week. Stephanie will join me once we know when the funeral service is scheduled."

"So, we aren't on the special task force anymore."

Kruger shook his head. "The task force has been suspended until further notice, by order of the president."

"What about Sandy and Jimmie?"

"They'll be joining us in DC day after tomorrow."

"Good." JR returned his attention to the window.

After an extended length of silence passed between the two friends, JR said, "Any ideas where to start?"

"I'm going to look through Alan's bureau and personal files. I want you to do a deep dive into his office and personal computer. I'm told the bureau has all of those items locked away waiting for us. My first inclination is to assume he stumbled onto something he wasn't supposed to, and it cost him his life."

"You don't think it was random?"

"No, I'm positive it wasn't random. The fact someone stole a Ford Explorer and ambushed him in the area of the park with the least amount of CCTV security worries me. This was carefully planned and executed. We'll start there."

JR nodded.

***

At 6:45 the next morning, the J. Edgar Hoover building was abuzz with activity, most of which centered around the investigation into the murder of Deputy Director Alan Seltzer. In the midst of this maelstrom of activity, Sean Kruger and JR Diminski entered the conference room next to the office of the Director of the FBI. Milling around the room, Kruger saw Scott Lambert who was the Executive Assistant Director for the Criminal, Cyber, Response and Services Branch, Dr. Teri Monroe, Executive Assistant Director for Science and Technology Branch and numerous individuals he did not know. He also saw Joseph Kincaid, the current National Security Advisor for the President of the United States. JR made a beeline toward him while Kruger talked to Lambert and Monroe.

As he shook her hand, Monroe said, "I haven't spoken to you since the Randolph Bishop affair. It's good to see you, Sean."

"Good to see you too, Teri. Congratulations on your promotion."

With a shrug, she blushed. "I don't get to do things I enjoy any more, like working with agents such as yourself."

Kruger gave her a smile. "How's Charlie Craft?"

"He's now one of my assistants."

"When you see him, congratulate him for me."

"You can do it yourself. He's been assigned to this investigation."

"Good, I haven't had the pleasure of working with him for a while."

Turning to Lambert, Kruger said, "It's been awhile since I last saw you too, Scott. Wish the circumstances were better."

"I agree."

Their conversation lasted a few more seconds before Kruger noticed JR and Joseph approaching. After shaking Joseph's hand, the older man leaned over to speak quietly to Kruger.

"When was the last time you spoke to Alan?"

After blinking a few times, Kruger replied, "I hate to say this, but it's been several months. Why?"

Joseph took a deep breath. "Look at his personnel files. My nephew told me about a theory he had but didn't have enough evidence to take it to Paul yet."

"What was it?"

"I'm not going to taint your perspective. You'll find it."

At that moment, Paul Stumpf entered the conference room and sat at the head of the table. Everyone found a seat and the room grew quiet.

"Thank you all for being here early this morning. This will be a short meeting. There are a few organizational matters we need to attend to." He looked around the room; everyone remained quiet, waiting for him to proceed. "First and foremost, the individual in charge of the investigation into Alan Seltzer's death will be Special Agent Sean Kruger."

Everyone nodded and shot a glance at Kruger.

"You will give him your fullest cooperation at all times, no delays or push backs. Is that clear?"

Again, everyone nodded.

"Now that we have that settled, Dr. Monroe, would you present the findings your team found yesterday?"

Teri stood and walked to a laptop at the opposite end of the conference table. She pressed the side of a mouse and a screen on the wall lit up with a still image. She said, "This is a security camera view from the First Virginia National Bank near Alan's home. Pay attention to the left side of the screen." She clicked the mouse again.

From the left side, a bike rider could be seen pedaling hard as he crossed the fisheye lens' focal range. Two seconds after the cyclist disappeared, a dark SUV followed the same route. She paused the video when the Explorer was halfway across.

"We believe this is the SUV involved with the shooting."

She pressed the mouse again. The scene jumped to another view of a residential area. "This is a view from a doorbell camera on a home two blocks from the park. Note the Explorer is following closer in this view."

Everyone in the room watched as the bicycle moved from the left to right of the screen, the Explorer now only twenty or thirty feet behind the rider. When the short video finished, Teri pressed the mouse. "The next shot is disturbing, but necessary to watch. Our technicians have cropped the shot and enhanced it as much as possible."

She clicked the mouse again. There was not a sound in the room as the events unfolded in front of them. From the right side of the screen, the Explorer passed the bicycle and suddenly stopped, blocking the road. The rider slowed the bike and attempted to turn around. At that moment, the door to the SUV opened and a figure emerged.

She stopped the video. "We apologize for the poor quality of the video, but beyond this, enlargement pixel count is compromised." She started video again.

A figure emerged from the SUV and pointed an elongated pistol at the bike rider. The cyclist collapsed to the pavement and the gunman walked slowly toward the fallen man. Once he stood over the body, he pointed the pistol at the prone figure's head. An audible gasp sounded throughout the room. At this point the gunman turned and walked back to the Ford and drove away.

Teri ended the video and faced the group. "Preliminary autopsy indicated Alan was already dead before the fifth bullet was fired at pointblank range." She sat next to the laptop.

A hushed silence fell over the room as Stumpf let the effects captured on video sink in. After several moments of silence, he continued, "This was not a random act of violence. This was an execution of a senior member of the FBI. We all knew Alan. We all respected Alan and considered him a friend. He was also a valued member of this organization and I will not allow whoever did this to go unpunished."

Heads nodded around the table.

Stumpf stood. "I want to see Agent Kruger, Agent Diminski, and Joseph Kincaid in my office. The rest of you know what needs to be done. Dismissed."

CHAPTER 3

Arlington, VA

Stumpf held out his hand to JR. "I am really glad we finally have a chance to meet, Mr. Diminski. I wish it was under better circumstances."

"I do, too."

"I also wanted to thank you for the assistance you have provided this agency over the past several years."

JR tilted his head as he shook the director's hand. "I've never been called, Agent before."

"Technically, you aren't. But I wanted to make sure the individuals in that room gave you the respect you deserve. You've helped solve more investigations than the majority of the men and women in that room ever have."

"Thank you, Director."

Stumpf turned to Joseph. "Thank you for being here this morning. I'm sorry about your nephew. I hope the video was not too hard to watch."

Without responding, Joseph gave the director a grim smile.

As he shook Kruger's hand, Stumpf said, "Where do you want to start?"

"JR's going to dig into Alan's home laptop and I want to look through his personal and bureau files. I realize some of them may be classified, but there could be answers within them."

"What about his office computer?"

"If he was uncertain about his assumptions, I don't believe he'd put any information there."

"That makes sense."

JR said, "There are ways to hide files on a networked computer. Do you think Alan possessed the knowledge?"

Joseph nodded. "I would look at it. Alan's abilities with a computer were one of his strengths."

Stumpf replied, "No objections on my part." He turned to Kruger. "Do you have a theory?"

"Not really, but I agree with something you said in the conference room—he was targeted. *Why* becomes the first question we have to answer." He looked at Joseph.

After clearing his throat, Joseph said, "Paul, Alan and I had a conversation several weeks ago. He suggested there were similarities between a number of FBI investigations around the country. When I asked for more details, he told me he wasn't ready to discuss it yet."

"No details?"

"None. He did indicate he would bring them to your attention in the next few weeks. Apparently, he didn't feel he had enough evidence yet."

After turning to Kruger, Stumpf asked, "Were you aware of Alan's concerns?"

"No, sir." He took a deep breath and let it out slowly. "I—uh—I haven't spoken to Alan for several months and then it was only to talk about taking our wives on another cruise." His voice trailed off as he muttered, "Guess I should have called him…"

"Okay, gentlemen." Stumpf crossed his arms. "You

have a starting place. Where do you want to headquarter, Sean?"

"Not here."

"Why?"

"Too many distractions. Too many well-meaning individuals stopping by to offer their suggestions and assistance every five seconds. We'll get nowhere."

"I agree. Where?"

"I'd like somewhere close to Quantico, if possible."

"Any particular reason?"

"Several, but the main one is the accessibility to the lab."

"Consider it done. I want to be kept up-to-date—"

"Paul, that's the problem. Everybody who thinks they are the least bit important will want to be kept-up-to-date. If I'm constantly updating everybody, well…"

Stumpf frowned and started to say something but stopped. Joseph covered a smile with his hand and JR looked at the ceiling.

Kruger continued. "But I agree, Paul. You need to be kept up-to-date, but not hourly."

The director placed his hands on his hips and glared at Kruger. He, again, started to say something, but his expression softened. "Me, only, and it needs to be twice daily."

Kruger crossed his arms and tilted his head.

With a sigh, Stumpf nodded. "Daily."

"That I will do, thank you."

The meeting lasted another five minutes as they discussed the location for the team. As JR and Joseph left the room, Paul Stumpf said, "Sean, can I see you in private?"

"Sure."

As the door closed, Kruger looked at Stumpf. "Is this about the updates?"

With a smile, the director shook his head. "No, this is

about a personnel problem."

Kruger gave the director a sly smile. But remained quiet.

"You have a birthday coming up."

"Oh, that. Yes, I'm very much aware of it."

"According to FBI mandates, a field agent's fifty-seventh birthday is their designated retirement date."

"I'm aware of that as well."

"What are you going to do?"

"I really don't have much of a choice."

"Yes, you do."

"Oh?"

"You can take a well-deserved promotion into management."

"I'd have to move. No, thank you. Stephanie loves teaching at the university, the kids are comfortable in their school and my oldest son, Brian, and his family are there. It's not about me anymore. I have to think of them first."

Stumpf gave him a thoughtful nod and said, "Will you at least consider it?"

With a sigh, Kruger nodded.

***

Their assigned space at Quantico turned out to be an old conference room in an out-of-the-way corner of the facility. The space contained a long table with sixteen chairs. At Kruger's instructions, the table was removed and the chairs stayed in place. His second act was to commandeer five eight-foot folding tables from the commissary and place them against the walls. JR discovered a large chalkboard in a storage area and brought it to the room. By five p.m., two desktop computers and four telephone landlines were in place.

JR frowned as the technicians left the room. "Sean, what the hell are we going to do with landlines?"

"The FBI still has the mentality of a twentieth century

bureaucracy and those types of phones were the hallmark of that era. We can use them to order pizza."

With a chuckle, JR nodded and started setting up the desktop computers.

At 5:23 p.m. an FBI agent by the name of Robert Shaw delivered Alan Seltzer's bureau files and laptop, plus his personal records and computer. As Kruger signed the transfer of evidence receipt, the agent said, "Agent Kruger, may I ask you a question?"

Handing the paperwork back, Kruger said, "Sure."

"Alan Seltzer was the reason I joined the FBI. Do you believe this was a random act of violence against a black man?"

Kruger gave the agent, who was African American, a grim smile. "No, I don't."

"Did you know him?"

"Very well. He and I graduated from the Academy together and I considered him a personal friend."

The young agent nodded. "Three years ago, he gave the commencement address to my graduating class at Rutgers. His words inspired me to join the FBI." He paused and stared at Kruger. "Please find who did this." With those words, the young man strode out of the room and closed the door.

JR walked up to Kruger. "No pressure there."

As he kept his gaze on the recently closed door, Kruger nodded. "Alan had an impact on a lot of young men and women during his career." He turned to JR. "I know for a fact that young man is only one of dozens of agents who were persuaded to join the bureau because of Alan. I do not plan to let that legacy die."

Thirty minutes later, JR looked up from Alan's laptop. "I'm making progress here. Why don't you use one of those landlines and order some pizza?"

"What kind?"

"Don't care as long as it's not pepperoni."

Kruger chuckled. "Why no pepperoni?"

"I lived on it in college and now it's the only pizza Joey will eat. So, anything with veggies and a protein that's not pepperoni will work for me."

"Got it. How about a veggie with Italian sausage?"

"Yummy."

***

After eating in silence, Kruger left the conference room. Knowing their new workspace would be bustling with activity the next day, he drove to a local Costco. There he purchased a Keurig coffee unit, multiple gallon jugs of water, a variety of coffee pods and multiple packs of disposable coffee cups. He anticipated several days of brainstorming with his team and the consumption of coffee by the gallons.

JR watched Kruger set up the coffee service. He said, "I thought you hated Keurig machines."

"I do, but it will be easier for everyone to make coffee if they want it."

"You fussed at me for years about the Keurig on my credenza."

"It worked, didn't it? You have good coffee now." He pointed at the new machine. "That is temporary—we aren't going to be here forever."

JR rolled his eyes and turned back to the computer. He pointed to an Excel spreadsheet displayed on the screen. "Look at this."

After putting on his half-readers, Kruger leaned over and said, "Looks like a column of dates followed by numbers, a city and a state."

"The dates, city and states I get, what I can't figure out is the pattern of the numbers. I'm guessing they reference something. What that reference is?" He shook his head.

Kruger straightened and took his glasses off. "Huh."

"I found it on his bureau-issued laptop in a partitioned segment of the hard drive. From what I can tell, this particular partition is not visible to the bureau server. Also, note the file name."

"Book 1. So?"

"Excel assigns that name to any newly created file until it is saved under a different one."

"Even I know that, JR."

"Think about it for a second. We find a partition on his bureau-issued laptop that's invisible to the LAN. Located in this partition is a file, with a generic name, with dates, numbers and locations."

Kruger leaned over again. "Do you think this might be what Joseph was talking about?"

JR nodded. "That would be my guess."

Kruger glanced at his wristwatch. "It's almost eleven—let's call it a night and get back here early. Charlie will be here tomorrow. Maybe he'll know what the numbers mean."

"Good idea. I'm fried."

CHAPTER 4

Quantico, VA
The Next Day

Charlie Craft, a pencil-thin thirty-something with slightly stooped shoulders, smiled at his former mentor. His rimless glasses and now-thinning hair made him look older than his true age. As he shook Kruger's hand, he said, "I'm really looking forward to working with you and JR again. I wish the circumstances were better."

"I know, Charlie. Really glad to have you on board. JR can use the help." He paused. "How's the family?"

"Michelle is great and the boys are growing fast."

"Boys, like in plural?"

Charlie nodded. "Boys like in three."

Kruger smiled. Charlie Craft had been a young, shy forensic technician when they'd first met. A serial murder investigation in St. Louis, more years ago than Kruger cared to think about, was the reason. After that case, he'd taken Charlie under his wing and shown him, by example, what kind of evidence an investigator really needed. Afterward, Charlie flourished within the agency and was now a senior technician at Quantico. During one particular investigation of a series of high-profile assassinations, Charlie traveled to Springfield and worked directly with JR. The knowledge he obtained during those two weeks cemented his status within the bureau and a series of promotions followed.

JR shook his old friend's hand and the two wandered off toward the area now designated as the computer lab.

Standing next to the Keurig, Kruger watched the two men discuss the file JR found the previous evening. The two computer experts used a language as foreign and incomprehensible to him as Mandarin. As his coffee cup filled, his thoughts turned to his upcoming birthday. He would miss the thrill of discovering the first important clues, fitting the disjointed puzzle pieces together, the chase and the suspect's apprehension. But more importantly he would miss the people he worked with.

He also realized he would not miss the travel, the incredibly boring and lonely nights in a motel room, the constant quest to find healthy food on the road, or the long hours.

As his thoughts wandered, he realized something else. Apprehension about the future. A feeling he seldom experienced. The unknown of what lay beyond retirement gave him pause. For two and a half decades, his status as an FBI agent provided a purpose and a sense of pride. And now, a simple inevitable birthday would strip him of his personal mission.

Well-meaning individuals kept offering advice every time the subject came up. While he listened, none offered a solution. The only person who understood his dilemma was Stephanie. Several years ago, after Kruger was seriously wounded in a confrontation with a serial killer, she'd begged him to retire and teach. He did and grew bored almost immediately. After his return to the agency, she'd told him she would support any decision he made about his future with the FBI. Now with his fifty-seventh birthday rapidly approaching, the decision to retire was being made for him.

Realizing his cup of coffee was cold, he made another and got to work.

***

By mid-morning Kruger finished sorting Alan's personal files from his home office. Tax and household files were separated, boxed and considered unimportant for now. This left a complete bank box of work-related files he would need to carefully go through.

JR interrupted his concentration. "Hey, Sean. You need to see this."

As he approached the two computer specialists, he saw Charlie pounding away on one of the desktop units while JR pointed to a laptop. Kruger asked, "What'd you find?"

"The list I found last night was the Rosetta Stone. Charlie recognized the numbers as case files and he's downloading them right now. We are probably going to need a couple more desktops so Sandy and Jimmie can help review them."

"Okay. What's special about the files?"

JR stared at Kruger with eyebrows drawn together. "Each file is of an unsolved investigation."

"There are more than a few of those, JR."

"I know, but Charlie has a theory."

"Which is?"

Charlie turned in his chair and looked at Kruger. "Each of the files are an unsolved murder case of a prominent or high-profile person. Some are men and some are women."

"Got it, so?"

"All of the victims are either African American, Asian,

or Jewish, no Caucasians."

Kruger stared at the younger man for what seemed like a minute. "You're telling me Alan was investigating hate crimes?"

"Not sure I would characterize his involvement as investigating. He was more or less looking at abnormalities within the investigations."

"FBI investigations?"

JR shook his head. "No, all of these files are in the National Crime Information Center. A few are FBI, most are municipal or state investigations. Alan was doing a search and recording the case numbers."

"Did you find anything about his assumptions?"

Both JR and Charlie shook their heads. JR said, "All we found were the files he was checking on. If he made any assumptions, they aren't on his computers."

"Hmmm…." Kruger looked back at the bank box of Alan's files. "Let me look through his personal files. Maybe he made handwritten notes instead of putting them on a computer."

JR grinned. "Want some help?"

Kruger kept his attention on the bank box. "Yeah, two pairs of eyes are better than one."

***

The box yielded the answer to their question by mid-afternoon. With his feet propped up on one of the tables, Kruger leaned back in a chair studying the contents of a thick file. Halfway through it, he found several handwritten pages stapled together. After reading the first three sentences, he put his feet on the floor and sat straighter.

He looked at JR. "I believe I found something."

JR stood in front of a bank box, sorting files into stacks on the table. "What?"

Kruger handed the pages to JR and said, "He did suspect

a series of hate crimes."

Glancing at the pages, JR flipped through them. "Really."

Nodding, Kruger looked further into the file he held. "I need to go through the rest of this, but from what he writes on those pages, he thinks one person is responsible for all of the unsolved murders on the list you found."

"Yeah, but the locations are all over the country."

"I know—that puzzled Alan as well and probably the reason he hadn't brought it to anyone's attention." He pointed to the pages. "The last paragraph on the last page suggests he was going to take his findings to the director and then get me involved at some point."

"Does he give a reason?"

With a half-smile, Kruger said, "During the early years of Alan's career with the FBI, he was a brilliant investigator and researcher. Where he struggled was using the information to identify a suspect. We worked several cases together and he always handed that part off to me. Looks like he was going to do it again."

Returning his attention to the pages, JR asked, "What's our next step?"

"I haven't read any of the files Alan referenced, but my guess is he found a pattern within each of them. What that pattern is, he doesn't mention in his notes. Our next step is to find the pattern."

JR nodded but did not comment.

"We need to start going through all of those unsolved cases he identified."

***

Charlie Craft used his influence and secured the team two additional desktops. Special Agents Sandy Knoll and Jimmie Gibbs arrived late in the afternoon eager to get started. By nine o'clock, Kruger felt he saw a pattern emerge from the cases he reviewed. Not wanting to prejudice the others, he kept his thoughts to himself.

The group returned to the conference room at seven the next morning, and by eight-thirty, Kruger told everyone to get a fresh cup of coffee and join him at their makeshift conference table. Everyone brought their chair and gathered around an eight-foot table in the center of the room.

Curious as to what the others had found, Kruger placed his chair at one end and asked, "We've all had about six hours to look through the cases you were assigned. Let's start with Sandy. What did you find?"

Benedict "Sandy" Knoll, a retired Special Forces Major and now a special agent with the FBI, was a large man with bulging biceps. They stretched the sleeves of an untucked black polo shirt that hung over faded blue jeans. He kept his dark blond hair cut short allowing the streaks of gray to appear above his ears. His handsome, weathered face, permanently tanned from too many tours of duty in Iraq and Afghanistan displayed a frown. This morning, his normal mirrored Ray-Ban sunglasses were replaced with a pair of bifocals.

"The only pattern I saw was geographical clustering."

Kruger nodded. "Go on."

"Kind of like drawing a circle around a big city and spreading out like spokes."

Without commenting, Kruger pointed to Jimmie. "What'd you see?"

Jimmie Gibbs' swimmer physique provided a sharp contrast to Knoll's bulk. Swimming was a passion for Gibbs and he still held several Seal Team records for endurance and distance.

After retiring from Seal Team Six, he'd allowed his black hair to grow long and kept it in a ponytail extending past his shoulder blades. As a native Southern Californian, his usual dress was surfer casual, cargo shorts, linen shirt and sandals. Today was no exception. Blue eyes rounded out his handsome features. The retired Navy Seal was now married with a one-year old son. Kruger prized having Jimmie on his team because of his poise and level-headedness during investigations, especially when events got dicey.

"In two of the clusters, the victims were African Americans. The west coast cluster contains persons of Asian or Pacific Rim descent. The cluster in New York was all Jewish. I also noticed every single one of the victims possessed a college or higher degree. Plus, they were well off financially and were highly visible in their communities."

Kruger nodded. "Good observations. Anyone else?"

JR looked over his coffee cup. "Want to tell us what you saw?"

Kruger displayed a half grin. "Sandy and Jimmie are correct. I saw those patterns as well. I also saw something else." He paused for a moment. "Did anyone notice the timings of the murders?"

Knoll and Gibbs glanced at each other but shook their heads. Charlie frowned and JR grinned.

"All the incidents occurred during the traditional time of a college or university semester break."

CHAPTER 5

Hendrick University

Adjunct professor Dorian Monk walked through the center of campus, head down, hands in his pockets, ignoring students on his way to his next class. The scuffed brown leather satchel, hanging by a strap over his left shoulder, contained class notes and a Samsung Galaxy Tablet. Considered one of the best mathematics instructors at the school, his anti-social behavior was overlooked by his department head and the university's administration due to his status as a part-time lecturer and a non-tenure track member of the faculty. This allowed him an opportunity to earn a living without the need to become involved in campus politics.

Now in his late forties, he wore his thinning brown hair swept back and kept in a short ponytail. Perpetually smudged wire rim glasses sat on a hawk nose too large for his slim face. When traveling from one campus building to the next, he kept his dark brown eyes glued to the sidewalk in front of him. The only students who greeted him were freshmen unaware of his general disdain for students and social interaction.

Of average height and below average weight, he dressed his slim frame in jeans and untucked long sleeve shirts rolled up to his elbows. During cooler weather, a tattered brown Carhartt jacket kept the chill off.

With his official university mailing address registered as a P.O. box, no one knew where he lived. He did not socialize with any of the other professors, nor did he take part in student-related functions. He was there to draw a paycheck. His brilliance in the classroom and a long list of published papers kept him employed.

School officials and his department head considered him just another odd professor who taught upper level classes other members of the math department could not. His classes were always full with a waiting list each semester.

Within this backdrop, Dorian Monk harbored a secret—a burning hatred for his fellow human beings. It had been there since his first recollection of consciousness. He learned early to squelch it and bottle it up inside. The study of numbers and the logical solutions of formulas kept him sane. Somewhere in his late teens, he realized it was the randomness and unpredictable nature of human interactions he detested.

As Monk prepared for his 10:00 a.m. Ring Theory class, Harvey Copeland, head of the mathematics department, walked into the classroom. With his perpetual smile he said, "Good morning, Doctor Monk."

Monk stared at him. "Morning."

"I know you have a class in a few minutes, but I wanted to run something past you."

"Okay."

"The university has been asked to host a symposium the week after the semester is over."

Monk continued to stare at him but said nothing.

"The whole campus will be filled with law enforcement

professionals from all over the country."

Monk stiffened as his eyes narrowed. "Why?"

"One of the assistant directors of the FBI is an alumnus. Since he was in charge of putting on the symposium, he chose our campus."

"Lucky us."

"Yes, it is an honor."

A couple of students walked into the room and took their seats. Monk glanced at his wristwatch. "What's the symposium about?"

"There will be numerous guest lecturers from other universities here, plus they have asked for a select number of our faculty to contribute as well."

"Doctor Copeland, you didn't answer my question. Besides, what does this have to do with me? I'm just a part-time lecturer."

"By choice."

"Yes, by choice. But you still haven't told me what the symposium is about."

"It will be used to present the latest developments in computer technology used for law enforcement and security to those in attendance."

Monk blinked several times. "I'm not a computer expert. Again, what does this have to do with me?"

"Your recent paper on computer algorithms is of interest to the Cyber Crimes division of the FBI. They want you to lead a session."

"I don't conduct sessions."

"Dorian, I am aware of your reluctance to participate in these types of activities, but they are offering to pay participating professors six thousand per session. That's more than you make for teaching one class during the semester and this is only for four days."

More students filed in as the time approached 9:57. Monk looked at the students, then back at Copeland. "Okay, but I need more details."

Copeland smiled. "Great, I will put you down as a yes."

***

After the Ring Theory class, Monk left campus to eat at a small diner he frequented. His final class for the day would not start until one, so he sat at a table in the rear of the dining room, his back to the front entrance. Coffee and a small salad with dressing on the side comprised his daily lunch. He never ate on campus.

The coffee was hot and the salad limp, as usual. The one reason he liked this particular restaurant was few students cared for the blue-collar atmosphere. He could think in peace without having one of his students challenge him to a debate.

Today, his thoughts swirled around the news of a gathering of law enforcement officials on campus. Plus, if the FBI Cyber Crime division was involved, that meant there would be FBI agents as well. While the money was good for four days of work, the thought of interacting with those types for any length of time unsettled him.

While these thoughts intruded on his conscious, he sipped coffee, stared at the wall and lost track of time.

At 12:45 p.m., the waitress stood next to his table with a coffee pot in hand. "Professor Monk?"

He blinked several times and turned toward her. "Yes."

"Do you know what time it is?"

The blinking continued and he remained silent.

"It's fifteen till one."

His eyes widened as he glanced at his wristwatch. "Oh, dear." He threw a ten-dollar bill on the table and practically ran out of the diner.

CHAPTER 6

J. Edgar Hoover Building
Two Days Later

JR and Kruger sat at the conference table reviewing their notes as the meeting's attendees shuffled in and took their seats. Muted conversations filled the room while they waited for Paul Stumpf. Everyone stood when he entered and took his seat at the head of the table.

Without preamble, he said, "What can you tell us, Sean?"

Kruger walked to a laptop at the far end of the table and inserted a flash drive. When the computer recognized it, he clicked on a PowerPoint file. "Our assumption Alan was specifically targeted appears to be correct."

The room remained quiet.

The projector displayed the first slide of Kruger's presentation, a picture of Alan Seltzer and another black man. "We discovered files in Alan's personal computer indicating a multi-year search. In 2015, an African

American by the name of Roger Johnson was murdered in Atlanta. Murders happen all the time in Atlanta, but this one was different. Like Alan, Mr. Johnson was a lawyer— the two met and became friends in law school. They kept in touch over the years. While Alan took his law degree to the FBI, his friend went the corporate route and worked for The Coca-Cola Company. He worked normal hours and usually returned to his family every evening around the same time. One night in late May of 2015, Roger Johnson did not come home.

"He was found shot to death in his car located in a ditch two miles from his house. A Ram 1500 was later found abandoned and identified as the vehicle that forced Roger off the road. No one was arrested and there are no current persons of interest in the case. It's a cold case in the Atlanta Police Department. I spoke to one of the detectives who investigated the incident and he does not think Roger's murder will ever be solved."

Kruger paused and changed the PowerPoint slide. The next picture was a professional head shot of a middle aged African American woman. "This is Ramona Sturgis, a heart surgeon, wife and mother of two teenage girls. She was also the past president of the Atlanta chapter of the American Heart Association. She was murdered in her office one night while working late. Hospital security does not know how the assailant got in, nor do they have any clues of who it was." He paused and swept his gaze around the room. "The security cameras on that floor of the hospital were not functioning that night. Someone had disabled the system.

"The Marietta Police Department lists this as a cold case. The incident occurred the January before Roger Johnson's death in May."

Stumpf cleared his throat. "How many unsolved murders did Alan find?"

"Twenty-one."

A groan spread throughout the room.

"Over how long of a period?"

"Five years."

Teri Monroe asked, "Why weren't they flagged as the work of a serial killer?"

With a grim smile, Kruger changed to another PowerPoint slide. A map of the United States appeared with four circles surrounding four major cities. "Because the individual or individuals responsible never killed anyone twice in the same city. They branched out to other municipalities. All of Alan's research came from the National Crime Information Center. We have identified four clusters with the following cities in the center—San Jose, California, Albany, New York, Atlanta and Cincinnati. Different ethnic groups were targeted in each cluster. All are unsolved, all were basically an execution. Alan's murder is the only one we can find here in the DC area. We think he was targeted because he was getting too close."

Stumpf shook his head slowly. "Why do you think he hadn't brought this to our attention?"

"From his notes, we know he was preparing to bring it to you, Paul. And he was going to suggest giving it to me."

Scott Lambert crossed his arms and frowned. "Did he mention why?"

Kruger nodded. "He knew my forced retirement was approaching and he felt I would be motivated to solve it prior to my birthday."

Lambert snorted. "Kind of high on yourself, aren't you, Agent Kruger?"

Stumpf shot from his chair and leaned over the conference table, his palms flat on the surface. "May I remind you, Assistant Director Lambert, that your department has almost one hundred agents investigating Alan's death with zero—and I mean absolutely zero—results. Agent Kruger's team of five took less than two days to discover a direction. So be careful of your insinuations."

Teri Monroe sat back in her chair, trying to hide her smile. JR did not cover his; others in the room studied their notes intently and Kruger remained stoic.

An uncomfortable minute passed as Stumpf straightened and returned his attention to the PowerPoint slide and Kruger. "I believe we have the right personnel in place." Stumpf paused and then nodded at Kruger. "Sean, please tell your team I appreciate their dedication."

The Director's gaze fell on each of the individuals at the table. "If I hear of anyone questioning Agent Kruger's discoveries, it will be their last question with the FBI. Is that understood?" Everyone stared at Stumpf, afraid to move. "Good, get back to work." He turned toward his office and walked out of the conference room.

As Kruger watched the Director disappear through the door to his office, he muttered to himself. "I hope you don't regret that decision, Paul."

***

On the trip back to their makeshift headquarters at Quantico, JR turned to Kruger, who was driving. "You think this is the right direction?"

After a quick glance at his friend, he said, "The lizard part of my brain tells me it is. The analytical part believes there are too many unanswered questions to agree with the lizard part."

"What kind of questions?"

"The pattern for one. Five unsolved murders in four clusters. Each cluster representing a varying period of time. Each period concentrating on a specific ethnic group. And the weirdest one of all, each murder corresponds to a break in an academic year."

"I noticed you didn't share that piece of news this

morning."

"Nope. I didn't want everyone to finally come to the conclusion I'm crazy."

JR stared ahead at traffic. "What if we're right? What are the implications?"

Kruger shook his head. "Even I can't believe what I'm going to say. We have a serial killer who is an academic, moves to a new college or university every year or so, likes to prey on ethnic groups and…"

With a frown, JR turned to look at his friend. "You just thought of something, didn't you?"

"JR, who were the victims in each of the cases Alan identified?"

"Men and women of different ethnic backgrounds."

"Yes, but what else?"

"There really wasn't a pattern that I could see. Why?"

A half smile appeared on Kruger lips. "They were highly visible as leaders in their community." He shot a quick glance at JR. "That's the common denominator. They had a media presence. Our killer identified his victims from local news broadcasts."

Silence filled the rental car as they drew closer to Quantico. After five minutes, JR said, "I don't have the software here to do what I need to do next."

"Kind of what I thought."

"I'm not sure how many colleges and universities are within each of the clusters, but I bet the total number will be over a hundred."

Kruger nodded.

JR continued. "I would need to compare names of the faculty in each of the schools over the course of the past eight, maybe ten years."

"Yes, you would." Kruger now grinned. "Can Charlie help you?"

"No, I like Charlie, but he's too straitlaced and doesn't have an ounce of larceny in his bones. Alexia, however, does."

"That's an even better idea."

"This will be one of the largest hacking attempts I've ever tried."

"You sure you want to do it?"

"Hell, yes. I love a challenge."

"Good. Alan's funeral service is tomorrow. Steph's coming in this afternoon. Were you planning to stay?"

"I hate funerals."

"So do I."

"But Alan was your friend and mine. Plus, he was Joseph's nephew. I'll stay and leave immediately afterward."

***

Kruger tried several times to tie the necktie properly. During the last year, his wardrobe had seldom included suits so he rarely wore a tie. The suit still fit, but the tie was frustrating him. He stopped and looked at Stephanie. "You would think as many years as I wore a necktie, I would still have the muscle memory to tie one correctly."

She smiled as she slipped on her dress. "One would think so."

He tried again and finally got the length correct.

Stephanie turned her back to him. "Zip me up, please." As he did, she said, "Why didn't you agree to give one of the eulogies?"

"I hate funerals."

"I know. We've discussed that before. But Alan was your friend."

"I know. I agreed to be a pallbearer. I didn't feel the need to do both." He paused for a second. "Besides, I don't like eulogies. They try to summarize a person's life in one thousand words or less. It really minimizes the person who died. Everyone's life is worth more than a thousand words,

I don't care who you are."

When he stopped, she turned to look at him. "Sean, what's the matter?"

Moisture pooled in the corners of his eyes. "It's the finality of it, Steph. Alan didn't deserve to have his life end this way."

She reached up and placed her hand on his cheek. "You, of all people, know how unfair life can be. You have to celebrate the time you had with him."

He blinked as a tear slid down his cheek. Pulling her into an embrace, he remained quiet.

***

Kruger and Stephanie stood behind the seated family members at the graveside services. Those individuals included Linda, Alan's widow, his grown children, Frederick and Racheal, their spouses and the only grandchild, Racheal's one-year old son. Joseph and Mary Kincaid sat next to Linda, Mary holding her hand as the Methodist minister spoke words Kruger did not hear.

Like during the church service, Kruger held Stephanie's hand tightly, his thoughts wandering. He stared at the casket perched above the empty grave, the opening obscenely covered with a blanket of artificial turf to hide the fact it was just a hole in the ground. Alan Seltzer had been a fixture in Kruger's life for more than two decades. The constant travel to different FBI Field Offices allowed him to make numerous friends and acquaintances within the bureau, but none were there on a permanent basis like Alan Seltzer.

These thoughts made him squeeze Stephanie's hand tighter. She looked up at him and whispered, "Are you okay?"

He nodded once, afraid if he spoke his voice would crack.

After the graveside services concluded, Kruger led Stephanie back a few steps to let the other attendees pay their respects to the family. He stood there wondering what he could say to Alan's widow, but nothing came.

As the crowd dispersed, the two of them approached Linda Seltzer. She and Stephanie hugged and exchanged words Kruger could not hear. When Linda turned to Kruger, she stared up at him, tears rolling down her cheeks. All she could say was, "Oh—Sean."

As they hugged, he whispered into her ear. "I will find the person who did this. I promise."

CHAPTER 7

Springfield, MO

Alexia Montreal Gibbs' world consisted of three elements—her husband, Ex-Navy Seal James Gibbs, their one-year old son, Thomas, and her status as one of the world's best computer hackers who now worked for JR Diminski's computer security company. After spending a decade hiding in Mexico City with no family or friends, she felt comfortable with her new life.

Standing five-feet-nine, Alexia was tall by Western European standards. She was born in Spain to parents who were staunch supporters of Catalonia and harbored deep distrust of the government in Madrid. After completing her studies at the University of Barcelona, she worked for an ISP provider as a security analyst until she discovered a more lucrative vocation. Hacking.

During the early years of her hacking career, she joined an invisible group of revolutionaries working toward the demise of the Madrid government. At the time, she'd called the Latin Quarter of Paris home. She liked the bohemian atmosphere and was able to blend into the culture with ease. However, greed got to her one night, drawing the unwanted attention of the French General Directorate for Internal Security, the DGSI. After a hastily arranged midnight flight out of Charles de Gaulle International airport to Mexico City, she settled in the La Condesa district.

There she'd endured a self-imposed isolation by keeping a low profile and earning a meager living using her computer hacking skills. During this period, she wore her tousled black hair short, maintained a pencil-thin physique and when in public, wore loose-fitting clothes to hide her gender. As a naturally pretty woman, she'd disguised herself during her rare excursions into public with black Buddy Holly style glasses and a Chicago Cubs ball cap.

She lived alone. No cats or dogs—too much trouble if she had to disappear quickly. Then ten years after her exodus to Mexico she made a huge mistake. She unknowingly became involved with a group of Russians. The incident caused her to fear for her life. Then in a daring daylight raid she was spirited away from under the watchful eyes of her Russian nemesis by a group of FBI agents and a computer hacker.

Now two years after the incident, she wore her black hair long and flowing. Her clothing emphasized her slender athletic body, which she maintained with the help of her husband by swimming in the lake near their home on a daily basis. Her time was now spent doting over her son, her husband, their new house and helping JR's company become one of the premier go-to computer security companies in the world.

With JR in Washington, Alexia handled his duties in the Springfield office. This included meeting with client companies experiencing computer breaches, supervising the day-to-day operations and getting a new division of the company started. On the last day of JR's trip, she received a phone call from one of their client service representatives out in the cubicle farm on the second floor.

"Good morning, Jeremy." Alexi still retained a Spanish accent, though not as thick as it once was.

"Alexia, we have a problem with one of our clients this morning."

"What's the matter?"

"I have the CFO of Martinez's and Associates on the line. She believes they've been hit with a ransomware attack."

"How big of a company is it?"

"Our profile shows them to have five branch offices in the central United States and an additional one hundred remote sites. All of the remote sites are infected. Uh, by the way, they're also one of JR's first clients. Do you want to talk to her?"

Alexia smiled. "The CFO is a woman?"

"Yes, a very rude woman."

"Okay. Send her call to my phone and stay on the line so you can listen in."

"Got it."

Alexia ended the internal call and waited for the transfer to her phone. When Jeremy indicated the calls were joined, she said, "This is Alexia Gibbs. May I help you?"

"Who's in charge there?"

"I am. May I ask who I am speaking to?"

"Where's JR? I've always dealt with JR."

"I'm sorry, he's out of town at the moment."

"Then who are you?"

"I'm his assistant. May I ask who I am speaking to?"

"Julie Martinez. Are you sure JR's not there?"

"Yes, ma'am. He's due back tonight. Now, what can we help you with?"

"Our computers are not allowing us to open any files."

"We'll need to get one of our technicians into your system."

Jeremy said, "Alexia, we're already in their server. All the files are encrypted."

"That's unfortunate."

Julie Martinez started stammering. "Wh…Wha…are you—talking about? Encrypted?"

Alexia kept her voice calm. "Julie, it means someone has hacked your system and made your files unreadable. Normally there will be a *Read-Me* file in each of the folders. Did you see any of those, Jeremy?"

"Yes, ma'am."

"Did they say what they wanted for the encryption key?"

"No, it said they would be in touch."

Alexia said, "Julie, your company is going to need to let us start working on your server immediately."

"We never had this kind of trouble when JR was around."

"I will call him immediately and let him know. Expect a call from him."

"Very well."

The call ended and Alexia stood. She navigated the cubicle farm until she found the one occupied by Jeremy. "Can you show me one of the encrypted files?"

"Sure." A few seconds later, she saw the ending file identifiers, trying to hide her surprise. She leaned over and stared incredulously at the computer screen.

"Oh, dear." She straightened and hurried back to her own cubicle.

With her hands shaking slightly, she sent a text message to JR and waited for him to call her back.

***

JR looked at the text message as he waited in the departure gate at Dulles International Airport. He smiled. It was the first time since arriving in Washington that Alexia had reached out to him. He dialed her number on his cell phone and heard, "When are you going to be back?"

"I'm at the departure gate. What's wrong?" She rattled something off in Spanish JR did not understand. "English, Alexia."

"Sorry. Do you remember a computer virus you described in a dark web chatroom a number of years ago?"

He hesitated. "Yes, why?"

"And you told us you never used it, right?"

"No, I never did."

"Someone used your ideas to infect the files of Martinez and Associates."

After a few moments of quiet, JR said, "Julie wanted to talk to me and only me, correct?"

"Yes, very insistent. Please call her."

"I will. How do you know it's like the program I talked about?"

"Because it's not only affecting the files—it got into the programs and firmware."

JR paused for a moment and closed his eyes. An old memory made him shudder. "How much do they want?"

"We don't know yet. How big of a company is Martinez and Associates?"

"Fairly large. I know they operate in thirty states. Why?"

"My guess is they will want a sizeable sum for the decryption key."

"Can we rebuild the system?"

She hesitated. "Uh—one of the more malicious aspects of this program was it waited to encrypt the files just before their scheduled backup occurred. Now even the backup files are infected."

"What about an older version of back-up?"

"I'm afraid it will be the only way, but the company will lose a day or so of data."

"I'll be back by six."

***

Alexia stood behind JR as he sat in his cubicle. She asked, "Does that resemble what you proposed?"

He nodded.

"And you never released it into the wild?"

"No." He glanced at the clock in the lower right of the screen. "It's getting late, Alexia. Don't you need to pick up your son at daycare?"

"Yes, but I wanted to talk to you about this first."

"Okay, we've talked. Now go." He turned and gave her a smile. "It's okay. I'm sure somebody took my idea and designed a virus around it."

"I am sorry, JR."

"Don't worry. We can fix this. It'll just take time."

She nodded and walked toward the staircase.

After she left, he returned to his chair and studied the data on his screen. He leaned back with a furrowed brow. "Ah—shit."

***

Mia Diminski's stature could best be described as petite. Her Chinese and Texas ancestry helped produced long black hair normally worn in a ponytail. Tonight, it flowed around her shoulders as she leaned over to study the computer monitor closer with her brown eyes. "Are you sure, JR?" Her Texas drawl remained intact even after living more than half of her life outside the Lone Star State.

He nodded. "Yeah, I'm sure."

"When did you write it?"

"Originally, I was going to use it against P&G Global, then I met you, Joseph, and Sean. Things worked out differently after that. When P&G self-imploded, I decided the virus was too malicious to release into the wild, so I shelved it and, to be honest, forgot about it."

"Then how did Alexia recognize it?"

JR stared at her and blinked several times. "Uh—well..." He took a breath and let it out slowly. "During that period, I used to spend a lot of time in chat rooms, there were always discussions going on about how to create the perfect virus. In one that Alexia and I frequented, I shared my thoughts on how to code it. At the time I didn't know if she was male or female. She remembered the discussion apparently and recognized it."

"But JR, you never used it."

"I know."

"Then how did someone get the code?"

"That, my dear, is a question without an answer."

"Could someone have hacked one of your computers a long time ago without you knowing about it?"

JR pursed his lips. "Maybe, but for the life of me I don't see how."

She stopped standing and sat next to him, still studying the screen. "What if it happened during the Russian DDS attack on your server two years ago?"

His eyes widened as he stared back at her. "Oh, boy. I didn't think about that. It's the only time our system has ever been exposed." He stopped and looked back at the monitor. "But how would someone know about it? I never told anyone I actually wrote it. I just discussed how it would..."

Mia titled her head slightly. "How it would what?"

He was silent as he stared at the screen. Finally, he turned back to her. "How it worked."

"I've seen that look before. What did you remember?"

"As you know, we've always kept a complete backup of our system off-site without any direct connect."

She nodded.

"What if during the DDS attack, a Trojan horse was inserted into our system and I missed it? If that's the case, it would have provided someone the opportunity to find our back up files. We would never know about it and someone could have taken their time snooping around."

"Wouldn't you see something like that?"

"Not if they just looked around and copied files." He looked back at the screen. "Why don't you and Joey go on home? I have a few more things to do here tonight."

CHAPTER 8

Washington, DC / Springfield, MO

JR's departure the previous afternoon left Charlie Craft in charge of dismantling the phones and computers in the temporary war room at Quantico. Kruger, Jimmie and Sandy determined which files they needed for the next phase of the investigation and which ones to pack for storage.

Gibbs turned to Kruger. "I have an appointment with a San Francisco FBI agent tomorrow morning."

"Was she involved with any of the investigations?"

With a nod, Gibbs placed a lid on a white bank box. "Yeah, she investigated the one near Almaden Lake Park in San Jose. When I told her you were involved and suspected four other unsolved cases might be involved, she blurted out, '*about damn time.*'"

"What's her name?"

"Rachel Lee. She hasn't forgotten about the case. The victim was a professor at San Jose State University. Apparently, Lee took several of her classes while in college."

Kruger remained quiet for a few moments as he studied Gibbs. "How was she involved?"

As Gibbs finished taping the lid on a storage box, he said, "According to Alan's notes, she was brought in after the San Jose Police Department asked for help."

"Did she mention which cases she felt were related?"

Gibbs shook his head. "No, I thought I'd discuss that when I got there."

The elder FBI agent gave his young protégée a thoughtful nod. "I'll be curious as to what she tells you."

"Me, too. I'll keep you posted."

"If you run into any resistance from any of the local police jurisdictions, let me know. The SAC is an old friend of mine and owes me a favor. He can intervene if we need him to."

Gibbs carried the sealed bank box to a corner and stacked it on top of others already there. He returned to where Kruger stood and gave him a smile. "Sean, I've successfully dealt with warlords in Afghanistan. I think I can handle a few police chiefs."

"My dear Jimmie, you have no idea."

***

Stephanie sat next to her husband, flipping through a magazine while he read emails on his cell phone. They were sitting in the departure gate at Dulles International waiting for their flight back to Springfield. If all the flights were on time, they would be home by 10 p.m.

"Sean?"

He took his eyes off the phone and looked at her.

"What happens if you don't solve this before you have to retire?"

Returning his attention to the cell phone, he said, "That's not going to happen."

She placed her hand on his arm. "I understand how you feel—"

"I can't think that way, Stephanie." He shot her a glare. "I…" He closed his eyes, took a deep breath and shook his head.

"Sean, you're putting too much pressure on yourself."

With a harsh tone, he said, "Well, who the hell else is going to get it done?"

She smiled. "Last I knew, about fourteen thousand other special agents who work for the FBI."

He stared at her and blinked several times. After a while he chuckled. "Thank you."

"For what?"

"Allowing me to see how absurd I'm acting."

"That's what a wife is for, to point out when her husband is being absurd." She chuckled as well.

"To be honest with you, I don't know what I will do if I have to retire before we find Alan's killer." He raised his hands and dry rubbed his face. "All I know is I have to try before I do."

"Now that's the Sean Kruger I fell in love with."

He patted her hand and leaned back in the uncomfortable seat. "Jimmie's going to San Jose, California tomorrow and Sandy to Atlanta. I'm hoping they learn enough to give JR a direction. At least that's the plan."

She nodded. "What are you going to do?"

"I'm going to dig into Alan's old case files before he went into management. Something from his past may have sparked his behind-the-scenes investigation. Possibly something he left undone and couldn't get off his mind." He paused. "There's a reason he started looking into cold cases again."

"Alan went into management a long time ago, Sean. How far back do you think this goes?"

"Not sure—the cold cases he identified only go back

five years. That's why I want to look at his old cases." He paused. "Maybe something's there."

She started to reply, but a sudden announcement for their flight interrupted her.

***

The next morning, Kruger was in his office before sunrise accessing case files on his laptop from the bureau archives.

Stephanie appeared at the door to his home office with a cup of coffee in her hand. "Did you forget you made coffee?"

He looked up, blinked a few times and gave her a slight smile. "Apparently I did. Is that one mine?"

She nodded and placed it on his desk. "Any luck?"

"Not yet. I thought I would start with his unsolved cases. He didn't have that many, so it won't take too long to go through them."

"What if it wasn't an unsolved case? What then?"

He took a sip of coffee. "It's possible. Hell, Steph, I'm not even sure what I'm looking for. It could have been something he ran across recently. He hasn't been out in the field for fifteen years."

"So, you're basically looking for a needle in a haystack."

Kruger studied the black liquid in his mug. "I have to start somewhere."

"What about his notes?"

With a shake of his head, he said, "We went through them very carefully. None of us found a reference to why he started looking at these specific cases. Alan's investigative notes were always precise, succinct and written in non-literary prose. His conclusions were based on logic without speculation."

"So, in other words, he didn't include opinions."

"Only on rare occasions."

"Then look for the rare occasion."

With his coffee halfway to his lips, he stopped and stared at his wife. A grin appeared and he took a sip. "That is an excellent idea."

After helping Stephanie get the kids fed and dressed for their day, he returned to his office and started reviewing the downloaded files. The house was quiet with the kids in school and Stephanie at the university. It was mid-morning when he found the first hint of why Alan Seltzer had started looking at the cold cases that led to his murder.

***

Kruger parked his gun-metal gray Ford Mustang GT in an angled slot in front of a nondescript brick two-story office building on the southwest side of Springfield. The time approached noon and the surrounding area was busy with pedestrian and automobile traffic.

Kruger exited the car and stood on the sidewalk in front of the building taking in the surroundings. On the west side stood a high-end restaurant and to the east, an office with the names of four lawyers. Across the street was an urgent care facility and an expensive-looking daycare center.

Walking through the front door, he waved at the receptionist and headed toward the staircase leading to the second floor. At the top, the din of multiple one-sided conversations from the cubicle farm assaulted his senses. Kruger frowned. Normally, the sound of JR's technical staff discussing computer problems with clients did not reach this level of intensity.

He worked his way around the outside wall toward JR's personal cubicle next to a soundproof conference room. As he approached, JR pointed toward a chair next to him.

As he sat, Kruger said, "What's all the commotion about?"

"We had an influx of new clients while I was in DC." He gestured toward the room. "This is the result."

"Any particular reason?"

"Yeah. Let's go into the conference room, I'll explain."

Before entering the room, Kruger filled a cup at the coffee service next to JR's cubicle. When he shut the door, the sudden quiet lay in Shark contrast to the commotion outside. After a sip of the brew, he asked, "Do I need to come back when you aren't so busy?"

JR shook his head. "Alexia is handling it. What've you got?"

Kruger handed JR a small flash drive. As he watched the computer genius insert the device into a laptop and access the files, he asked, "So, why all the new clients?"

JR looked up and pushed his rimless glasses up the bridge of his nose. "Remember when we first met, I was dealing with Abel Pymel by myself?"

Kruger nodded.

"I wrote a rather nasty computer virus I planned to use on his company's computer system. I can't remember the reason, but I decided not to let it into the wild, never used it and completely forgot about it."

"There's a *however* in there somewhere."

"Yeah—there is. That virus is now on the internet infecting computers. How it got there is the question I've been trying to answer all morning."

"Maybe someone else wrote it."

"Nope." JR shook his head. "It's mine. I've been looking at the code all morning and it's exactly like I wrote it eight years ago."

"Huh."

"That's what I said when Alexia brought it to my attention."

"That still didn't answer my original question about why the influx of new clients."

"Word of mouth."

"That's not an answer."

"I know. I don't have an answer. Neither does Alexia."

"Any speculation?"

"On the influx of clients, no. On the virus, we think someone got into our system during the DDS attack two years ago. Looked around, found the virus and stole it."

"Wouldn't they have needed to know what to look for to find it?"

JR shook his head. "Not if they already knew it was there."

"So, what are you saying, JR?"

"I'm speculating here, but we know the Russians were behind the DDS attack, right?"

"That's what you told me."

"They were, trust me. It is also common knowledge that Russian hackers participate in dark web chatrooms all the time."

"Oh, boy. I'm not going to like this, am I?"

"Probably not. I wrote the thing as an experiment during the last few months I lived in New York. After I moved here and before I met you and Joseph, I rewrote it and made it even more malicious. It became more of a mental exercise in programming. I used it as a topic for discussions in dark web chatrooms on various occasions. What I'm thinking is I got careless at some point and a Russian hacker figured out who I was. Whoever that person was became involved with the DDS attack on my company two years ago and found the virus."

Kruger frowned. "You can't be serious. You're speculating."

"It's the only explanation I can come up with."

"Are you saying your company is the only one getting all this new business?"

JR shook his head and snorted. "I'm not that egotistical. No, I think someone figured out there's a lot of money to be made and had the perfect tool to do so. Most companies just pay the ransom, get the encryption key and move on. Others don't and probably spend more money fixing it than they would by just paying the ransom."

Kruger crossed his arms. "You're making a lot of assumptions with few facts to base them on."

"Yes."

"Think about all the coincidences your assumptions involve."

JR smiled. "Kind of makes you crazy, doesn't it?"

His answer was a long hard stare.

CHAPTER 9

San Jose, California

Jimmie Gibbs shook Rachel Lee's hand. He noted a firm and calloused grip. Her appearance matched his expectations from their conversations on the phone. Short black hair, piercing dark almond-shaped eyes, a slender athletic body and an air of confidence.

"Agent Gibbs, how can I be of assistance?" Her tone hinted at reserve and caution.

"Thank you for agreeing to see me, Agent Lee. As I said on the phone, I'm on a taskforce looking into five unsolved murders here in the San Jose area."

Having driven separately, the two FBI agents met at the location where the college professor's body had been discovered. Gibbs continued, "We believe all of these cold cases are related."

Lee nodded and referred to a Samsung tablet she carried. "I've reviewed my case notes from the one in Almaden Lake Park. Per your request, we checked with the four other municipalities and have their case notes also." She looked up at Gibbs. "I suspected the same thing, but I don't see a pattern here, Agent."

As they started walking toward the spot where Lee indicated the victim's body had been found, he said, "Please call me, Jimmie."

She smiled and nodded. "I'm Rachel." She pointed to a spot under a tall cottonwood tree. "Professor Ming was found there. No sign of a struggle and no blood. We believe she was killed elsewhere and dumped here." She handed the tablet to Gibbs.

He swiped the screen to change the pictures. "This report doesn't mention a location for the murder. Any idea of where she was killed?"

Lee shook her head. "Never determined. Some of us believe it was in the faculty parking lot at the university."

Gibbs raised his eyes from the tablet. "Why?"

"She was last seen walking from her office on campus toward her car, which, by the way, has never been located."

"Huh."

"This was in between semesters in January. So, it gets dark around five o'clock here. Her partner filed a report with the San Jose police after she failed to return home after work. Something she never did."

With a nod, Gibbs said, "How long before the body was found?"

"Local police got a call around nine that night about a body in the park."

He nodded again. "Why was the bureau called in?"

"Because Professor Ming was of Chinese descent and gay, the SJPD declared it a hate crime and handed it over to us."

"In other words, they couldn't figure it out and dumped it into the bureau's lap."

"Pretty much."

Gibbs studied the tablet. "What about the other cases I told you about? Any similarities?"

Lee shook her head. "None that jump out at me."

"What about the victims?"

"Two females and three males."

"What about ethnicity?"

"Excuse me?"

"You mentioned Professor Ming was Chinese—what about the others?"

"I'm not sure. I didn't look at that aspect of it. Let me see the tablet."

He handed it back and watched as she scrolled through the files. After five minutes she looked up at Gibbs. "One Chinese, one from South Korea, two from Japan and one from Vietnam, all from the Pacific Rim. All first generation born here or in the case of the victim from Vietnam, brought here as a child."

Gibbs nodded. "If you look at the time of the murders, they all occurred in between semesters or when a university had a break in classes."

She was rapidly swiping the screen. "Damn, you're right." She looked up at Gibbs. "What else?"

"I doubt this information is in the files, but we think there is a connection between the five individuals. Probably a university."

She crossed her arms. "Come clean, Jimmie. What do you guys think is going on here?"

"At the moment our premise is the suspect may be an academic and at one time worked for a college or university in the area. All of his victims are highly educated professionals and of similar ethnic background. We don't know for sure, but we think all the victims have something in common. What that is, we don't know yet. We also believe the suspect changes universities frequently."

"How the heck can you determine that?"

He gave her a half smile. "As my boss calls it, old fashioned detective work. I start at San Jose State and get a list of professors who were only at the university during the time period of the murders."

"What if you don't find anyone like that at San Jose State?"

"Then I'll have to check some of the other schools in the area."

"So, is all of this related to the murder of Deputy Director Seltzer?"

Gibbs nodded.

"Count me in. Our SAC told me to give you all the help you needed."

***

It took two days and a trip to twelve area colleges before they had a list of five possible suspects. Jimmie Gibbs stared at his notes while Rachel Lee drove him back to his hotel. She glanced at him. "What's our next step?"

"I'm not sure. I need to talk to Sean Kruger and get his ideas."

"What's he like to work for?"

Gibbs smiled. "Best boss I've ever had and that includes some excellent ones in the Navy."

"You were in the Navy?"

He nodded. "Ten years."

"What'd you do?"

He hesitated, not sure exactly how to answer. "Uh— special forces."

She glanced at him again with wide eyes. "You were a Navy Seal?"

"Yes."

"Did you know Gary Lee?"

"Yeah, I did. Great guy. How do you know him?"

"He was my brother."

"Was?" Gibbs paused. "What happened?"

She stared ahead and just shook her head.

"I'm sorry, Rachel. I didn't know. When?"

"Last summer. We were never told where he was when it happened."

Gibbs was quiet. Finally, all he could think to say was, "Yeah, that's pretty standard."

Silence permeated the car's interior as Rachel Lee navigated the afternoon traffic.

When they pulled into the hotel parking lot, he turned to her. "I'd like to talk to Professor Ming's partner. Do you think she would meet with us?"

"I can ask. When do you want to do it?"

"Tonight, or first thing in the morning. I'm flying home tomorrow afternoon."

Lee nodded. He stepped out of the car and as she drove away, he dialed Sean Kruger.

"Kruger."

"Sean, it's Jimmie."

"Did you find anything?"

"Maybe. We've identified five individuals who worked for area universities and were only here during the year and a half the murders occurred."

"Is there a way to check to see if there are any connections between those individuals and the victims?"

"I want to talk to one of the victim's partner before I head back. I'm curious to see if any of the names mean anything to her."

"That's a good idea. Can you send the names to JR tonight?"

"Yeah, I'm back at the hotel and will email them in a few minutes."

"When do you get back tomorrow?"

"Very late."

"Yeah, I've made those flights from the west coast. Not fun. Let's talk on Friday."

***

Gibbs followed Rachel Lee into the apartment once occupied by Professor Yuan Chen and the woman they were meeting. Maria Simms was petite in stature, mid-fifties with gray streaks in her dark brown hair. She was dressed professionally and Gibbs noticed a laptop sitting on the kitchen table.

Lee introduced them. "Maria, this is Special Agent James Gibbs. He is looking into Yuan's murder."

The small woman blinked several times and extended her hand. "It's been four years, Agent. Why is the FBI suddenly interested?"

"I'm not at liberty to discuss details at the moment, but I can tell you the case is being reopened."

Her eyebrows rose and she gave him a lopsided smile. "I'm an appellate court judge, agent. I can keep a secret."

Gibbs hesitated for a few moments and then gave her an overview. When he was done, she remained quiet for several moments. "I see. So, you don't think it was random."

"No, ma'am."

"Let me see the names of the other victims."

He handed her the list as she put on half-readers. She remained quiet as she studied the list. A frown appeared and she pointed to a name. "Nguyen Minh."

"How were they connected?"

"Yuan and she collaborated on a paper about a year before her death. Minh was a math professor at the University of California at Santa Cruz."

Gibbs nodded. "Really?"

"Yes."

Putting the list back in his sport coat inside pocket, he said, "Minh was killed the next summer. He was the last one in California."

Maria Simms stared at Gibbs but remained quiet.

He continued, "And you didn't recognize any of the other names?"

"No."

He pulled another piece of paper from his coat pocket. "Does the name Dorian Monk mean anything to you?"

A shake of her head was his answer.

He returned the paper to his pocket. "Thank you, Judge. You've been very helpful."

***

The boarding gate for his flight back east was crowded. Jimmie Gibbs leaned against the glass wall across from the gate and away from the other passengers, a cell phone pressed to his ear. Kruger was on the other end of the call.

"Sean, here's the thing. There's a connection between the victims. Rachel Lee is checking with the families of the other victims to see if they recognize any of the other victims' names."

"Good work, Jimmie. JR is using the names you sent him. He should have something by tomorrow, he thinks."

"Have him check the name Dorian Monk."

"Why?"

"A feeling."

"Want to explain?"

"I believe if there are any connections between the victims it will be professional or situational. If that's the case it's also the reason no one has connected the dots."

"That makes sense."

"Two of the victims were mathematicians."

"Okay, go on."

"Dorian Monk is the only math professor on our suspect list."

"I'll have JR check on him first."

The boarding announcement for his flight interrupted their conversation. "I have to go, Sean. I talk to you tomorrow."

"Sounds good." He paused. "By the way, nicely done."

CHAPTER 10

Springfield, MO

Pointing to the computer screen, JR said, "Of the five names Jimmie sent, that is the only one without a LinkedIn page or a social media presence."

Kruger put on his half-readers and leaned over. He straightened and turned to Jimmie. "Dorian Monk, just like you suspected?"

Gibbs remained quiet as he listened.

JR continued, "I've conducted multiple searches for all five names. All five are currently teaching at different universities across the country. All but one has been at their current school for more than three years. Monk hasn't. He's registered with the American Mathematics Society and has numerous papers published in academic publications. The address given to the AMS is a post office box in Covington, Kentucky. He lists his current position as an adjunct professor of advanced mathematics at Hendrick University in Kentucky."

Kruger placed his hand on his chin and tapped his lips.

"Is he still on the faculty?"

"Yes."

Turning to Kruger, Gibbs asked, "What's an adjunct professor?"

"Think of it as a contract professor, someone who only works part-time and is hired on a semester to semester basis. They are generally on a non-tenured career track and go from college to college, depending on what they teach. A lot of the ones I've known had day jobs and taught night school." He paused and asked, "Where is this Hendrick college, JR?"

"Across the river from Cincinnati in northern Kentucky." He paused. "Smack dab in the middle of the most recent cluster Alan found."

"Sandy is due back from Atlanta this afternoon. That was the first cluster Alan identified." Kruger pursed his lips. "He told me he couldn't find any connections between the victims. To him it felt like a dead end."

"Not necessarily." JR was staring at what appeared to be an ID photo on his monitor. He pointed toward it. "Look at that."

Kruger focused on the picture. "I'll be damned. What college?"

"Brighten University in Atlanta."

On the screen was an agitated young man who had probably protested having his picture taken. The name on the ID read D. Monk, Mathematics Department.

Kruger crossed his arms. "That puts him in three of the four clusters. How many years was he at Brighten?"

"He was only there for two semesters." He paused, turned toward the two men standing behind him and smiled. "Our Dr. Monk spent four years at Carlton State University in Morrow, Georgia. The first murder occurred there and just before he moved to Brighten."

As Kruger studied the picture, his expression remained neutral. "Okay gentlemen, I want to know everything we can learn about Dorian Monk, PhD."

Jimmie Gibbs nodded. "I'll start with the military and see if he ever served."

"Good."

JR returned his attention to his computer screen. "I'll find out where he got his PhD and backtrack from there."

With a nod, Kruger said, "I'll have the bureau do a deep dive on him." He paused for a second. "Guys, keep it low-keyed. There's always the possibility he isn't our suspect and I don't want some rookie FBI agent finding out and rushing over to Hendrick College to arrest the guy."

Both JR and Gibbs said in unison, "Got it."

***

Barbara Whitlock's position as an analyst for the FBI stretched back as far as Kruger could remember. Having worked with her on numerous cases, he knew her results to be exceptional. She was also discreet. Scrolling through his list of contacts on his cell phone, he found her direct number—a number only a select group of agents possessed—and pressed the send icon.

The call was answered on the fourth ring.

"Well, if it isn't Sean Kruger. Is this a social call or business?"

Kruger smiled. Barbara always asked the same question when he called. "Can't I call just to say hello?"

He heard a deep sigh. "You can but you never do. You never call unless you want something."

"That isn't fair, Barbara. I don't always call needing something."

"That is just so much BS, Agent Kruger." She chuckled. "What can I do for you this morning?"

"I need background on someone."

"As you always do. Who is it this time?"

"A man named Dorian Monk. He's a mathematics

professor currently teaching at Hendrick University in Kentucky."

"Do you have a social security number for him?"

He read off the number.

"How do you spell the name?"

Kruger told her.

"What all do you need on him?"

"Any and everything you can find. I need to know if he's ever been arrested, and if so, for what."

"Is this related to Alan's death?"

"Yes, Barbara, it could be."

"Glad you told me. I'm a week behind and this request just jumped to the top of the pile. Say hello to that lovely wife of yours, Sean. Tell her everyone in this department is still jealous of her."

"I will, Barbara, and tell Bob hello for me."

The call ended and Kruger sat back in his chair in the conference room. They were making progress, but time was slipping away and that was one commodity he did not possess in ample quantities.

***

JR and Kruger leaned against the railing on Kruger's back deck. Both nursed beers as they watched darkness descend over the back yard.

"There's not a lot of information out there on Dorian Monk, Sean."

"I was afraid of that. I talked to Barbara Whitlock today. She called back late this afternoon and told me he doesn't have a criminal record either as a juvenile or adult. What did you find?"

"Not much. I did find his early student records. He attended an elementary school in Casper until the age of ten, but there's a gap after that until he goes to college."

"What kind of gap?"

"I can't find where he went to high school."

"Do you think he was homeschooled?"

"It would make sense."

"What about his parents?"

Shaking his head, JR said, "I found their obituaries. They died a couple of years apart, after he went to college. Cause of death was not stated."

"Where did Monk do his undergraduate work?"

"Full scholarship to Northwestern University, got his BS in mathematics in three years."

Kruger whistled softly. "What about his post-graduate work?"

"MIT."

"I take it he's smart."

JR nodded. "MIT rated his IQ at over 160."

"Damn."

"There was also a notification in his student file about his antisocial tendencies."

Turning to look at his friend in the dark, Kruger asked, "How antisocial?"

"Lived alone, no roommates, didn't join study groups or associate with anyone away from classes. He very seldom met with his advisor until time to complete his PhD."

"Not unusual for someone that smart, but I'm curious about what prompted the note in his student file."

JR shook his head. "There wasn't any explanation, just the notations I mentioned."

"Huh."

"One other thing."

"What's that?"

"There's a symposium at Hendrick College next week. Guess who is heading up one of the sessions?"

Kruger's eyebrows rose. "Monk?"

A nod was JR's answer.

"What's his topic?"

After taking a sip of beer, JR said, "Apparently, he

published a paper on computer algorithms that attracted the attention of the FBI Cyber Crimes Division."

"I thought you said he's a mathematician."

JR nodded. "He is."

"I think we need to crash this little party. You still have your FBI credentials, don't you?"

"Of course."

"Then I think we need to have a chat with Doctor Dorian Monk."

"Kind of what I thought you'd say."

"How do we get invited?"

"Already taken care of. We're both registered for his workshop."

"I won't understand any of it, JR."

"You don't need to."

***

Kruger opened the door to Kristin's room and checked to make sure she was asleep and properly covered. Being a restless sleeper, she sometimes kicked the covers off before falling asleep. He quietly entered the room and adjusted the sheet and blanket. As he stared down at the sleeping little girl, he felt a momentary pang of guilt at the amount of time his upcoming out-of-town trip would require.

Satisfied she was sleeping and comfortable, he exited, leaving her door slightly ajar. His next stop was Mikey's room. A complete opposite of his sister, he could sleep through a violent thunderstorm without moving a muscle. Kruger adjusted his blanket and went to his and Stephanie's bedroom.

She was already in bed with the covers pulled up to her chin. As he entered, she said softly, "Shut the door."

He smiled, closed their door and slipped under the sheets. She scooted over and placed her arm over his chest and her head on his shoulder. As he wrapped his arm around her, he felt bare skin.

She said, "How many more trips do you think you'll need to make?"

"A few. Why?"

"Just curious. While I'm not looking forward to your retirement, I am looking forward to not having you gone anymore."

He remained quiet as he rubbed her bare back and stared at the dark ceiling. "Steph?"

"Yes."

"Paul wants me to think about taking a promotion so I don't have to retire."

She stiffened but did not pull back.

"I told him no."

Raising her head, she looked at him. "Why not?"

"We'd have to move to DC and I refuse to do that."

She put her head back on his shoulder. "If it keeps you with the FBI, it might not be so bad."

"No, it would be horrible. I detest DC. Besides, it would disrupt *your* new career. While I'm sure there are good neighborhoods available, I don't want to raise the kids there."

Without responding, she slipped her hand under his T-shirt and caressed his chest.

He continued, "I'm not sure what I want to do yet, but the more I think about it, the more I know I don't want to move. This is our home. Brian and his family are here—the kids are happy in school and you're just getting started with your teaching career."

"I am." Her hand moved lower to his abdomen.

"Like I told Paul, it's time I thought of my family first and what I want to do second." He kissed her lips as she slipped her hand inside his boxer shorts.

CHAPTER 11

Hendrick University

"I see no need to meet with anybody from the FBI."

"It's not a request, Dorian. The President of the University is involved—it's more of a requirement for renewing your contract. He was hoping you would agree without resorting to threats."

"Maybe I don't want my contract renewed."

Harvey Copeland took a deep breath. Monk was an asset to the department, but sometimes his complete lack of cooperation with anything outside of the classroom was simply not worth it. "That would be up to you, but I'm told the FBI agent is with the Cyber Crime division and would like to consult with you about one of your recent papers."

"Will they pay for the consulting?"

"I doubt it. You can add it to your resume; consultant, Federal Bureau of Investigation."

"Hmmm…"

"Yes or no, Dorian?"

"Very well, I will meet with him. But I do it under

protest."

"Which is your prerogative."

"Where will we be meeting?"

"I've scheduled the faculty meeting room."

***

Dorian Monk, PhD walked into the room to find two individuals waiting for him. One was tall and in his late fifties, the other in his mid-forties, of average height and weight with thinning hair and wire rim glasses. Both wore casual slacks—the older a navy sport coat over a white oxford shirt, the younger man an untucked black polo shirt.

The older of the two offered his hand, which Monk ignored.

Instead he stared at each with a blank expression. "I'm Doctor Dorian Monk. Who am I addressing?"

With a sudden understanding of the type of personality they were dealing with, FBI Profiler Sean Kruger nodded toward his friend. "This is JR Diminski. He's with the FBI Cyber Crime Division and I'm Special Agent Sean Kruger."

Monk squinted and stared at JR. "Your name is familiar, have we met."

JR shook his head. "Can't say that we have."

"I don't forget names. We've met somewhere."

"Possibly. Do you attend Black Hat?"

"On occasion, when they ask me."

"It could have been there. I attend every year."

"Maybe." He folded his arms. "What area of Cyber Crime is your specialty, Agent Diminski?"

JR said with a sly smile, "Computer attacks and security."

Monk did not respond right away. Instead he tilted his head slightly. "Where did you go to school?"

"MIT."

"As did I. That's probably where I heard your name."

"Maybe that's it." JR smiled slightly. While at MIT, JR had been known by a different name.

As JR hid his surprise, Monk's attention turned to Kruger. "What are your qualifications for attending this conference, Agent Kruger?"

The older FBI agent's expression remained neutral as he hid his amusement at the mathematician's attempt to control the meeting. "Doctor Monk, I have a PhD in Clinical Psychology and twenty-five years of experience as a profiler with the bureau. JR and I are currently working on an investigation I can't discuss, but it involves computers and algorithms. That's why we're here, to learn as much as possible about the subject."

Monk looked at JR and then back at Kruger. With a slight nod, he said, "Very well. What did you want to discuss?"

JR smiled. Round one to Kruger.

The room contained a conference table with eight chairs. Kruger and JR sat across from the professor as Monk placed his backpack in front of him erecting a subconscious barrier between the two FBI agents and himself.

JR started the conversation. "Dr. Monk, I read your recent paper on Machine Learning Algorithms."

Monk nodded.

"Do you believe your model can be used to help a computer learn the strengths and weaknesses of any given security firewall?"

"That was the purpose of the paper, agent. Modern society has become too dependent on computers and the internet."

"I don't disagree. But, if your assumptions in the paper are correct, they would make most computer firewalls obsolete."

A glare was his first response. "They are *not* assumptions. They are mathematical expressions. But you are correct in your assessment of their importance."

"Aren't you letting the proverbial genie out of the bottle?"

"My dear FBI Agent, the genie was let out of the bottle in the late 1960s when the US Department of Defense developed packet switching to allow multiple computers to communicate on a single network."

JR tilted his head slightly. "Do you believe developing the internet was a mistake, Doctor Monk?"

"A mistake, yes. Was it inevitable? Yes. Someone somewhere would have developed it. Mankind is in a race to see who can design the last invention that will destroy us all."

Pausing, JR narrowed his eyes. "That's a little dark, don't you think, professor?"

Monk shrugged.

Kruger suddenly realized JR knew something about Monk's paper he had not revealed. He sat back and listened, understanding only parts of the discussion that followed.

After Monk left the meeting, JR remained quiet as he placed the small computer he took notes on into his backpack. Without saying a word or looking at Kruger, he exited the conference room and hurried toward the first door leading to the outside.

Kruger caught up with him twenty yards from the building. "Kind of quiet, aren't you?"

"Thinking."

Kruger nodded and followed.

When they reached the rental car, JR placed his backpack in the rear passenger seat and slid into the front one. Kruger got behind the wheel and started the car.

"Okay, what are you thinking about?"

JR turned to his friend. "Before I answer that, what was your impression?"

"He has an elevated opinion of himself."

"Yes. What else?"

"His opening salvos of verbal back and forth were meant to inform us of his importance. Without going into psychological details, he has a serious issue with authority and believes himself to be the smartest person in the room. What did you think?"

"He reminded me of one of the hackers I used to encounter in a dark web chatroom."

"How so?"

"Same ideas, same verbiage. In fact, some of it was verbatim."

"Which one?"

"There were several statements he made, but the main one was about an invention that would destroy man. I've heard that more than once."

Kruger kept his attention on JR and sat back in the driver's seat, the car's motor running, but still in Park.

JR nodded. "If he is, he's as good with a computer as he is with mathematics."

Without comment, Kruger placed the car in *reverse* and backed out of the parking slot. "You suspect something else, don't you?"

"Yeah."

"What?"

"I'm still sorting it out, but when I was at MIT, I was known by my birth name, John Zachara. I didn't change it until I moved to Springfield." He paused and turned his attention to his friend. "How would he have heard it at MIT?"

Kruger shot a quick glance at his passenger. "Spit it out, JR. What do you suspect?"

"If I'm right, we have a larger problem than we first suspected."

Rolling his eyes, Kruger said, "Just say it."

With a slight smile, he turned to his friend. "Who instigated the DDS attack on my computer system?"

"The Russians…" He stopped and quickly glanced at JR. "You think…"

"I'm speculating, but what if Monk is the hacker I think he is? That means he was present during the discussions about the concepts of the virus code I wrote." He paused. "I need to talk to Alexia and see if she remembers this guy."

**

JR called Alexia from his hotel room. "Any updates on the virus?"

"There haven't been any additional instances, if that is what you are asking."

"Good. There's another reason for my call. Do you remember a hacker who went by the name Chronos?"

"Yes, I always found the name pretentious."

"Why?"

"Taking an alias that is the god of time and the father of Zeus is silly."

"I think I met him today."

There was silence on the call for a few moments. "Where?"

"Hendrick College. A math professor named Dorian Monk. Ever hear of him?"

"No, but then I have tried to forget those years I spent in isolation. What makes you think this is the same person?"

"Sean and I had an interview with him today. He wrote an obscure paper about machine learning algorithms two years ago."

"I have not read it."

"I hadn't either until I read it on the plane coming here. I only understood a quarter of it. The rest was very esoteric, but it did propose that algorithms could be used to help AI learn to penetrate any firewall."

Alexia was quiet. Finally, she said, "You didn't answer my question on why you think this Monk person is

Chronos."

"Two things. First, he said he knew my name. Second, he made the following statement, and I quote, 'Mankind is in a race to see who can design the last invention that will destroy us all.'"

"That sounds familiar. But then, I may not have had that much communication with him. Why would he say he knew your name?"

"That's where I started to question who he was. He indicated he might have heard my name while at MIT."

"You attended MIT under your birth name."

"Exactly, I didn't change my name to JR Diminski until later."

"What do you need me to do?"

"Use your old alias and see if Chronos is still haunting the Dark Web. My guess he is. See what you can learn and we'll talk about it when I get back."

"Is this person involved with the death of Sean's friend Alan?"

"Don't know, but Sean is pointing a finger at him."

"I will see what I can find out."

***

JR knocked on Kruger's hotel room door. When it opened, he saw Kruger with a cell phone pressed to his ear. The FBI agent silently motioned him inside.

There was silence in the room until Kruger said, "Thanks, Barbara. I know you tried. There just isn't a lot about this guy out there."

More silence.

"No, move on to other projects. What you gave me will help. Thanks." Kruger ended the call and looked at his friend. "Our Professor Monk doesn't seem to have a financial presence in the real world outside of a bank account and his IRS filings. She found an account used by the college to pay him, but he only uses it to collect his pay and then transfers it out. He files his taxes with the 1040EZ form and always by e-file. He doesn't own a house, a car or any sizeable asset she can find."

JR nodded. "Makes sense. He probably has an alias he's using."

"Is there a way for you to find it?"

"Not without some hint as to the direction. I can try the bank account, but my bet is he is taking cash out and depositing it in another account using a different name. That's how I'd do it."

Kruger nodded. "And since the deposit wouldn't be over ten thousand dollars, the bank doesn't have to file form 8300 with the IRS. Think we spooked him today?"

"Can't say. With his big ego I kind of doubt it."

"I agree. What did you find out?"

"Alexia remembers him. If Monk is the guy I think he is, he went by the alias of Chronos. She's going to see if he is still active in some of the chat rooms we used to hang out in."

"I need to know where this guy lives and have a look around inside."

"Got any ideas? The college only has a PO Box as an address."

"The only way I know is to follow him home."

"Need me to stay a day longer?"

"No, attend the seminar like you planned and fly out late tomorrow. Jimmie's flying in to help me keep an eye on him."

JR nodded.

CHAPTER 12

Hendrick University
The Next Day

Kruger stood and offered his hand when the department head approached his table at a small cafe near campus. As Copeland shook it, he said, "I appreciate meeting off campus grounds, Agent Kruger. I didn't expect to see you again now that the seminar is over."

"To be honest with you, neither did I."

After the two men gave their lunch order to a waitress, Copeland looked at Kruger over his glasses. "Does this have anything to do with your interview with Dorian Monk?"

"It has everything to do with his interview."

"When I got your call, that was my first thought. I hope he's not a suspect in something."

Keeping his expression neutral, Kruger clasped his hands on the table in front of him. "Not at the moment."

Placing a hand on his forehead, Copeland took a long

breath and sighed. "Oh, dear, what does *not at the moment* mean?"

"It means not at the moment. Do you have concerns, Dr. Copeland?"

The department head paused as the waitress placed their iced teas in front of them. When she was gone, he said, "Everyone in the department has concerns about Dorian Monk, including the administration."

The comment was not what Kruger expected. "How so?"

"We keep Monk as an adjunct professor for one reason. His classes are always full with a long waiting list. Not because the students like him, actually, it's quite the opposite. But because he is a brilliant mathematician. It also doesn't hurt that many of his academic publications are considered required reading in certain mathematical circles. His presence on campus has been amazing for recruiting top students."

"He hasn't been here that long, Doctor Copeland. How can he be helping with recruiting?"

"Word gets around fast in the world of mathematics."

"I see."

"But I must tell you, outside the classroom, he is a serious pain in my behind."

"Care to elaborate?"

"He's been accused of harassing students and minorities off campus, writing editorials to the Cincinnati Enquirer critical of just about everything in the world, which thank God they don't publish. Plus, on numerous occasions, has told the president of the university to go to hell or some other vulgar suggestion."

"Other than the harassment charges, none of those activities would draw my interest, Doctor."

"What has?"

"Before I answer that question, answer one for me. When did you hire Monk?"

Copeland looked at the ceiling and let out a breath. "Oh, let's see. About this time two years ago."

"From where?"

"San Jose State University."

Kruger nodded. "Why did he leave?"

"His contract was up with them and he wanted a change of scenery. Or, at least that's what he told me."

"Did you talk to anyone at San Jose State about him?"

With a nod, Copeland took a drink from his glass of tea. "I spoke to the department head."

"And?"

"She told me Monk was always on time to class, his classes always had a waiting list and…"

With a smile Kruger sipped his iced tea. "I take it you just figured something out, Dr. Copeland?"

"I just realized she was describing the same situation we have here. If I am ever asked about him from another school, I would have to give the same answer."

"Uh-huh."

"Oh dear. Can you answer my question yet?"

With a slight smile, Kruger said, "From what we have been able to piece together, he stays about a year or two in an area, sometimes at the same college or university, sometimes more than one. It depends on the needs of the schools. He's never been offered a track for tenure and seems to migrate from place to place. He doesn't seem to have a problem when it comes to getting a new contract somewhere else."

"We knew that."

"He also has zero presence in the digital world, Doctor."

"I'm not following you."

"He doesn't keep a bank account—"

"He has to—the college only pays with direct deposit."

"He only uses it to collect the money and then withdraws it immediately. He does not use it for transactions."

"Oh…"

"He doesn't own any significant assets that the FBI can find and since we don't know where he lives, we can't interview his landlord."

"The university should have his address on file."

"He uses a PO Box."

"Oh, dear." Copeland paused for a few moments. "Agent, you still have not answered my question about why the FBI is interested in Monk."

"Where was he four weeks ago?"

He paused. "What date?"

Kruger told him.

Copeland closed his eyes. "He told us he had a death in the family and left campus. Why?"

"Dorian Monk has no family. Do you remember reading about the murder of the Deputy Director of the FBI, Alan Seltzer?"

"Vaguely, why?"

Pausing for a second to keep his emotions in check, Kruger continued, "Those were the dates Alan was stalked and murdered. I'm the lead agent on the investigation."

"Surely, you don't suspect Dorian Monk."

"He's currently a person of interest."

"Oh, dear." Copeland stared at Kruger without blinking for almost fifteen seconds. "I know Dorian is a pain in the ass, but—murder?"

"Like I said, Doctor, he's a person of interest."

"Surely the timing of the Deputy Director's death has to be a coincidence, agent."

Kruger shrugged. "Maybe, but I have learned over the course of my twenty-five-year career with the bureau, there are no coincidences, only connections. There's more."

Copeland only blinked.

"Alan Seltzer discovered a total of twenty-one unsolved murders in twenty-one different locations. Each of those twenty-one murders occurred within fifty miles of a school

Dorian Monk taught at. He's been in four geographical locations during that length of time and each locale, except one, has five murders."

Copeland only blinked.

"All of the victims were highly educated and professional individuals of varying ethnicities."

"That's not proof that Monk did it, agent."

"No, I would have to agree, but there is one other fact that joins the cases together."

"What?"

"They all occurred during the normal times a university or college is on semester break. We checked and the timing matches the semester breaks for each of the colleges Monk taught at."

"Still…"

"Connections, Doctor Copeland. Now all I have to do is prove it."

Blinking rapidly, Dr. Copeland stared at Kruger. Both men drew silent as the waitress placed their lunch orders in front of them. When she left, Kruger said, "Is Monk still on campus today?"

Nodding, Copeland glanced at his watch. "Yes, he has his last session at one today. He will probably be on campus until at least three. Why?"

"Thought I might pay him a visit off campus. Do you know where he lives?"

Copeland shook his head. "I try not to socialize with Dr. Monk."

"Wise."

They continued their conversation until both finished their lunch. During this time, Kruger learned Monk was always seen walking on campus, no bicycle. The one additional fact he learned was that Monk always walked off campus to the south. As he emptied his glass of tea, he decided his next task would be to follow Monk to his place of residence.

***

Dorian Monk left Barrington Hall and took his normal path crossing the main east-west thoroughfare at a pedestrian crossing on the southern border of the college. Parked on a side street in his rental car, Kruger watched and followed the man's progress as he continued south along the street.

Ten blocks from campus, Monk stood under a sheltered bus stop and ignored a woman already there. Kruger watched the mathematician concentrating on a pad of paper, making notes occasionally. Five minutes later, a bus arrived and Monk stepped on board, butting in front of the woman. Putting the car in gear, Kruger followed.

Forty minutes later at a bus stop in a seedy section of Covington, Monk departed the bus and entered a run-down apartment building. Noting the address and time, Kruger smiled and drove the rental car back to his hotel.

Once in his room, he took his cell phone and dialed a number from memory. The call was answered immediately.

"What'd you find out?"

"How hard would it be for you to trace the ownership and tenant list of an apartment building if I just gave you the address?"

"Where's the apartment building?"

"Covington, Kentucky."

"Don't know. Hour, maybe. Maybe less. Why?"

"Our Professor Monk is a mysterious individual. He won't give the college his physical address and since he's part-time, they don't care."

"Huh."

"That was my reaction, as well."

"Give me the address. I'll have to hack into the Kenton County building permits to get started."

"How did you know what county it's in?"

"I can do more than one thing at a time, Sean. Google is a wonderful tool."

Chuckling, Kruger said, "I'm going to meet with Jimmie. Call me back if you find anything."

"Got it."

The call ended and Kruger dialed another number.

"Hi."

Hearing Stephanie's voice on the phone always made Kruger smile. "Hi, back."

"When are you coming home?"

"Tomorrow."

"Early or late?"

"Late."

"Do you want me to save you some dinner?"

"Don't worry with it. I'll get something during my layover in Memphis."

"You sure?"

"Yes." He hesitated. "Are you still okay with taking a trip to South Dakota after I retire?"

"Of course, I am. If I remember correctly, it was my idea."

He smiled and took a deep breath. "Good, I'm already starting to look forward to it."

"Good. You should. Call me tomorrow."

***

The Next Morning

"Sean, I didn't find anyone at the apartment under the name Monk."

"Not surprised. Jimmie's here. We—uh, actually, he will be doing the research this morning."

"Remember the name I mentioned he used on the internet?"

"No."

"Chronos."

"Just one name?"

"Yes."

"Okay, I'll tell Jimmie."

Standing in Kruger's hotel room, Gibbs watched as his boss ended the call. Displaying his perpetual smile, he asked, "Research?"

"Yeah, gotta be careful what you say on a cell phone."

A chuckle was his response.

"JR thinks he might know the name Monk is using at the apartment."

"Good, what is it?"

"Chronos."

Gibbs nodded.

Two hours later with the sun a third of the way up a cloudless sky, the day promised to be warm. Kruger and Gibbs sat in the rental car three blocks from the apartment building Monk had entered the previous afternoon. Jimmie said, "Any idea when he leaves?"

"The seminar was over yesterday. Copeland thinks he'll be on campus until around one today. After that he's done for the semester."

"Once he's on the bus, I'll do my research."

Kruger said, "I'll follow the bus and make sure you're not disturbed."

"Got it."

They waited ten more minutes before Kruger pointed at a lanky figure exiting the apartment complex. "That's him."

Gibbs looked through Nikon Trailblazer ATB compact binoculars. "Huh—why do the weird ones always look so ordinary?"

With a smile, Kruger shook his head. "Welcome to my world."

Lowering the binoculars, Gibbs watched the man get on the bus. As it pulled away from the curb, the retired Seal opened the car door and slipped out. He bent over before shutting the door. "Let me know if he turns around."

"You got it."

***

Gibbs secured his wireless earbud in his left ear and shuffled over to the apartment complex. He found a bulletin board just inside the building's entrance which announced several vacant apartments. It gave directions to the manager's office, which he followed. Office hours were posted on the door indicating the manager would be there from nine in the morning till noon. He checked his watch and noticed it was two minutes after nine and knocked.

The door opened and an elderly heavyset woman opened the door. Her disheveled gray hair fell haphazardly over a wrinkled forehead. She stared at him with dull gray eyes behind blocky black rimmed glasses.

"Yes?"

"I saw you have several apartments for rent."

"Only have one, it has two bedrooms."

"Can I see it?"

She glared at him for several moments and nodded. "I'll show you where it is. If you're interested, get back to me."

She left the front door open and led him to a table in the middle of the front room. On the table resided an architectural blueprint of the apartment complex. Multi-colored Post It Notes identified the occupant of each unit. As she pointed to a corner apartment on the diagram, Gibbs quickly scanned the names. One was of interest and he made a note of the apartment's location. He returned his attention to the older woman. "Looks interesting. Mind if I look around first?"

"Sure, just don't bother the other residents."

"Wouldn't dream of it."

After exiting the manager's office, he made his way toward the apartment and listened as he passed other doors. He heard TVs, conversations, yelling, crying babies and a variety of other sounds.

When he arrived at the apartment of interest, he knocked gently. He heard only silence from the interior. This was the apartment belonging to T. Chronos, according to the Post-It-Note on the landlord's architectural drawing.

He extracted a slim flat wire from his billfold and held it like a key. He quickly scanned the door frame and did not find anything that would tell the occupant the door had been opened during his absence. It only took ten seconds for Jimmie to conquer the cheap door lock and slip into Dorian Monk's home.

CHAPTER 13

Covington, KY

The room smelled of Pine-Sol and chlorine. He stood perfectly still, listening. The only sounds he heard came from adjacent apartments. The one where he stood remained silent.

Once his eyes adjusted to the gloom, he noticed the furnishings appeared old and threadbare. A sagging sofa with a chipped pressed-board coffee table dominated the space. An old floor lamp from the seventies stood next to the sofa, offering the only option for light in the depressing area.

Boxes were neatly stacked near the door. Gibbs slipped on latex gloves retrieved from his jeans pocket and opened the top box. Books. He extracted one and looked at the first page. With a smile, he read the neatly written hand note. *Property of DR. DORIAN MONK.*

Satisfied, he ventured further into the apartment. Three rooms occupied the space within. The living area, which joined a small kitchen separated by a breakfast bar made up the front space. Gibbs checked the cabinets and only found a few plates, cups and glasses. The refrigerator contained even less—a head of lettuce, a bottle of ranch dressing, orange juice, a carton of eggs and a few tomatoes.

In the freezer compartment, boxes of Lean Cuisine entrées were neatly stacked within the space. Gibbs shook his head at the austere life of the apartment's tenant. Toward the back of the apartment, he found one bedroom with a small bath next to it. The chlorine smell detected earlier emanated from this area. As he stood at the entrance to the bedroom, his eyes searched for anything of interest. The only furnishings were a neatly made twin-size bed and a nightstand with a small digital clock and a lamp on the top. More boxes were stacked against one wall.

He approached a door he assumed was a closet. Within the space he found five shirts hung exactly one inch apart. Five pairs of jeans, also separated by the same amount of space, were next. He took a picture with his cell phone. At the bottom of the closet he found two rolling suitcases which were heavier than they should be. With a slight grin, he took both out of the closet.

The smaller one contained files and bank statements. He checked the files and only found pages of mathematical formulas. He photographed several of the bank statements and then took pictures of the contents of several files. Once everything was repacked, he opened the larger case.

Inside were men's undergarments, socks, and a folded Carhart jacket. Gibbs took pictures of these as well. At the bottom, under the folded jacket, he found a bank bag. He unzipped it and stared at the contents. Cash—lots of cash. There were five bundles of one-hundred-dollar bills, plus loose currency. These Gibbs spread out on the floor and photographed. He counted the unbundled bills and determined there was two-thousand dollars in a variety of denominations. Replacing everything exactly where he found them, he closed the closet door and looked under the bed.

What he saw made him dial Kruger's number.

"What's wrong, Jimmie?"

"I've got a Glock 17 with a suppressor, a Glock 30, a Remington 700 with a scope and a Savage MSR15. Lots of ammo for all of them."

"This is the guy, Jimmie. What else did you find?"

"Bank records, files and a lot of cash."

"Take pictures and get out of there. I'll head back and pick you up."

"See you in a few."

***

"How much cash?"

Gibbs stared out the front window of the rental car as they drove back toward campus. "Right at fifty-two thousand. Sean, the guy's apartment looked like he could bolt in five minutes. There isn't much there."

"Yeah, but he doesn't know we know it. Okay, with the information you photographed, we'll see if JR can trace him better. Did you see any other IDs?"

Shaking his head, Gibbs said, "No, and I was looking."

Kruger nodded. "Okay, now we have to figure out a legal way of getting into his apartment."

"Got any ideas?"

"Not at the moment, but I'm working on it."

***

From the backseat of the bus, Dorian Monk observed the white Chevy Malibu slow and turn into a parking lot. It reversed its course and headed in the opposite direction. His concern increased as the car disappeared into the morning traffic. The older FBI agent he interviewed with drove the car. He suddenly realized why the car would back track. He stood and waited for the bus to arrive at the next stop.

As he stepped off, he removed a small prepaid cell phone from his leather satchel and dialed a local taxi service.

Thirty minutes later, he opened the door to his apartment and turned on the lights. He was surprised to see the apartment exactly the same as when he had left earlier in the morning. He hurried to his bed and peered underneath. Nothing appeared missing. Taking a deep breath, he opened the closet and took inventory. Everything was there and looked undisturbed. He started to relax until he noticed the suitcases were not properly placed. Their current location did not match the indentations left in the carpet.

He stood and closed his eyes. Taking several deeper breaths, he tried to calm himself. He'd always known this moment would come, but he was not ready to give up just yet. He opened the suitcase with the cash and extracted one of the small bundles.

The taxi driver, an overweight middle-aged woman, remained outside the apartment building nervously waiting for him to return. When he did, he asked her to take him to an address in Cincinnati just over the river.

By noon, Monk was loading his boxes, gun cases and suitcases into the back of a 2008 Chevy Equinox purchased for five thousand dollars in cash. With the vehicle packed, he made one last trip through the apartment. Satisfied all of his important possessions were out of the apartment, he left his key on the coffee table and returned to the SUV. Once out of the parking lot, he drove west.

***

Kruger paced the hotel room, his cell phone held in his hand on speaker. Gibbs sat quietly near the writing desk and listened.

"I understand that, Don. There has to be a way to get a search warrant for this guy's apartment."

"Not with the evidence you've told me so far, Sean." Don Meacham, a bureau attorney who Kruger knew personally, did not comment further.

"What if Jimmie and I are knocking on his door and we both smell smoke?"

"Iffy at best. The problem with a scenario like that is a good defense attorney will shoot a hole through it because there is no fire. Now, if there truly was a fire, any evidence gathered would be admissible."

"You're not making this easy, Don."

A chuckle sounded through the speaker. "It never is with you, Sean."

"Okay, what if—"

When his cell phone beeped, Kruger glanced at the screen and said, "I've got to go, I'll call you back, Don."

"Okay, in the meantime, I'll look for legal precedents."

Kruger touched a button. "This is Kruger."

"Agent, this is Harvey Copeland. I was just informed that Professor Monk did not show up today.'"

"What do you mean, didn't show up?"

"I just left his office and it appears he has not been there. It's past one and he hasn't turned in his class summaries for the next semester."

With a frown, Kruger glanced at Jimmie who was now standing next to the desk, his brow furrowed.

"So, no one's seen him today?"

"Not that I can find."

"Has he ever done this before, just not show up?"

"Never."

"Okay, thank you Dr. Copeland, we'll check on him."

The call ended. Kruger smiled and looked at Jimmie. "That's our ticket. Wellness check."

Gibbs smiled as the two men left the hotel room.

***

Jimmie Gibbs knocked on the apartment door for the third time. "Dr. Monk, FBI. Can we talk to you?"

Silence was their only response.

Gibbs put a latex glove on his right hand and tried the doorknob. It turned. With raised eyebrows, he glanced at Kruger, who nodded, his service Glock in both hands and pointed at the ground.

Withdrawing his Sig Sauer P226 with his left hand, Jimmie carefully opened the door. "Dr. Monk, we're coming in."

Both men rushed in and covered both sides of the room. It was empty except for the furniture.

"Shit." Jimmie hurried to the bedroom followed by Kruger. Each man stood on either side of the opening, guns still in hand, pointing up. Jimmie stole a quick glance into the room and holstered his Sig Sauer. "He's gone, Sean."

Kruger glanced into the room and saw the closet door open with nothing inside. He too, holstered his gun.

Jimmie bent down and glanced under the bed. "Nothing there either."

Taking out his cell phone, Kruger rapidly punched in a number. When it was answered, he said. "Paul, I need a forensic team ASAP."

He listened.

"Covington, Kentucky." Kruger gave him the address.

A pause.

"Yeah, on the other side of the river south of Cincinnati."

More listening.

"We found him, Paul. We know who killed Alan."

CHAPTER 14

Springfield, MO

Kruger leaned against the credenza behind JR's cubicle and sipped coffee.

The computer hacker stood next to him, pouring a cup for himself. "So, what did the forensic team find?"

"Not much. Jimmie told me he smelled chlorine when he first entered the apartment. Apparently, Monk maintained a ritual of wiping the surfaces around the apartment to rid it of fingerprints."

"Did they find any?"

Nodding, Kruger took another sip. "A few. We have an index finger from his left hand and three fingers on the right. They've run them through the database." He paused and sipped coffee. "He's never been fingerprinted."

"What about DNA?"

"Lots of it."

"What else did they find?"

"They found trace elements of gunpowder and gun lubricants in the carpet under the bed. We have proof he stored guns there. Other than the DNA, fingerprints and the residue, they didn't find much else."

JR nodded as he tasted his coffee. "Any idea where he went?"

"None. We do, however, have a few names I want you to research."

Raising an eyebrow, JR looked over his rimless glasses.

"Jimmie's found evidence, during his first excursion into Monk's apartment, that he uses a couple of aliases in the financial world. He rented the apartment under the name Timothy Chronos. My bet is he has an ID with that name. We also think he uses the name Dorian Marshall."

"You think, you're not sure?"

"It's the name he used to open the bank account where his paychecks from Hendrick College were deposited."

"How'd that work?"

Kruger shrugged. "We're not sure. Jimmie is still at Hendrick looking into it. Lots of questions. Unfortunately, everyone in administration seems to have contracted a severe case of amnesia concerning Dorian Monk. Even Doctor Copeland."

JR scratched his chin. "So, the bank was able to give you the social security number he opened the checking account with?"

With a nod, Kruger pulled a folded piece of paper from the inside pocket of his sport coat. "Before I left yesterday, Jimmie and I stopped and met with them. This is a printout from the bank. You'll find the social and a history of the account after I—uh—asked them nicely."

"I'm sure you were very diplomatic when you requested this information."

After another sip of coffee, Kruger shook his head. "No, I wasn't. They were too busy covering their ass and I got tired of it. Something about a bank audit came up. They got very cooperative after that part of the conversation."

With a chuckle, JR took the page and looked at it. "Only

deposits and a withdrawal after each deposit." He looked up. "That's it?"

His answer was a nod.

"Huh."

"I've got other agents at all the colleges and universities Monk's taught at over the years. They're checking to see if he was paid with direct deposits or checks."

JR said, "Direct deposit's been common since the eighties, Sean."

"We're hoping we'll get lucky and find more names he's used." He paused for a moment. "What I can't figure out is how he moved so fast. We got back to his apartment by 1:30 and he had already packed everything and left. What did he use for transportation?"

Staring off at a spot only he could see, JR sipped his coffee. After almost half a minute, he said, "Are there any truck rental places close to his apartment?"

"No, we thought of that and couldn't find any."

"Have you checked taxi services? Uber and Lyft?"

Kruger nodded. "No one by the name Dorian Monk was picked up."

JR tilted his head. "Sean, think about what you just said."

Kruger's eyes widened. "Shit…"

"Uber and Lyft only take credit cards. Monk doesn't have a credit card in his real name. Taxis still take cash."

Pointing at JR's computer, Kruger asked, "Can you find out what taxi services operate in Covington?"

JR's fingers danced on the keyboard. "There are several, most service Cincinnati and the airport."

"Email the list to Jimmie." As he punched in a number on his cell phone, the FBI agent looked at JR again. "Taxi companies will have a record of the destination of who they pick up, regardless of how the fare is paid."

"They should."

When the call was answered, Kruger said, "Jimmie, JR

is emailing you a list of taxi services in and around Covington. There's a chance Monk used one to get back to the apartment."

Kruger was silent for a few moments. "Yeah, I know, it's a long shot."

More silence.

"Are you still at the college?" A pause. "Good, prevail on Dr. Copeland for a copy of Monk's faculty ID picture. Maybe we can figure out how he got his stuff out of the apartment so fast."

The call ended and Kruger looked at JR. "Think back on when you deleted all of your public records and disappeared from the radar. How would Monk do it now?"

"You said he has cash."

"At least fifty thousand dollars."

"That's not really a lot, but it's a start." He paused. "Did Jimmie find a computer in the apartment?"

"No. If he has one, he had it with him."

"I think we have to assume he does."

Kruger nodded.

"My guess is he bought a car with cash somewhere. If he did, the car lot probably provided him temporary registration. If you can find the lot, they'll be able to give you details about the vehicle." He paused and sipped his now-cold coffee. "The problem is, he's had a couple of day's head start and could be anywhere by now."

"I know."

"It's a big country, Sean."

"Tell me about it. I've flown over it way too many times."

"Once you get past the Mississippi River, there's plenty of isolated locations between there and the west coast. He could disappear with ease."

"That's what I'm afraid of. What if this guy digs in and hides for a while?" He paused for a heartbeat. "I'm running out of time."

***

Jimmie Gibbs showed the picture to Bobby Ray Clayton, the owner of Your EZ Ride car lot in Southern Cincinnati.

The man stared at the picture through smudged glasses. "Yeah, that's him. Sold him a white 2008 Chevy Equinox with 98,000 miles on it. Sweet SUV, the best one I had on the lot."

Gibbs smiled. "I'm sure it was. How did he pay for it?"

"Cash."

"How much?"

"I'm embarrassed about this, but he got me down to five thousand."

"Why are you embarrassed?"

"I should have gotten at least six for it."

"Why?"

"Low miles, clean and it even had newer tires on it. But he was waving the money in my face. That happens on slow days. I sell vehicles too cheap."

"I see. Can I see the paperwork on it?"

"What's he done? Am I in trouble, Agent?"

"He's just someone we need to talk to and, no, you're not in trouble." Gibbs paused and grinned. "Unless the car was stolen or you rolled the mileage back?"

Clayton raised his hands, palms toward Jimmie and shook his head. "No, no, no, no, I'm a legit dealer."

"Can I see the paperwork?"

Nodding rapidly, the man turned and shuffled to a filing cabinet in his office. As he flipped through the filing cabinet he said, "My wife and I run this lot, Agent Gibbs. I buy my cars from an auction house and we offer a loan assistance program to people who have challenged credit histories." He stopped and turned toward Gibbs. "The guy paid cash—he didn't look like a criminal."

"I understand, Mr. Clayton. We just want to ask him a few questions. Don't worry—this won't come back on you."

"I hope not. We try to run a clean lot here."

"I'm sure you do."

"Ah, here it is." He pulled a file out of the cabinet and handed it to Gibbs. "My wife still likes to do the paperwork the old fashion way."

"How's that?"

"By hand."

Jimmie nodded as he flipped through the file. The third page produced one of the items he needed. A photocopy of a driver's license. The next item he needed appeared right after the page with the photo—the registration paperwork. He extracted the pages. "Can you make a copy of these for me?"

***

Back in his rental car, Jimmie did a Google search on his phone. What came back brought a knowing smile to his face. He scrolled to a number on his contact list and hit send. The call was answered immediately.

"Kruger."

"It's Jimmie."

"What'd you find?"

"He has an Ohio DL under the name Timothy Chronos. I looked at the address on Google Maps."

"And?"

"Empty lot."

"Okay, wrap up what you are doing and give a copy of everything to the Cincinnati Field Office. I need you back here."

"Got it. See you tomorrow."

PART TWO

THE SEARCH

San Francisco, CA
One Month Later

By October 1, 1949, when Mao Zedong declared the creation of the People's Republic of China, two refugees were already on a ship bound for their new country, the United States. Because China had been an important ally during World War II, Chinese immigrants were afforded benefits denied to other Pacific Rim inhabitants. Due to this and after more than sixty years of discrimination, President Franklin Roosevelt signed legislation repealing the Chinese Exclusion Act on December 17, 1943. This allowed the once predominantly bachelor society of Chinatown to become more assimilated and attract families with children.

Into this newfound freedom, Deng Wu and his wife Li emerged as prominent members of the Chinatown political elite. Their son, Chiang—named after the famous Chinese general Chiang Kia Shek—grew up and attended the California Institute of Technology. There he graduated with a doctorate in the up-and-coming field of computer electronics. He married a girl from his old Chinatown neighborhood and on the 4th of July, 1965, gave birth to a son, David.

Fifty-five years later, David Wu was rich in his own right after establishing several high-tech companies in the Silicon Valley region. He was also the college roommate and lifelong friend of the current President of the United States, Roy Griffin.

To say they were close would be an understatement. Their relationship was more like two brothers. Both led busy lives, which prevented getting together very often. But when they did, it was like the passing of time did not exist.

David's relationship with the president was not only personal—he was also his most fervent supporter and campaign contribution organizer. That is why when David Wu asked to see the president, he was granted immediate access.

The meeting took place in Griffin's San Mateo, California home during a week of R&R for the president.

Slender and tall, Wu wore his black hair in a ponytail which displayed evenly dispersed streaks of gray. He spoke English with a non-descript American accent, Cantonese like a native and was becoming fluent in Mandarin. The two friends embraced briefly, causing Griffin's Secret Service guards to hold their breath even though they knew Wu was not a security risk.

"How've you been, David?" Griffin smiled as he looked at his friend.

"Like yourself, busy." Wu lowered his voice. "I need to talk to you in private, Roy."

Griffin frowned. "This must be serious."

"It's a personal matter. One I don't want your

bodyguards to know about."

With a chuckle, Roy nodded and pointed to his library. He then turned to the lead agent of his protection detail. "Bob, David and I need a little privacy. We're going to the library. Please position someone outside the window so you can feel like you're doing your job."

Bob Wray gave the president a grin and nodded. He pointed to Judy Poindexter. "Please make sure the president doesn't escape out of the library window."

She smiled and headed for the front door.

Once the door to the library was closed, Wu sat in one of the room's leather wingback chairs. Griffin sat across from him and made a steeple with his hands. "What's this about, David?"

With a sigh, Wu studied the carpet for a few moments before returning his attention to the president. "It's about my sister."

Griffin said. "Have they still not found a suspect?"

"No." He paused. "I don't think they're trying anymore, nor do they seem to care."

President Roy Griffin took a deep breath and debated telling his friend what he knew. Friendship won out. "David, I can assure you, the FBI still cares."

Wu flashed the temper Griffin remembered from their college days. Through narrowed eyes, Wu said, "Do not give me a politically correct speech. We've known each other too long and been through too much for you to lie to me."

"I'm not lying."

Crossing his arms, Wu looked defiant. "Want to try again?"

"Your sister was not the only one."

Blinking rapidly, Wu uncrossed his arms and leaned forward. "What do you mean, not the only one?"

"Just what I told you. I am sure you heard about the death of FBI Deputy Director, Alan Seltzer over a month ago."

"Yes."

"His death led to the discovery of a series of seemingly unrelated unsolved murders across the United States."

Wu remained quiet.

"One of the FBI's top profilers started looking into them. His efforts were successful in identifying a person-of-interest in your sister's murder. However, the agent uses a different term for this person."

"What is it?"

"He calls him a serial killer."

His eyes widened. "Holea was murdered by a serial killer?"

"Yes. Along with twenty other individuals of varying ethnic backgrounds across the country."

A tear rolled down Wu's cheek.

"I'm sorry, David. It wasn't random like you were told. All of the murders appear to have been committed by one person. The FBI believes this individual chose his victims carefully and stalked them before—well, you know."

Silence filled the room as the two men stared at each other. Finally, Wu said, "Is there anything I can do to help?"

Griffin started to shake his head but stopped. He blinked several times and then a smile came to his face. "The agent I just mentioned is a trusted friend of Cheryl's and mine. Remember the two agents who saved our lives from the sniper after my mother-in-law's funeral?"

A nod was his answer.

"One of them is the man who made the connection. He has spent the last twenty-five years successfully identifying and chasing down serial killers all across this country. Unfortunately, he is also very close to the mandatory retirement age for an FBI agent. There's not much I can do about the regulation, but there may be a way around it."

"What's that?"

"How serious are you about helping?"

"I would spend every cent I have to find this person."

"I don't think we need that much, but I just thought of something you can do."

"I'm listening."

"I have the authority to form any organization or commission I want by executive order. What I can't do without Congressional approval is fund that organization. In today's political climate I could probably get it done in a year or so, but that's not going to help us right now."

Wu smiled. "What if this organization was privately funded?"

"That's what I was thinking."

"Tell me more."

***

Paul Stumpf listened to President Roy Griffin outline his proposal. As he listened, a grin appeared. "I think it has merit, Mr. President."

"Would Sean do it?"

"I can't answer that without asking him first. But I do know he's getting nervous. Dorian Monk has disappeared off the face of the earth and Sean is two weeks away from his birthday and retirement. He's not someone you want to be around right now."

"My plan would only be temporary. The commission would only last until Monk is found and arrested."

Stumpf nodded. "Is your friend aware of the costs involved?"

Griffin smiled. "David is a very wealthy man. He could fund this project for a year with pocket change."

"If he accepts, Sean will want to keep his team together."

"I explained that to David Wu. He wants this to work; he told me to give Sean carte-blanche authority to hire anyone he feels is needed. The bottom line is he wants the murderer of his sister and the others brought to justice. He doesn't care about the costs."

"Then I'd better talk to Sean."

***

Despite the fact the Agency sent a Gulfstream G280 for his flight to Washington, DC for a brief meeting with Paul Stumpf, Sean Kruger fumed. A state he found himself in more and more as his birthday loomed.

He turned to the young agent who drove the vehicle that picked him up at the airport and said, "Do you have any idea what this is about, Tom?"

Thomas Shark was taller than Kruger's six feet by three inches. He was still high school skinny, with an angular face and closely cropped brown hair. They had worked several cases together over the course of Kruger's career and he held a lot of respect for the younger agent.

"No, sir. All I was told was that Director Stumpf personally asked for me to meet you at the airport." He glanced at the senior agent and smiled. "I was more than happy to do it."

The tension in Kruger's voice eased. "I'm glad you could. Where are you assigned right now?"

"Here in DC, I'm—uh—in training."

Kruger raised an eyebrow. "Care to be more specific?"

With a slight grin Shark said, "I'll be taking over the Denver Field Office as Special Agent in Charge as soon as the current SAC retires. They want me here until he leaves."

"Congratulations, Tom. That's the best news I've heard in a long time. You deserve it."

"I learned through the grapevine it was due to a recommendation you gave to Alan Seltzer six months ago."

Silence fell over the two occupants as Kruger looked out

the passenger window. Finally, he nodded. "I remember the conversation. It was one of the last times I spoke to Alan."

"I'm sorry, Sean."

"Me, too." He paused. "Alan was a good man. He didn't deserve what happened."

Shark didn't respond.

Kruger continued, "I doubt what I told him resulted in your promotion. Your performance and abilities are the reason."

"I learned a lot during the times we worked together. I always appreciated your input."

"Glad to do it." He returned his gaze to the window and watched Washington, DC pass by. His excitement about the younger agent's promotion moderated by the realization his own career would soon be over.

***

When Kruger entered the conference room next to Paul Stumpf's office, he found the president's National Security Advisor, Joseph Kincaid, already sitting and waiting. He stood as Kruger entered and smiled when they shook hands.

Kruger asked, "What are you doing here, Joseph?"

"I bring a message from the president."

Rolling his eyes, Kruger frowned. "This isn't some command appearance about my upcoming retirement is it?"

His response was a slow shake of the head.

The door to Stumpf's office opened and the Director of the FBI entered, smiled and offered his hand to Kruger. "Glad you could make it, Sean."

Tired of the theatrics and wasted time, Kruger did not return the greeting. "What the hell is this about, Paul? I'm on a short timeline and coming to DC is not helpful."

Stumpf's smile broadened as he motioned Kruger to sit. "When we explain the reason for your trip, I'm sure you'll find it worth your time."

"Whatever." Kruger sat and clasped his hands in front of him, alternating his attention from Joseph to Stumpf, his glare intensifying with each second.

Joseph started. "Were you aware that one of President Griffin's best friends is a man named David Wu?"

Kruger shook his head.

"Do you know who David Wu is?"

"Only that he's one of the richest men in the United States. Other than that, no, I don't."

"Griffin and Wu were college roommates and still close friends."

"Good for them."

Stumpf brought his hand up to cover his smile.

With a sigh, Kruger said, "Get to the point, Joseph."

"Think back on the names of the five victims you believe Dorian Monk killed around San Francisco."

Blinking several times, Kruger's eyes widened. "Holea Wu. The third victim."

Both Stumpf and Joseph nodded.

"I take it she was related to this David Wu."

"His sister."

"Ah—geez."

Stumpf asked, "Is the picture getting clearer?"

Kruger nodded.

"Sean, your retirement date is set in stone. No one can change that." Stumpf paused and glanced at Joseph, who nodded. "We have an alternative for you."

Leaning forward, Kruger stared at the director. "I'm listening."

Joseph took over. "The president signed an executive order this morning creating a special task force to investigate the unsolved murders discovered by Deputy Director Alan Seltzer." He paused, and when Kruger didn't respond, continued, "The commission is slated to start the 23rd of this month. You will be the Special Agent in Charge and will have complete control of its activities and who you want on your team."

"Who's paying for it?"

"David Wu."

"For how long?"

"As long as it takes."

"Is this legal?"

Both Stumpf and Joseph nodded.

"I can pick my own team?"

They both nodded again.

"If I choose someone that's currently with the FBI, will it negatively affect their career?"

Stumpf answered, "It will only enhance it."

Kruger took a deep breath and sat back in his chair. One hand remained on the tabletop and he drummed his fingers on the surface. "What happens after we find Monk?"

"It will dissolve after his conviction, sentencing and incarceration."

"What if we find him and he's not willing to surrender?"

"Same thing—the commission will be dissolved."

"Who do I report to?"

Stumpf pointed to Joseph. "To the president through him as his liaison."

"I accept."

CHAPTER 16

Washington, DC / Springfield

After the meeting with the director and Joseph, Kruger spent a few hours with the Human Resources Department signing paperwork for his pending retirement. By four in the afternoon, he again sat in the passenger compartment of the Gulfstream, typing out a group text message to JR, Jimmie and Alexia Gibbs, Sandy Knoll and Ryan Clark. All were to be in JR's conference room by 7:30 a.m. the next morning, except Clark. He would join them via a conference call. All responded with an affirmative text message.

At 6:34 p.m., Kruger walked into the kitchen of his home in Springfield. Stephanie, having heard the garage door open, was standing next to the kitchen island with a worried look on her face. Kristin and Mikey stood next to her, their normal habit of running into his arms forgotten as they reflected their mother's concern.

With a smile, he knelt and spread his arms. Both kids ran to him and he gave them a big hug. Once they were satisfied all was normal, they both ran off to another section of the house with their usual laughter.

Standing, Kruger went to his wife and gave her a tight embrace.

She asked, "What happened?"

"I signed all the paperwork, so I don't have to do that later. I get my final paycheck at the end of the month. There will be a lumpsum check included for all my unused vacation and my pension will start in July."

"So that's it?"

He nodded. "As far as the FBI is concerned. There's more."

With a frown, she pushed away and stared at him. "What?"

"As of June 23rd, I work for the President of the United States as the Special Agent in Charge of a commission looking into the murder of Alan Seltzer."

She started to smile but stopped. Her forehead furrowed. "Is this a good thing, Sean?"

"Yes, a very good thing."

Now smiling, she returned to his embrace and put her head against his chest. "Good. Maybe you won't be so grumpy."

"Maybe."

***

JR arrived at his office a few minutes after six the next morning. The only illumination on the second floor came from lights in the soundproof conference room in the far corner. Years before, Kruger received his own key to the building and his own code to arm and disarm the security system. His name was also on file with the Springfield Police and Fire Departments as an alternate contact in the case of emergency. Seeing his friend already in the conference room this early did not surprise him.

Turning on a few select light switches near his cubicle, JR noticed a pot of coffee already prepared and waiting for him. He poured a cup and opened the door to the room. "You're here early."

Kruger smiled and looked up from his laptop. "Lots to do."

"Thought you were retiring."

"I am, but not today."

Sipping his coffee, JR tilted his head. "Excuse me?"

"That's why I called a meeting. We're not done searching for Monk. I got a reprieve."

"Let me guess—Joseph got involved."

"He did, but the president actually came up with the idea. Little did I know six years ago when Ryan and I kept him from being shot by a sniper, he would come to my rescue."

"I'm not following you."

"Let's put it this way. I officially retire from the FBI on June 23rd. On June 24th, I become the Special Agent in Charge of a task force created by the president for the sole purpose of finding, arresting and convicting Dorian Monk for the murder of twenty individuals and Deputy Director Alan Seltzer."

"Since you mentioned a task force, I take it the rest of us are involved."

"Yes. I'll get to the details during our meeting. But our team is intact, and we have a mission to carry out."

"Just us?"

"No, the FBI still has an active investigation into Alan's murder. Their focus is now on searching for Dorian Monk. Unfortunately, they also have other investigations they need to conduct. Our team will have no other duties. We are to concentrate on this to its conclusion."

"Then what?"

Kruger smiled and shrugged. "Guess I'll finally get a chance to sit on the front porch in a rocking chair."

JR snorted. "I seriously doubt that." He set his coffee cup down and went to his cubicle to retrieve a laptop. After returning, he sat next to Kruger and opened it. "I discovered something yesterday."

"Oh?"

"I got to thinking about the bank accounts used by the colleges and universities to pay Monk over the years. Knowing where he taught allowed me to find the ones used to pay him. Most of them are closed or inactive."

"Kind of what we suspected."

"Yes, however, I found one we didn't suspect."

One of Kruger's eyebrows shot up. "Really?"

With a nod, JR pointed at the now-active laptop. "It appears Dorian Marshall had an account with well over a quarter million dollars in it. I found it yesterday in a large bank in San Francisco, California."

"Had?"

"I'll get to that in a second."

"Are you sure it's the same guy?"

JR nodded. "One of the first mistakes I've seen him make. He used the same social security number for this account as he did for the college accounts. What concerned me about this account was the amount of money. That's a lot for a professor, not to mention a part-time one."

Kruger was quiet as the stared at the computer screen. "Yes, it is." He paused. "How did an adjunct professor accumulate that much cash?"

With a smile JR said, "I asked myself the same question. He's considered a mathematical genius, correct?"

"Yeah."

"He's also very clever with computers from what I can determine. I checked the deposits and found something strange."

"What?"

"All the deposits were from internal transfers within the same bank."

"Wouldn't the bank notice that?"

"One would think so, but apparently it didn't."

"So, what are you saying?"

"Dorian Monk hacked into the bank and placed an algorithm into the system which rounds up any transaction to the next penny. Those pennies are automatically transferred to a variety of accounts and when the totals reach a random amount, they are transferred to the account for Dorian Marshall."

"A penny? That's not a lot."

"No, it's not, and when you think about it, more than likely unnoticeable. But when done over millions of transactions it can add up fast."

"JR, wouldn't a bank audit or a business account audit find something like that?"

"Yes, but only after the fact. If the money is transferred out and the account closed before the audit, well…"

"It could be extremely difficult for the bank to get the money back."

"Exactly, particularly if the money is transferred numerous times afterward. Besides, bank accounts are covered by FDIC insurance. The banks blame it on a software glitch, files a claim, reimburses the affected accounts, keep their mouths shut and no one knows any different."

"Did that happen?"

His answer was a nod.

"Do you think he's done it before?"

"I have no proof, but I would say yes. If he's done this in numerous banks over the course of five or six years…" He shrugged.

"There's no telling how much money he has stashed away."

"I would say that's a fair statement. There's something else."

"What?"

"I haven't been able to stop thinking about the virus I wrote being out in the wild."

Kruger folded his arms and waited.

"Let's assume Monk is the Chronos from the chatroom where the virus discussions occurred."

"Okay, let's."

"Monk also recognized my name during our interview, right?"

"Yeah, I thought it strange."

"So, did I. When I attended MIT, I used my birth name. Plus, we didn't meet at Black Hat either. I've checked—none of his known aliases have ever registered for the conference."

A frown appeared on Kruger's face, but he remained silent.

"So how did the Russians know to look for the virus during their DDS attack?"

"What about other hackers in the chatroom?"

"Possibly, but I believe we have to assume it was Monk."

"I hate assumptions."

"I know, so do I, but they sometimes lead to conclusions."

Kruger folded his arms and smiled. "I will assume you have a conclusion."

JR nodded. "Dorian Monk isn't a loner—he's part of a larger organization."

Kruger was quiet for a while. His gaze locked on JR. "Let's suppose you're correct. Can you follow the money from the bank in San Francisco?"

JR shrugged. "I think so. What are you thinking?"

"If he's connected to a larger group, we need proof."

"Let me see if I can follow the money trail."

"By all means try. This may be the first break we've had since he disappeared."

***

By 7:25 a.m. Kruger's team was present with Ryan Clark talking to them through a Polycom SoundStation in the middle of the conference room table. While he was outside getting a fresh cup of coffee, Kruger smiled and watched the individuals in the room interact. He considered them friends and would miss working with them after the conclusion of the Dorian Monk affair.

He took a deep breath and let it out slowly. Time to get this new phase of the investigation started.

The room went silent as he sat at the head of the table, all eyes on him and expressing a note of concern. He started, "Thanks for coming in early."

Nods around the table.

"I was in Washington yesterday."

No one spoke.

He continued, "I have good news about the investigation."

Sandy Knoll said in his gravelly voice, "About damn time."

"Yes, it is Sandy. As you all know, I have a birthday coming up in less than two weeks and will be forced to retire from the FBI."

From the speaker phone, Clark said, "That policy sucks."

Everyone at the table agreed with a nod.

Knoll smiled. "I've seen that look in your eye before, Sean. You got something up your sleeve?"

"As a matter of fact, I do. As of June 24th, I will become the SAC of a special task force looking into the murder of Deputy Director Alan Seltzer."

Smiles erupted around the table. JR folded his arms and sat back to watch everyone else.

They heard Clark from the speaker. "Where does that leave us, Sean?"

"Right there with me."

Everyone clapped.

Kruger proceeded to go over the details as he knew them and then said, "Any questions?"

Jimmie Gibbs spoke for the first time that morning. "What happens when this is over, Sean?"

Clasping his hands in front of him, Kruger studied them for a few seconds. With a sad smile, he said, "All of you who are with the FBI will go back to your previous assignments with the agency. Alexia will return to her duties with JR's company and JR will do what JR normally does. I will retire and spend more time with my family."

Jimmie stared at Alexia and she stared back. He turned to Kruger. "I'm not moving."

"That's your decision, Jimmie. But the agency will take a dim view of it."

"Don't care."

Knoll cleared his throat. "Don't worry about it, Jimmie. Things have a way of working out."

"Yeah, they do."

Kruger noted the knowing looks between the two men and almost smiled.

CHAPTER 17

Somewhere in the Western United States

Dorian Monk stepped out of the rustic log cabin onto the wood-plank front porch. Located within the tree line of the Rocky Mountains in western Wyoming, the isolated cabin usually helped Monk resolve problems. But after a month of solitude, he was no closer to a solution.

Built before the start of World War II by his mother's big-game hunting father on land owned by the family since the late 1800s, the cabin provided a getaway for members of his family for decades. The one-room cabin possessed few modern amenities. A fireplace for cooking and heating, a twin mattress and frame for sleeping, an elevation that kept temperatures comfortable in the summer, a recently added chemical toilet and a spring-fed hand water pump. This far into the mountains, access to electricity remained elusive, which was fine with Monk. The lack of power kept the cabin off the grid and away from prying eyes.

Shopping for supplies and trips to a WIFI spot in Lander, Wyoming were the only times he ventured from the cabin. During his isolation, he'd allowed his beard and hair to grow. With a hat and dark aviator sunglasses, he no longer resembled the individual who shuffled from classroom to classroom at Hendrick College.

A thick stand of trees surrounded the area. After decades of visiting the cabin, he could name each tree species found on the property. They included Colorado Blue Spruce, Douglas-Fir, Lodgepole Pine, Cottonwoods, Ponderosa Pine, Rocky Mountain Juniper, and White Fir. Firewood was plentiful just from fallen trees in the surrounding woods. East of the cabin were the lowlands and to the northwest, the higher elevations of Yellowstone National Park.

If not for the fact the FBI knew about him, he would have relished this length of time isolated and separated from mankind. Normally, he would stay less than two weeks several times a year at the cabin. In the past, the solitude helped him solve mathematical problems which normally led to a published paper. However, solving the equation of how the FBI found him continued to elude him.

This mental exercise occupied most of his waking hours. Recalling each and every one of his exploits, the only misstep he could identify occurred during the last one. Eliminating the Deputy Director of the FBI had taken meticulous and detailed planning. Knowing where the security cameras were located and timing his attack precisely to avoid them, at first glance, seemed to work perfectly.

Unless…

He gathered his laptop and placed it in his satchel. The drive to Laramie, Wyoming would take over four hours. He knew of several privately owned motels in and around the area which still preferred to be paid in cash. He would stay a few days and use their Wi-Fi to do the research to answer the question of how the FBI found him.

***

The time approached ten-thirty p.m. as JR prepared to shut down his computer and return home. The only light still illuminated on the second floor was located above his workspace. The normal sounds from the cubicle farm would commence again at seven in the morning and last another fourteen hours.

His company now had over a hundred associates spread across the country. While others managed the day-to-day administrative duties, his role in the company remained the same He was the individual who assessed and identified computer problems for new clients. Once his assessments were complete, others took over for implementation of a solution. A key figure in this implementation was one of his better hires—Alexia Montreal Gibbs, wife of retired Navy Seal and current FBI agent Jimmie Gibbs.

Weariness swept over JR as he thought about the coming retirement of his friend Sean Kruger. The man's status as a legendary FBI agent, in many respects, had helped grow his business. Assisting Kruger's investigations had also helped him maintain his edge as one of the better computer hackers in the country.

As he looked up, he saw Alexia approaching his cubicle.

"What are you doing here this late, JR?"

"I could ask you the same question."

She smiled and raised her backpack. "Jimmie and I actually had a date tonight. We went to a movie and then a late dinner. I left my computer here while we were out. I'll be working from home tomorrow. That's my excuse. What's yours?"

"This Monk character has me stumped. I can't get a line on him at all."

"Did following the money not work?"

JR shook his head. "It hasn't so far."

She nodded. "Where do you think he is?"

"That's the key question right now. We don't know."

"You know where he isn't, don't you?"

"What do you mean?"

"He doesn't have a presence on the internet, right?"

JR nodded.

"What if he has a presence on the dark web?"

With a frown, JR tilted his head and stared at her.

"I've been thinking, and this is pure speculation, what if he's not acting alone like everyone thinks?"

"It's a possibility we've been considering."

"When I first thought about this, I looked up some statistics from the FBI Uniform Crime Report. Fifty percent of all murders are committed by someone unknown to the victim. Here is another surprising fact—of the total numbers of murders in 2017, forty percent went unsolved. Which means of the 15,129 murders committed in 2017, 4,292 were for unknown reasons, were committed by unknown persons and went unsolved."

JR continued to stare. "Where did all of that come from?"

"I just told you, The FBI Uniform Crime Report. It's called the UCR."

With a thoughtful nod, he said, "So, you think there's a group that communicates with each other on the dark web who are randomly murdering people of color or ethnic backgrounds and are getting away with it?"

Alexia frowned. "When you put it that way, it sounds silly."

"It doesn't sound silly. It connects dots Sean and I couldn't connect."

She glanced at her cell phone. "I've got to go, JR. We can discuss this further tomorrow. Remember, I'm working from home."

"Okay."

She left and JR turned to stare at the three flat screen monitors on his desk. "No, Alexia, it doesn't sound silly. It just might be the direction we need to look at."

***

The Next Morning

"You're saying Alexia figured this out?"

"Yes."

Kruger stared at a spot on the far side of the cubicle farm and sipped coffee. "What do you think?"

As JR poured a fresh cup from the coffee service, he said, "After she left last night, I started digging around. While there are a lot of websites on the regular web that spew white nationalist propaganda, it's nothing like what I found on the dark web."

"Such as?"

"You'd just have to look at it. I find it repugnant to discuss. But suffice it to say, there's a lot of it and it's very violent."

With a slight smile, Kruger glanced at his friend. "You used to be a denizen of the dark web, if I remember correctly."

"Yeah, but never those types of chat rooms."

"Do you think you can find him in one?"

With a shrug, JR sat behind his desk. "Don't know. Maybe." He paused and looked up. "What happens if I do find him?"

"Once you've located him, I send in the Cavalry."

JR glanced at the clock and date displayed at the bottom right side of his middle monitor. "Your birthday is two days away. Got any plans?"

"Steph and I are going to have dinner at our favorite restaurant. It's just another day, JR. No big deal."

"Right…"

CHAPTER 18

Springfield, MO
Two Days Later

Kruger stared at the empty wine glass in front of him on the white tablecloth. Stephanie continued their conversation but he concentrated on the emptiness of the stemware.

She stopped and frowned. "You're not listening to me, are you?"

He looked up. "Of course, I'm listening to you."

"Sean Kruger, don't lie to me, you're horrible at it. Tell me what I said."

He blinked a few times. "I was listening. I just didn't hear what you said."

She reached for his hand and squeezed it. "Where were you?"

He held up the wine glass in his free hand and nodded at it. "I was thinking about how empty this glass is. How only minutes before it had a purpose. To hold my wine. Now, it's empty, useless and taking up space on the table. Kind of the way I feel today."

"We're all getting older. Birthdays can make us melancholy at times."

"I know, but that's not it. It's something else."

She gave him the smile he'd fallen in love with the first time they met. "Is that something your retirement?"

With a grim smile he nodded. "I know I've retired a couple of times. But deep down inside I knew I could always go back to the agency if I wanted to." He paused and shook his head. "This time it's different. I can't go back."

Without responding, she took his hand in both of hers and touched her cheek with it. "We both know there's nothing I can say to make you feel better so I won't try."

Their waitress stopped at the table. "Have you two made your selections for dinner?"

Kruger shook his head and held up his wine glass. "Not yet, but I would appreciate it if you could give this wine glass a purpose again."

Stephanie chuckled and the waitress tilted her head and pursed her lips. "Beg your pardon?"

"Sorry, I'll have another glass of wine. Then we'll order."

***

After picking up their children at Brian Kruger's house, Sean and Stephanie returned home and got the kids settled for the night. As the time approached eleven, Kruger was already in bed with his hands behind his head, staring at the ceiling. He could hear Stephanie, still in the bathroom, humming to herself.

He got out of bed, closed the bedroom door and slipped back under the sheets. When she emerged, she wore a long sheer nightgown that allowed light from the bathroom to perfectly outline everything underneath. She glanced at the closed bedroom door and smiled. With the bathroom door shut, two battery operated flameless candles provided the only illumination in the room. In the soft glow of the light, she pulled back the covers, lay down next to him and snuggled.

Kruger wrapped his arm around her shoulders, kissed her forehead and said, "I like what you're wearing, but I wonder how long you think you'll keep it on."

"Not long—I hope."

***

Kruger's mood appeared noticeably brighter the next morning. On his first full day of retirement, he made breakfast for the kids while Stephanie got ready for a faculty meeting at the university. She would return before ten and the family would travel thirty miles south to Silver Dollar City near Branson, Missouri for an afternoon outing.

At nine-thirty-seven a.m. a UPS truck stopped in front of Kruger's house and the driver walked to the front porch with a small padded envelope in his hand. After ringing the doorbell, he didn't walk back to his truck like normal. When the second ring sounded, Kruger went to the front door and experienced a momentary twinge of concern because the driver remained on the porch. Through the glass storm door, he saw the normal driver assigned to the route. He held the package up and said, "I need a signature, Sean."

After opening the door, he took the tablet-like object and signed his name where the driver indicated. As he handed it back, he said, "This is kind of unusual isn't it, Jerry?"

The driver shrugged. "Happens once in a while for important deliveries. It always puts me behind."

Kruger took the package and then watched the driver hurry back to his truck.

After closing the storm door, Kruger glanced at the

shipping label. The return address was Joseph Kincaid's residence in Arlington, VA.

Curiosity grew as he took the package back to his office on the western end of the house. It opened easily and after peering inside, he smiled.

Several objects were inside—an ID wallet, a badge mounted on a thick leather badge holder with a steel spring loaded clip on the back, a laminated ID badge with lanyard and a letter. Kruger examined the badge. It looked similar to his FBI one, including the words SPECIAL AGENT across the bottom. In the center was stamped the seal of Homeland Security with a U on the left and an S on the right. Across the top he saw the words; *Homeland Security.*

He opened the letter and read the following:

By Order of the President of the United States.

> *The position of Homeland Security Special Agent has been bestowed upon retired FBI Agent Sean Kruger for the specific purposes of investigating crimes committed against the United States that are deemed outside the normal jurisdiction of the FBI, DOJ, Secret Service, US Marshal and any other law enforcement agency within the United States.*

> *It is hereby also determined that the National Security Advisor will have oversight of this new position and provide details of these investigations to the office of President of the United States.*

> *The holder of this office shall be afforded the cooperation of all agencies under the auspices of Homeland Security.*

> *So bestowed by order of the President of the United States this day:*

Below the proclamation, Kruger saw the signature of President Roy Griffin and the date the order had been signed. He also noticed there was no ending date. A small grin appeared as he reread the letter. He would have to talk to Joseph about the details, but the declaration seemed overly broad.

He opened the ID wallet and read his new title—Special Agent in Charge. He realized the picture on the ID was the same picture taken on his last trip to the J. Edgar Hoover building for his retired FBI agent ID.

He felt a presence behind him.

"What's that?"

Turning to see Stephanie standing in the doorway of his office, he said, "You're home early."

She shrugged and walked up next to him. He handed her the letter.

He remained silent as she read. When finished, she smiled. "Shall I kneel before you, oh great important, one?"

With a chuckle, he showed her the badge.

"Looks impressive." She paused. "So, exactly what does this mean, Sean?"

"It means I've been given *carte blanche* to find Dorian Monk."

***

The trip to Silver Dollar City, while fun and exciting for the kids, left everyone exhausted. After arriving home, Kristin and Mikey offered no resistance at bedtime. They were tucked away and asleep by eight-thirty. Afterward, Stephanie retreated to her and Kruger's bedroom to read, while Kruger took the opportunity to sit at his home office desk and check emails. Halfway down the list he found one from Joseph asking him to call him at his first convenience. Noting the time of the email, he glanced at his watch. Still early for Joseph. He found Joseph's number in his contact list and made the call. It was answered on the third ring.

"How was the first day of your retirement?"

"Exhausting. Took the kids to Silver Dollar City."

"Sounds like fun."

Kruger frowned; Joseph's tone did not possess its normal upbeat rhythm. "What's the matter, Joseph?"

"Nothing. It's been a long day."

"I can call back tomorrow."

"Nonsense. You're already on the phone."

"What did you want to talk about?"

"Your new status."

"Ahh… Any problems?"

"Nope, not in the long term." He paused. "Short-term, maybe."

Chuckling, Kruger said, "Let me guess, a turf-war erupted."

"Yes, unfortunately. Homeland Security Secretary Joan Watson found out about your appointment and is demanding you report to her. The president told her, in no uncertain terms, that wasn't going to happen."

"Well, that settles that little skirmish."

"Maybe."

"Joseph, you know I don't like getting involved with the palace intrigue."

"I don't think you'll have to. But if she whispers into the ears of Senator Jordan Quinn, things could heat up."

Kruger was quiet as he realized his newfound position might be the source of problems for the president. "I thought he was a friend of the president."

"As Truman said, if you need a friend in Washington, get a dog."

"Try to keep me out of it."

"I'll do my best."

"So, now can I put the team together?"

"Yes. Report to me and me alone. If anyone calls you, refer them to me."

"Got it. Looking forward to working with you again, Joseph."

"Me, too."

CHAPTER 19

Laramie, WY

After eight days in two different hotels in Laramie, Dorian Monk came to the conclusion he did not want to return to the mountain cabin yet. Since his departure from Covington, he'd found no evidence the FBI, or anyone else for that matter, knew his location.

With the realization he did not need to return to the isolation of the mountains, Monk chose to rent an apartment. One on the western outskirts of town which would allow a fast exit toward his cabin should the need arise.

Using Zillow, he found one featuring two bedrooms and a bath on the ground floor of a run-down complex just outside the town's city limit. He arranged to meet the property manager.

When the agreed upon appointment time came and went, Monk's contempt for his fellow man increased. Unfortunately, the apartment's location fit his needs perfectly—otherwise, he would have left. So, Monk leaned against the front of his Equinox and waited in the parking lot. Thirty minutes later, a dusty ten-year-old Ford F-150 parked next to his SUV. The driver stared at him for several moments before opening the door and lighting a cigarette.

She appeared to be in her mid-fifties and stood as tall as she was wide. Her face displayed a permanent scowl. "You Chronos?"

Monk nodded.

"I don't allow pets."

"Don't have any."

"No loud parties."

"I don't like people."

"How long do you want the place?" The lit cigarette darted up and down in her lips as she spoke.

"What's your shortest lease?"

"Twelve months."

"Then I want the place for twelve months."

She tossed him a set of keys, which he caught with his left hand. "Help yourself. I don't go into empty apartments with renters. The only one I have available is 3A. Bottom floor northwest corner."

He nodded and walked toward the building. When he opened the door his senses were assaulted by the stench of cat urine. He quickly looked around, decided he could do worse and returned to the parking lot.

"How much?"

"Three hundred cleaning deposit, seven-fifty per month if you pay by check, six-fifty if you pay with cash. Most of my renters pay with cash."

He nodded. "I take it you didn't get a cleaning deposit from the last tenant."

"What's that supposed to mean?"

"Place smells like cat piss."

"Don't allow pets."

He tossed her the key, which she grabbed out of the air. He said, "Go smell it yourself. You clean up the cat smell and I'll rent the place."

She frowned and stared at him a moment. "Wait here. I don't go into empty apartments with renters."

"You said that."

She did not respond and waddled toward the building. Five minutes later, she returned. "I'll have the carpets shampooed. When do you want to move in?"

"When they're clean."

She had apparently lit anther cigarette while in the apartment, because the one now dangling from her lips had an impossible length of ash at the end. Monk expected it to fall at any moment. Taking it from her lips, she dropped it on the parking lot and crushed it out with the heel of her cowboy boot. "I'll get the paperwork."

Two days later, a truck owned by a local secondhand furniture store unloaded its contents onto the newly shampooed and sanitized carpets of apartment 3A. Monk spent half the day arranging for utilities and internet service in the name of Timothy Chronos. He moved the small amount of clothing and personal items he'd brought from the cabin into his new space. As dusk turned to night, he opened his laptop and accessed the dark web.

***

JR Diminski's eyes snapped open. He glanced at the digital clock on his nightstand and saw it was two minutes past three in the morning. His cellular phone could be heard dancing on the mahogany top of the nightstand as it vibrated from an incoming notification. He put on his glasses and stared at the screen. Once he could focus on the display, he mumbled, "Shit." After jumping out of bed, he practically ran to his home office.

Mia opened her eyes, shook her head and rolled over. JR's nocturnal notifications meant he had a snooper program active. Normal procedure when he worked with

Sean Kruger.

***

Jimmie Gibbs, Sandy Knoll and Kruger leaned over JR's shoulder as he pointed to the middle monitor on his desk in the cubicle.

"A CenturyLink Wi-Fi connection for a Timothy Chronos went active yesterday."

Knoll asked, "Where?"

"Laramie, Wyoming. It's in an apartment complex on the western-most city limits. The utilities for the apartment were transferred from the LLC that owns the building to T. Chronos the previous day."

Kruger crossed his arms. "How'd you find that?"

"Once the Wi-Fi connection was discovered, it was just a matter of hacking into the utility company records."

With a nod, Kruger continued to study the monitor. "Anything else?"

JR shook his head. "No."

Jimmie crossed his arms as he stared at the monitor. "If he's in Laramie, the University of Wyoming is there. Do you suppose he is trying to get another teaching gig?"

Knoll and Kruger looked at him with raised eyebrows. Knoll said, "It would be kind of tough with a nationwide BOLO out on him."

Kruger shook his head slowly. "It might not even be him, gentlemen. The nationwide BOLO is for Dorian Monk. We kept the other names he uses out of it. He'd have a hard time getting a job teaching under his real name. Any cursory background check would raise red flags. Plus, I doubt he has teaching credentials under his other alias."

With a nod, Jimmie said, "Yeah, there is that. But we have to remember this guy's a loner. He vanished after leaving Covington and had to be somewhere. What if he owns a place in the mountains? Laramie is just east of the

Rocky Mountains."

JR stared at Gibbs and blinked several times. "Maybe." He turned to his computer and started typing rapidly.

Knowing JR would be in a zone for a while, the three other men poured cups of coffee and retreated to the conference room.

Once seated, Kruger showed them his new ID and badge. "You two are still officially with the FBI, but on temporary loan to Homeland Security for a special task force. You keep your tenure and pay-grade."

Gibbs and Knoll nodded.

"I, on the other hand, work for Homeland Security and report to Joseph." Kruger grew quiet as he took a sip of coffee. He then said, "Guys, I'm not sure how long this investigation will last. I want both of you to know how much I have appreciated your experience and assistance over the past few years."

Knoll looked embarrassed and Gibbs smiled as he sipped his coffee. Neither responded.

"That being said, I'm afraid we're going to need to do a lot of traveling for the foreseeable future."

"Wyoming?" This from Knoll.

A nod.

Gibbs pursed his lips. "My uncle ran a hunting lodge in Montana. Before my sister..." He paused, swallowed hard and blinked several times. "My dad and I started going there when I was ten. I learned to shoot during those trips. Good times." He paused again. "Wish Dad was still around. I'd like to have another trip with him."

Knoll asked, "Where in Montana?"

"Northwest of Bozeman. The place was extremely remote. The reason I mentioned it, Dad felt the place was isolated enough that few, if anyone, would ever bother it. He kept copies of important papers there in a safe under the floor."

"Huh." Kruger stared at the younger man. "If Monk has

a cabin, maybe he does the same thing. Good suggestion, Jimmie." Remaining quiet for a few moments, Kruger tapped his lips with an index finger. "I'd like both of you to head out to Laramie. Put the apartment building under surveillance and see if you can determine if this is our guy. I'll have Clark meet you two out there so all of you can take shifts. If it is Monk, I'll head that way. If he does have a cabin, maybe he'll lead us to it."

Both men nodded. Knoll said, "I take it we aren't going to enlist the help of the local FBI Field Office?"

"Not right now. Joseph told me the president wants our task force to accomplish this by ourselves. Why, I wasn't told. But for now, we keep it within our little group."

CHAPTER 20

Laramie, WY

Numbers swirled within the mind of Dorian Monk as he lay in his bed staring at the ceiling. Quadratic and Polynomial equations were his relentless companions during these occurrences, blocking out all other perceptions and thoughts. In more lucid moments, he knew one day the equations would take over and he would succumb to their allure. The episodes were becoming more frequent and longer. When they happened, he remained catatonic. Once they passed, the agony of the headaches left his eyes bloodshot and his body exhausted. Sleep an impossible occurrence.

A knock on the apartment door went unanswered as he watched the equations speed across the ceiling. The time was 4:23 in the afternoon and the visitor eventually went away.

After sunset and darkness prevailed, Monk sat on the side of the bed, exhausted and nauseous. He held his head with both hands as he leaned over trying not to retch. Tears streamed from his eyes as every neuron in his brain felt consumed by flames.

His distrust of doctors kept him from seeking professional help—plus he did not want to be placed under sedation for fear of revealing his identity. He would live with the agony for now. If, and when, it got worse, there was always the option of placing the Glock 30 under his chin and pulling the trigger.

***

Jimmie Gibbs walked through the parking lot of the Castleberry Arms Apartment complex. With the sun past its zenith and tenants going about their day, his interest in the vehicles parked around the buildings went unnoticed. He wandered nonchalantly among the parked pickups and SUVs looking for anything to identify their quarry. To his surprise, parking slots were assigned to the individual apartments. Sitting in the slot for apartment A3 sat a white 2008 Chevy Equinox with a Wyoming plate. After checking the VIN plate visible through the front windshield, he confirmed it was the one purchased in Cincinnati. He took a picture of the license and sent it directly to JR. With this accomplished he continued his casual walk around the parking lot.

Ten minutes after finding the SUV he sat in the passenger seat of a GMC Denali with Sandy Knoll behind the wheel. Gibbs stared at the message just received from JR.

"Got him. License is registered to Dorian Mathews with an address in Cheyenne."

Knoll nodded. "Okay, now the fun begins. We wait."

Gibbs glanced around, looking for an inconspicuous location to park. "Where?"

The area to the south of the isolated apartment building offered only an empty field for half-a-mile before turning into a small subdivision of single-family homes. To the east lay a large industrial building with few cars in the parking lot. Across the street, the land to the west held manufactured homes behind a privacy fence. A tract of modest single-family ranch-style homes were north of their location.

Twisting his head in several directions, Knoll shrugged. "I'm working on it."

Without a good solution to their problem, Knoll parked the rented Denali on Venture Drive next to the apartment complex. Ten minutes later, Gibbs watched a silver 2013 Chevrolet Silverado pull into the parking lot and stop in the slot next to Monk's Equinox. A tall, slender man in jeans, cowboy boots and an untucked white polo shirt walked toward Monk's apartment. The man's stride held purpose as he approached.

Both Knoll and Gibbs watched as he pounded on the door. After knocking several times, the man placed his hands on his hips and shook his head. He then looked in the window next to the door. A few moments later, the man returned to his truck and drove away.

"Now what do you suppose that was all about?" Knoll had placed his massive arms on the steering wheel and rested his chin on them.

With a grin, Gibbs said, "Don't know, but I'm going to find out. Why don't you follow the Chevy and I'll check Monk's apartment?" He slipped out of the SUV and walked toward apartment A3.

Knoll waited until the truck passed him to put the Denali in gear and follow.

Extracting a slim metal shim out of his billfold, Gibbs opened the cheap door lock on the apartment in less than fifteen seconds. When he was inside, he stood still and listened. The only sound he heard came from a refrigerator in the small kitchen next to the living area.

Darkness prevailed as the only illumination available

came from the window by the door. Cheap plastic blinds were closed and covered by a light-blocking curtain. But enough light seeped through the crack where the two panels met for him to see a hallway leading to the bedrooms. The apartment was small and orderly. The only furnishings in this room were two reclining chairs with an end table between them and a table lamp on top. Gibbs noted the absence of a TV. The kitchen was likewise sparsely furnished with a small wood dining table and two chairs. He spotted one of the objectives of his home invasion on the kitchen table—a cell phone.

Gibbs silently walked toward the hallway and stopped before going farther. The sound of a man breathing hard and fast could be heard. He withdrew the Sig Sauer P226 from its holster at the small of his back and held it in his right hand.

The light from the front window barely penetrated the apartment gloom, but there was enough for Gibbs to determine someone lay on a bed in the first bedroom. The breathing sounds came from this individual. As Gibbs' sight adjusted to the gloom, he could see the eyes were opened but unfocused. The man's chest moved up and down with rapid breaths. They would stop every once in a while and then commence again several moments later, only harder.

Medical training as a Navy Seal allowed him to recognize the man was having a seizure of some kind. His first inclination was to help, but after taking one step into the bedroom, he remembered the purpose of his intrusion. Taking his cell phone from his pocket, he backed up, steadied himself against the door jam and took a low-light picture of the figure on the bed.

Without making any additional sounds, Gibbs returned the Sig Sauer to its holster and went back to the cell phone on the kitchen table. He attached a small device to the charging port and counted to ten, just like JR instructed.

When he was done, he put the device back in his pocket and slipped out of the apartment.

As he passed the SUV parked in the slot marked for A3, he placed a device in the rear driver-side wheel well. With this accomplished, he made a call to Sandy Knoll.

"Our door knocker just entered a biker bar on the northern city limits. What'd you find out?"

"Monk's having some type of seizure."

"Should we call an ambulance?"

Gibbs was silent for a few moments as he debated the pros and cons. "If we do, he'll know someone was in his apartment and will probably disappear again. When I was going through EMT training with the Seals, we were taught that most seizures subside after a while and generally do not cause damage. If he had been convulsing, I would have called one, but he wasn't."

"So, you're saying, leave him alone."

"Yeah, guess I am."

Knoll chuckled. "I just heard from Clark. He's in town."

"Okay, I'm going to hang out here for a while and keep an eye on Monk."

"I'll keep an eye on Slim and have Clark join you."

"Sounds good."

***

As dusk turned to night, Gibbs opened the door of the Ford Fusion and sat in the passenger seat. Ryan Clark nodded and pulled away from the curb. "Good to see you again, Jimmie."

Clark wore his dark brown hair longer than FBI standards with the gray at his temples more prominent after each haircut. Now in his mid-forties, his handsome face held deep worry lines around his eyes which betrayed his lengthy career in law-enforcement.

At one time, a detective with the Arlington, Virginia,

Police Department, he and Kruger became acquainted during several joint investigations over the past two decades. Their friendship strengthened when they were teamed up on the Beltway Sniper case in October 2002. In 2016, they found themselves, once again working together, to chase a team of assassins across the United States. It was during this operation, while protecting then-Congressman Roy Griffin, that Clark was shot with a bullet meant for Griffin. Kruger then lobbied the director to make him an agent and after his recovery he joined the FBI. Since then, he had made a name for himself within the agency.

"Likewise, Ryan."

"Now what?"

"I've got a GPS tracking device on his SUV. He hasn't left the apartment and I haven't seen any lights or signs of activity since this afternoon. He's still there."

"Good."

"What's Sandy doing?"

"He's still sitting on the guy who knocked on the door. He wants you to go into the bar and see what's going on."

"Why me?"

"He said you fit in with the bar's clientele better than he does."

"Great. What about you?"

"I'll go back and watch the apartment."

***

Dorian Monk seldom felt the pangs of hunger. Normally, he ate small amounts of food off and on during the day and rarely, if ever, prepared a large meal. As the effects of his most recent migraine faded, he stared inside the small refrigerator and saw nothing he wanted to eat. He glanced at the clock on the stove and saw it was past nine. He turned his cell phone on and dialed the number of a local Papa John's pizza delivery.

***

Clark watched the young lady approach apartment A3 with the pizza box in hand. The door opened before she could knock. The gloom from the interior failed to illuminate the individual handing the money to her. After the pizza box disappeared inside, the door closed and the delivery person walked back to her vehicle. The transaction took less than fifteen seconds. When the college aged girl drove away, Clark sent a text message and waited for the return call. It came thirty seconds later.

Before Clark could say anything, JR said, What've you got, Ryan?"

"Monk just had a pizza delivered. That would mean he called it in or ordered online."

"He didn't order online, and I would have received an alert if he used the phone. Unless…"

Clark waited.

JR came back and said, "The phone must have been turned off when Jimmie tried to compromise it."

"And that means?"

"We still don't have access to this phone, only his internet activity."

"Jimmie's not going to like that."

"He'll have to try again."

CHAPTER 21

Laramie, WY

The headache from the seizure still lingered and sleep eluded Dorian Monk until four in the morning. The lingering odor of onions from the pizza added to his sense of nausea.

After numerous cups of coffee, he turned his cell phone on and checked text messages. Two new ones appeared. The oldest one admonished him for not answering when his contact had knocked and the second one told him to be in the apartment at noon.

He checked the cell phone clock and found the time to be ten-thirty-seven in the morning. He returned the message and told the sender he would be at the apartment all day.

***

Three FBI agents were now keeping tabs on the activity around Monk's apartment in shifts and separate vehicles.

Knoll, after taking the night watch, remained at their hotel to get a few hours of sleep. Clark kept tabs on Slim with the Silverado and Jimmie watched the Castleberry Arms apartment complex from across the street with a clear view of apartment A3's front door.

Gibbs' cell phone vibrated. "Yeah."

"It's Clark. Slim appears to be headed your way."

"Where'd he stay last night?"

"Hotel on the north side. He registered under the name Frank Smith. The Silverado is owned by an LLC called Freedom Rains."

"Have JR check it out."

"Already called him."

"You headed this way?"

"Yeah. See you in a few minutes."

Gibbs watched as the Silverado pulled into the parking lot and stopped next to Monk's SUV. The man sat in the truck for a long time, staring at the apartment building. When he got out, he wore a caramel-colored Carhart jacket with his left arm straight and held tight against his body. His casual pace toward Monk's apartment door belied his intentions.

Gibbs reached for his Sig Sauer and quickly exited the car. This was a move he had seen before. Now in a full sprint, he ran toward the man who now stood knocking on Monk's door.

Stopping twenty yards away, Gibbs pointed the Sig Sauer at the man and screamed. "FBI—FBI! Get your hands away from your body."

The man in the Carhartt jacket slowly turned around and smiled at Gibbs. He did not raise his hand, but quickly brought the sawed-off shotgun to a level position pointed in the young FBI agent's direction. Without hesitation, Jimmie pulled the trigger of the Sig Sauer twice. The man with the shotgun staggered as the shotgun went off.

***

Ryan Clark pulled into the parking lot and saw Gibbs, gun in hand, running toward the apartment. Extracting his Glock from its holster, he sprang out of the car and ran toward the coming confrontation.

He saw Gibbs plant himself firmly, point his gun at the man near Monk's apartment door and identify himself as an FBI agent. As the man turned to look at Gibbs, he brought up a small shotgun. Clark planted himself and aimed his Glock at the man just as Gibbs fired.

The whole incident lasted less than five seconds.

Clark shot a glance in Gibbs' direction and saw him advancing toward the man now lying on the porch in front of apartment A3. Clark reached for his cell phone and called 911.

***

The shotgun lay several inches from the prone man's grasp, so Gibbs kicked it away. The man's open, unseeing eyes were fixed on the cloudless sky above. Satisfied the cowboy did not pose a threat, Gibbs shot a quick glance at apartment A3. A man stood behind the window staring at him.

Clark appeared beside Gibbs and said, "I've called for backup. How'd you know he had a shotgun?"

"The guy must have served in Iraq or Afghanistan. He had a jacket on in this heat and his left arm was straight, holding a concealed weapon. I've seen this type of crap too many times while I was over there." He paused and looked at Clark. "Monk's been staring out the window. He now knows he's being watched by FBI agents. Better get Sandy over here."

Clark pulled his cell phone out again. As he waited for the call to connect, he stared at Jimmie. "You're bleeding."

***

By the time Kruger arrived in Laramie twelve hours later, Dorian Monk was being held in protective custody and the identity of the man Gibbs called Slim was known. The local police and sheriff's department continued to complain about three FBI agents being in town and not informing their respective departments.

Albany County Sheriff, Bud Wilkins, glared at Kruger. "Protocol demands that FBI agents announce their presence to local law enforcement, Agent Kruger."

"I agree, Sheriff."

"Then why didn't they?" Wilkins looked over his glasses at Kruger, his brow furrowed. He wore a neatly pressed long sleeve uniform shirt, faded jeans, dusty cowboy boots and was fence-rail thin.

Kruger smiled. "Because I asked them not to."

Wilkins blinked several times, his mouth slightly open. "You asked them not to? Am I hearing you correct?"

A nod from Kruger was his answer.

The sheriff pushed his black rim glasses up his slender nose as his face reddened. "Care to explain why?"

"Sheriff, Dorian Monk is suspected of being a serial killer. We don't have any hard evidence against him and the last time we tried to arrest him, he vanished for two months. We suspect he has a remote cabin in the area, and we were trying to determine the location. The incident that occurred at the Castleberry Arms apartment was totally unexpected. We had no intention of arresting anyone here in your county. We were here only to observe and follow Monk."

The sheriff was silent for a few moments. "So, you had no idea he was mixed up in this militia nonsense?"

Shaking his head, Kruger answered, "Wasn't even on our radar. But it is now."

"I've been dealing with them ever since I took this job ten years ago. They're not really a militia—they're more of an organized crime gang. They operate in the shadows and no one knows who belongs to the group."

"What about the cowboy with the shotgun?"

"Never seen him before. We think he was imported."

Kruger picked up the sheet of paper with the man's criminal history. "Billy Ray Washburn, twenty-eight, did a tour in Afghanistan with the Army, Dishonorable Discharge for assault of a superior officer, since then numerous assault charges and petty burglaries. Last known residence was Billings, Montana." Kruger looked up. "Nice guy."

With his face returning to its normal hue, Wilkins crossed his arms. "So, your team was only here to determine where this Monk fella disappeared to?"

"Yes, he just rented the apartment last week. We lost track of him in Covington, Kentucky over two months ago."

"He could have been in a hotel."

"He could have, but we have ways of checking. He wasn't."

"I won't ask how."

"Probably best."

"So now what?"

"Can I talk to him?"

"Don't see why not. Follow me."

***

Monk was escorted into the interrogation room by two deputy sheriffs. Kruger watched as the mathematician sat down across from him. Since Monk was in protective custody, handcuffs and shackles were not being utilized.

The math genius only stared at Kruger.

"You left Covington in a big hurry, Dorian. Why?"

"I want a lawyer."

"You haven't been charged with a crime. Why would you need a lawyer? Are you guilty of something, Dorian?"

"Then let me out of here."

"You're being held for your own protection. Who was the guy with the shotgun?"

"I don't know what you're talking about."

"Sure, you do. He wasn't at your apartment selling magazine subscriptions. He had a concealed shotgun and if you had opened the door when he knocked, well…"

"You're speculating, Agent Kruger."

"No, I'm not. Why was he there?"

Monk glared at Kruger with unblinking eyes. The former FBI agent returned the stare and displayed a slight smile.

Thirty seconds into the staring contest, Monk blinked and said, "Release me or let me have an attorney."

"If we release you, we can't protect you."

"I don't know what your game is, Agent, but I don't need protection."

"Then why did someone show up at your apartment to kill you?"

"He obviously had the wrong apartment."

"No, my team saw him at your place the previous day. He knew you lived there. He was a hired gun, Dorian. Someone hired him to kill you. Care to tell me why someone wants you dead?"

"Maybe a disgruntled student."

"Try again."

Monk leaned back, narrowed his eyes and crossed his arms. "I have no idea. Let me out of here."

"Why did you leave Covington in such a hurry?"

"I was done for the semester. Now, let me out of here."

Kruger stared hard at Monk and gave him a half smile. "Ah, I see. Done for the semester. Are you going back in the fall?"

"That is none of your business."

Keeping his eyes locked on the mathematician, Kruger stood, creating a loud screech as he shoved back the metal chair. "Very well. I'll talk to the sheriff."

***

The bandage above Jimmie Gibbs' left eye drew Kruger's scrutiny. He pointed to it and asked, "What's that about?"

Gibbs shrugged.

Clark smiled as he looked at Kruger. "When the shotgun went off, our friend, Mr. Gibbs here, took several pellets to the side of his face. He didn't even know he was hit."

Kruger walked closer to Gibbs and examined the bandage. "You could have lost your eye, Jimmie."

They were all meeting in Kruger's hotel room. Knoll stood off to the side, his huge arms folded over his chest. Clark sat on the corner of the bed as Kruger stared at Gibbs.

"Well, I didn't."

"How'd you know the guy had a shotgun?"

"I'd seen the move before in Afghanistan, the Taliban used to send guys into a crowd with a heavy coat on and a stiff left arm. The arm would be holding a sawed-off shotgun out of sight against the coat. This clown was doing the same thing."

"How many pellets hit you?"

"The doc said five."

"They get them?"

Gibbs nodded.

Satisfied Gibbs was okay, Kruger turned and walked over to the hotel room's window and stared out. "Monk is to be released tomorrow morning. Since he knows we're here, we don't have to be as secretive about watching him. Plus, the local sheriff has offered to have some of his deputies help with the surveillance."

Knoll spoke. "Do you trust him?"

The side of Kruger's mouth twitched. "For now. The positive side is it frees us up to check into this militia he told me about."

Clark frowned. "What militia?"

Returning his attention to his team in the room, Kruger frowned. "After I spoke to the sheriff about releasing Monk, he told me a little more about them. They call themselves para-military patriots, but the way the sheriff described them, they're more of a criminal gang. He thinks they started in Denver and migrated to Casper a few years ago. Drugs, human trafficking, stolen vehicles and cattle rustling are their preferred activities. No one knows who the leader is, but when they catch someone they suspect is a member, a well-paid lawyer from Casper shows up and the accused is bailed out immediately."

"Is the FBI field office in Casper aware of this group?" Knoll was now leaning on the small desk in the room.

Kruger nodded. "They are but don't have the resources to devote to an inquiry."

"How does this fit into our investigation of Monk?"

"Good question, Ryan." Kruger paused and looked at each man in the room. "JR and I have been batting around a few hypotheses. Monk has hidden his past fairly well, but JR found a few facts. We now know he was born in Casper and went to elementary school there. Beyond this information, there's a gap from middle school until he goes to college."

Clark said, "Homeschooled?"

"We think so. No proof of it, but it would make sense."

"So, what are you saying, Sean?" This from Gibbs.

"What if Mister Dorian Monk is a member of a militia group? During his schooling he was indoctrinated with their hatred and philosophy and then sent out into the world."

Knoll chuckled. "That's kind of farfetched isn't it?"

"Yes, it probably is, but why did Monk come back here, and why did someone try to kill him?"

CHAPTER 22

Wyoming

Since the furnishings and personal possessions within the apartment were sparse, the search did not take long. Albany Country sheriff detectives completed their task in a few hours and left the place ransacked. Monk opened the door to his apartment and froze. The beginning of a migraine thumbed behind his eyes. This signaled another seizure.

He quickly stripped off his clothes and stood under a cold shower, letting the cool water cascade over his face and head. Time slipped away as the headache transitioned into a seizure.

When he woke, he was sitting on the floor of the tub knees pressed to his chest, his arms wrapped around them. The water still cascaded over him. Disoriented and shivering, he turned the shower off.

After drying, he checked the time and discovered only an hour had elapsed. He quickly dressed, grabbed the keys to the Equinox, locked the door to the apartment and walked quickly to his SUV. Once inside, he found it undisturbed. Having his apartment searched gave him a sense of being violated. The normalcy of his SUV eased the feeling.

As he sat behind the steering wheel, he searched the parking lot for his watchers. An Albany County sheriff's car was parked next to the lot's exit. He could feel the eyes of the policeman boring into him as the man spoke into his radio.

Knowing the sheriff's car could not follow him out of the county, he started the engine and drove out of the lot.

***

"I appreciate you telling us, Sheriff. We can manage from here." Kruger listened in silence and after a few moments said, "Yes, thank you." He ended the call and moved toward the window of his hotel room. A cloudless sky and the sun at its zenith greeted him. After spending several minutes contemplating their next step, he left his hotel room and walked to Sandy Knoll's door.

When the big man opened it, Kruger said, "Monk just left the apartment. What's the range of the GPS unit?"

Knoll motioned him inside. When the door closed, he said, "You're thinking old school, Sean. The unit communicates with three geosynchronous orbiting satellites, which allow us to know where the SUV is, what direction it is traveling and how fast." He held up his cell phone. "All that information is relayed to an app I have on this."

"Huh, glad my parents didn't have one when I first started driving."

"Yeah, no joke. Mine would have taken the keys and locked me in my room."

With a grim smile, Kruger nodded. "Let's go find him."

The four men split into two teams, Knoll and Kruger, Gibbs and Clark. Since Knoll had the GPS app on his phone, he led the way.

Sixty minutes later, after traveling west on Interstate 80 for seventy miles, Kruger glanced at Knoll. "Where's he now?"

"About thirty miles ahead of us. He just made a turn to the north. Looks like he's on US 287."

"Where does that lead us?"

With a grin, Knoll said, "North."

"Ha, ha. Where north?"

"It's Wyoming, Sean. There isn't much out here."

Kruger nodded. "I can see that. Are we getting close to mountains?"

"Sean, we're in the high plains. The elevation of Laramie is almost two thousand feet higher than Denver."

Kruger shot Knoll a quick glance. "Huh. Didn't know that."

Knoll nodded. "We're actually descending by driving west."

"What about north?"

"About the same, until we get to the Shoshone National Forest or Yellowstone. The elevation increases there and yes, that means mountains. My guess is he's heading to Shoshone."

"How do you know so much about this area?"

"Did some winter survival training out here—about twenty years ago."

Kruger nodded and returned to staring at the barren landscape.

Five minutes later, Knoll asked, "Your status is temporary right now, isn't it?"

"Yes. Why do you ask?"

"Jimmie told me a few days before you officially retired, someone from HR contacted him and gave him a choice of three Field Offices that needed someone with his language skills. Phoenix, Houston and Santa Fe."

"All of those are good field offices. Is there a problem?"

"Yeah, he's not moving. Alexia makes good money with JR's firm and he doesn't want to leave their place. He told me since his sister died, he's never felt at home anywhere. Their place near Stockton Lake does. Plus, he wants to raise their son away from big cities."

"I take it you feel the same way."

With a nod, Knoll continued, "Yeah, Linda and I are tired of moving, too. When we were both in the military, we relocated constantly until we bought our place in Arlington. Then when we bought the condo at the Lake of the Ozarks, we started spending more time there. We put the place in Arlington up for sale about three weeks ago and had a contract on it within two days. Linda's in Texas now getting everything packed."

"Are congratulations in order?"

Another nod from Knoll was his answer.

"So, what are you trying to say, Sandy?"

Knoll shot Kruger a quick glance and smiled. "Neither one of us have any intentions of moving if the bureau tells us to."

"Not very conducive for career advancement."

"We both know that and, quite frankly, don't care."

"Okay." Kruger's attention was on the big man now, not the depressing landscape. "So, what does that mean?"

"Before I say anything, what are your plans when this Monk business is over?"

Kruger looked ahead and took a deep breath. "Nothing specific. We're going to take a family vacation to South Dakota."

Chuckling, Knoll asked, "What the hell's in South Dakota?"

"My college roommate. We've kept in touch all these years and haven't seen each other for almost a decade. He lost his wife to cancer about a year ago and I'd like to spend a few days with him. We want to show the kids Mount Rushmore and some of the other sights up there."

"After that?"

Kruger did not answer.

"Kind of what I thought. Jimmie wanted me to ask you a question."

"Seems we have some time on our hands right now."

"Now, remember, this is only in the conception phase. We haven't got the bugs worked out yet, nor do we know where to get the financing."

"I'm listening."

"You know that after Jimmie left the Seal's he worked for Joseph for a while, just like I did?"

"No, I didn't know that, but I always wondered about it."

"He really enjoyed it, as did I. The only reason we joined the FBI is because you asked us to."

Again, Kruger did not respond.

"We're thinking about setting up a private defense contractor company. I still have a lot of contacts with within the military who are at the Pentagon. So does Jimmie. Even Joseph agreed to help when he can."

"Sounds like a good plan."

Taking another quick glance at Kruger, Knoll said, "We'd like for you to join us when we do it."

Silence filled the rented GMC Denali as Kruger just stared at Knoll.

The big man continued, "We have a hanger located at the Springfield Branson National Airport we'll use it as our base of operations. We signed a six-month option on it last week. One of my military buddies is a pilot who agreed to join us when we pull the trigger."

"Do you have a corporate name picked out?"

"KKG Solutions. We already have an LLC set up as our corporate entity."

"This appears to be far beyond the conception stage. You two are serious, aren't you?"

"Very. We already have the board of directors

determined, a mission statement, we've filed with the Missouri Secretary of State and have an attorney identified as our legal counsel."

"Who is it?"

With a grin, Knoll said, "An ex-Seal Jimmie knows who got his law degree after he left the service."

"So, what's stopping you two from doing this?"

"You."

"Don't let me stop you."

"We aren't, but we also knew you wouldn't join us while still with the FBI. That, as they say, is just a matter of time now. You are an integral part of our plan. We want to offer services most private military contractors don't offer."

With a smile, Kruger said, "I've never been in the military."

"Doesn't matter. You have over twenty-five years with the FBI. We need your expertise."

"I don't know…"

"Like I said, we don't have the financial backing locked yet and we need to conclude this issue with Monk. We don't need an answer right now."

Kruger stared out the passenger window, his hand supporting his chin. Knoll couldn't see it, but the ex-FBI agent displayed the slightest of smiles. He knew where to get the financial backing.

CHAPTER 23

Northwest Fremont County, Wyoming

Nestled in a wooded area halfway between Lava Mountain Lodge and Fish Lake Mountain, the cabin could only be accessed on horseback or four-wheel drive. It remained in a trust created by Monk's mother. As the only remaining member of the family, Monk, in effect owned the cabin. The thought of the land passing into the hands of the state, should something happen to him, never entered his mind.

Monk parked the Equinox in front of the cabin and turned off the engine. His state of anxiety lessened as he stared at the structure. To him, this was home. The frequency of his seizures since leaving this oasis concerned him. No one could find him here, not even the men who had sent the cowboy assassin knew about this place.

There was nothing to retrieve from the back of the SUV after leaving the apartment without luggage. His tension from the previous few days melted away as he stood inside the quiet cabin. Taking a deep breath, he closed his eyes and relaxed. Time to get back to normalcy. First on the list, build a fire in the fireplace.

As he transferred the wood from the storage bin next to the hearth and arranged it inside the firebox, he heard the door to his cabin open.

***

Knoll pointed at his phone. "After he turned west off 287 it appears he drove another eleven miles before stopping. The vehicle hasn't moved for ten minutes."

Kruger looked at the phone. "How far?"

"The turn is a few miles ahead. It's starting to get dark, what do you want to do?"

Silence filled the Denali as Kruger stared at the screen of the satellite phone. "You're the guy with special forces training. What do you think?"

With a grin, Knoll said, "Keep going."

"Then by all means, Agent Knoll, proceed."

It took the better part of an hour for the four men to navigate the dark trail leading to the remote cabin using the tracking app. With Clark and Gibbs abandoning their rented Ford Fusion, Gibbs now sat in the front passenger seat guiding Knoll. When they were half-a-mile from the location indicated by GPS, they donned the tactical gear Clark had brought when he arrived in Wyoming.

The equipment included night-vision goggles, wireless headsets for their Motorola radios, utility vests, hiking boots, a backpack with evidence-gathering supplies, a shotgun and two AR-15 assault rifles. Clark took the shotgun with Knoll and Gibbs carrying the AR-15s. Kruger relied on his trusty Glock 19.

Knoll led the way on what could now only charitably be called a trail, followed by Gibbs, Clark and finally Kruger. The path surrounded by Lodgepole Pines with the occasional Spruce and Ponderosa Pine intermixed. As they approached a clearing, they could see a cabin in the green hue of the NVGs. Monk's Equinox was parked several yards from the front entrance. No lights were visible through the two windows on either side of the door.

When he saw the darkened cabin, hairs on the back of Knoll's neck tingled. He signaled everyone to halt and gathered them around. In as soft a voice as possible, he said, "It's too early for all the lights to be out. Something's wrong."

Clark whispered, "Maybe he was tired from the trip and went to bed early."

Kruger shook his head. "I'm with Sandy. Something's not right."

Displaying a crooked smile, Jimmie Gibbs, said, "I'll check it out."

Before anyone could protest, Gibbs took off in the dark toward the SUV. Using the vehicle to hide his approach to the cabin, he stopped and felt the hood. The engine compartment was cool. Keeping low, he dashed to the left side of the log structure and peered around the corner toward the front door. Through his NVG's, Gibbs could see the door slightly ajar. He keyed his mic. "Front door is open slightly. I'm checking it out."

He crouched and approached the door low enough not to be seen through the window. Once at the door, he stood and listened and only heard silence. With the door hinges on the side where he stood, he quietly moved to the right side of the doorway and pushed the door open with the barrel of his AR-15. The silence remained unbroken.

He whispered into the mic, "Interior's dark, no sound. Approach the right side for back-up."

His response came as two clicks in his earpiece. Ten seconds later, Knoll stood next to him with Clark and Kruger on the opposite side of the door. Jimmie held up his fist with three fingers extended. He lowered each one until he made a fist and bolted inside with Knoll right behind him.

In the after-action report Kruger would file later, his description of the scene inside the cabin was labeled as gruesome.

Monk was found bound to a straight-back chair. Numerous fingers littered the cabin floor where they dropped after being severed. His eyes were bound by a wide strip of cloth and his head hung at an odd angle, revealing a fatal slash across his neck. Blood covered the floor around him.

Knoll and Gibbs, having seen worse in their tours overseas, started looking for the utensils used for the torture. Kruger holstered his Glock and stared at the lifeless body. After glancing at his watch, he calculated the time they'd seen the vehicle stationary on the GPS monitor and the current time as just over two hours. He said, "Sandy, which side of Monk's car did you place the GPS tracker?"

"Driver's side rear wheel well, why?"

"A hunch. Come with me, Ryan."

Kruger found the unit Sandy had placed on the SUV and looked in each of the other wheel wells. Nothing. He slid under the Chevy and, using a flashlight, once again found nothing. Finally, he opened the driver's door and looked at the On-Star unit. With Sandy's satellite phone in hand, he punched in a number.

JR answered. "What'd you find?"

"A mess. Do you still have a backdoor into the On-Star system?"

"Yeah, why?"

"I need a vehicle traced."

"Give me the VIN number."

After JR had the number, he said, "I'll call you back."

Kruger ended the call and sat in the driver's seat. He looked around the interior of the vehicle and started searching the glove box, center console and all the other nooks and crannies of a modern SUV.

Ten minutes later, his phone vibrated. "Talk to me."

"The unit in that particular vehicle has been hacked, Sean."

"Go on."

"It's sending a continuous signal, which is not how it's supposed to work. To me, it looks like someone is holding the On-Star button continuously. You're rummaging around in the interior opening and closing the glove box, aren't you?"

"Yeah."

"Thought so. I can hear everything you are doing and what you are saying. Someone was using it to keep track of Monk."

"And someone is probably listening to me right now."

"That would be a good assumption."

Kruger stepped out of the SUV and made a call directly to Joseph Kincaid.

***

The first responders to the scene were Fremont County Deputy Sheriffs driving all-wheel drive Ford Police Interceptors and F-150 Police Responders. Clark and Knoll were the intermediators while Kruger and Gibbs waited to search the cabin. By midnight, FBI agents from the Denver Field Office arrived, along with a forensic technician and a medical examiner.

As the first hints of dawn began to illuminate the surrounding Lodgepole pines, Gibbs and Kruger were allowed into the cabin to start the search for any documents deemed important to the investigation of the late Dorian Monk. After the body was removed and on its way to Cheyenne, they donned latex gloves and started searching the interior. Thirty minutes later, Gibbs motioned for

Kruger to join him.

"What does that look like, Sean?"

Kruger bent and examined the floorboards. "Huh." He smiled. "A trap door hidden under a throw rug."

"There's dirt in the cracks. Doesn't look like it's been opened for a while."

Using his cell phone, Kruger took a variety of pictures before Gibbs utilized a flathead screwdriver to pry open the section of floor. A two-foot by two-foot space was exposed, one barely large enough for a man to pass. Once the door was off, the bottom remained obscured in the gloom of the cabin.

Using a Maglite, Gibbs lay on the floor and stuck his head and hand with the flashlight into the opening. "This thing's about five-feet-deep and ten-feet-square." He stood and prepared to lower himself down. "It's lined with banker boxes."

"Okay, let's get a few halogen lamps down there and see what we can find."

One of the sheriff's deputies offered a utility ladder from his truck and the FBI agents from Denver offered the halogen lamps. After pictures of the hidden chamber were taken, Kruger and Gibbs started removing the boxes.

The five-foot ceiling caused both to stoop over while lifting the heavy boxes through the small opening. Kruger's back screamed with discomfort as the constant bending stretched seldom-used muscles. But he chose not to tell anyone.

With the files now on the front porch of the cabin, Kruger and Gibbs started their search. The vast majority of the documents were spiral notebooks with mathematical equations and handwritten notes of their meaning. Also found were numerous notebooks containing the outlines for the various papers Monk had published. After digging through the last box, Kruger felt a note of frustration.

"There isn't anything here except the history and notes

of a professor who taught classes and published papers."

Gibbs remained quiet staring at one particular stack of boxes.

"What's the matter, Jimmie?"

"Not sure. I've got a feeling about something." He returned to the stack and opened the top box. Gibbs removed the contents. Three quarters of the way down was a flat piece of cardboard that created a false bottom. Gibbs looked at Kruger with a grin and lifted it. Underneath they saw manila folders bulging with papers. Kruger lifted one and started flipping through.

With a big smile, Kruger looked at Gibbs. "Bingo."

CHAPTER 24

FBI Denver Field Office

Thomas Shark energetically shook Kruger's hand. "It's good to see you again, Sean."

"Congratulations on your first assignment as a Special Agent in Charge."

"I had a good mentor."

During Shark's first year as a rookie agent, he had assisted Kruger in finding a serial killer who used his job as a substitute school bus driver to kill unsuspecting customers of a convenience store chain. All because the shooter felt the chain's stores were purposefully giving him lottery tickets that weren't winners. Shark had also worked with Kruger on the investigation leading to the attempted terrorist bombing of the Bud Walton Arena in Fayetteville, Arkansas. Shark was the individual who had single handedly kept Kruger alive until the paramedics arrived after the premature detonation of the terrorist's bomb.

Kruger blushed. "I never thanked you for what you did for me in Fayetteville."

"Nothing to thank me for."

"Yeah, well…"

"I understand you're now a Special Agent in Charge with Homeland Security."

"Urban legend. My current assignment is finding the person who murdered Alan Seltzer."

"Is this Monk character responsible?"

"We think he pulled the trigger. At first, the theory was he acted alone. But, with evidence gathered at his cabin, we now know he was receiving instructions from someone else."

Shark smiled. "I was told to offer you all the assistance you needed, which I would have anyway."

"That's kind of you, Tom." Kruger paused and folded his arms. "Do you have problems with survivalists here in Colorado?"

A quiet fell over the meeting. Taking a deep breath, Shark nodded. "It's more than a problem. While we have a lot of legitimate individuals who are preparing for a collapse of society, others are using it as a ruse to conduct gang-like criminal activity."

"Such as?"

"The usual stuff—drugs, prostitution, smuggling guns, protection rackets, et cetera. You name it, it's being done."

"Any problems with crimes against people with ethnic backgrounds?"

Shark nodded. "You have to remember Colorado is a fairly liberal-minded state, marijuana is legal here. However, as you venture further north up the Front Range Urban Corridor, attitudes change to a more libertarian disdain of any interference by government."

"What's the Front Range Urban Corridor?"

"The eastern side of the Rocky Mountains from Pueblo, Colorado up through Denver to Cheyenne, Wyoming. That encompasses about five million individual souls."

"So, why is that a problem?"

"I hate the term, but I would call the individuals involved white nationalists."

"How bad?"

"It gets worse the farther north you go. Lots of places to hide in the Rockies."

"You didn't answer my question, Tom."

"No, I didn't because, to be honest, we really don't know the extent at this time. When you get into certain regions of the mountains, it resembles another country. Witnesses are either afraid to talk or they secretly agree with the groups." He hesitated. "The bureau's lost a few agents over the years."

"Huh."

Shark nodded. "I was sent here to clean it up. So far, I'm not making much progress."

"Do the local authorities support your efforts?"

"Some do. Others shrug their shoulders and look the other way."

"Let me guess—the more rural counties."

"Not necessarily. If the sheriff's been in office for a while, the office is helpful. It's the newly elected ones who turn the blind eye."

"What about state government?"

"Colorado is on board. Wyoming, not so much."

"Why?"

"The previous SAC didn't have evidence, but he thought these groups were contributing tons of money to members of the state legislature. He felt the governor was being pressured by members of his party to lay off. Apparently, he tried to clean it up and then, all of a sudden, stopped."

"Is Paul Stumpf aware of this?"

Shark shook his head.

"Why not?"

"The previous SAC got frustrated with the problem and turned his attention to other priorities. I've only been here a month and everything I'm telling you is from discussions with other agents and from reading the retired SAC's files."

Kruger smiled and nodded. "Got it." He paused and walked to the window in Shark's office. He stood there and held his hands behind his back. "How many agents do you trust?"

There was silence from Shark.

Turning and glancing at him, Kruger raised his eyebrows. "That many?"

"I don't know them well enough to trust yet. I've got some eager-beavers here in Denver, but the ones up in Wyoming have been around a while."

With a smile, Kruger said, "Then it's time for them to be transferred."

"How's that going to happen?"

The corner of Kruger's mouth twitched. "Leave it to me. That way, you will have nothing to do with it and can start fresh with new agents of your own choosing."

Shark smiled and nodded. "Can you tell me what you found in Monk's cabin?"

"Not yet. Not because I don't want to, but because I don't completely understand it. What I can tell you is it appears he was part of a larger organization. An organization posing a serious threat to our country."

***

The death of Dorian Monk presented two options for Kruger. One, he could disband his team, end his tenure with Homeland Security and retire. Or, his team could delve into the documents found in Monk's mountain cabin and determine how serious the threat was. Kruger chose the latter.

Two days after his meeting with Shark, he was once again leaning against the credenza behind JR's cubicle, sipping a cup of coffee. The original Keurig machine Kruger fussed about for years had eventually stopped working and been recycled. Replacing the Keurig and occupying its own serving cabinet and storage area was a Bunn commercial coffeemaker with a brewing station and two warming plates. A local company serviced it on a bi-weekly basis.

Kruger looked at the new unit. "I like this new system Jody authorized for the second floor."

"I miss my Keurig."

"Why? The coffee sucked."

JR turned to look at his friend. "That's a matter of opinion. I could experiment with different styles of coffee with the Keurig. All you get with that monstrosity over there is a brownish-black liquid that tastes the same every time you make a pot."

"That's the point, JR. Consistency."

"Bah, humbug. Where's the excitement with consistency?"

With a grin, Kruger said, "You've got money, buy yourself a new Keurig."

"Don't think the thought hasn't crossed my mind."

"But…"

"I don't want to hurt Jody's feelings."

"Bullshit. You hadn't thought of it yet. Had you?"

A sheepish grin appeared on JR lips and he chuckled. "No, I really hadn't."

Both men laughed before the conversation turned serious. Kruger said, "Have you been able to find anything?"

JR stood and walked the short distance to the coffee service area, poured a fresh cup and returned. "They have a website I've been poking around in. It's crude and made by someone using a WordPress template."

"And…"

"Very amateurish. There's not much to it."

"You sure it's the same group?"

"I believe so." He paused and took a sip from his fresh

cup. "From experience, we both know cell phone reception in the remote parts of the Rockies can be spotty."

Kruger nodded. "I would think internet would be too."

"Exactly. That's why I believe the group isn't communicating through their website or with cell phones."

"Then how are they talking to each other?"

"With shortwave radio."

With a frown, Kruger tilted his head.

"That was my reaction at first. Have you ever heard of a numbers station?"

"No."

"During the Cold War, number stations were used by various governments to openly communicate with their intelligence officers in other countries. The idea was to broadcast a set of numbers which would be meaningless to someone without the key. If the listener knew the key, they could understand the message."

"Sounds like a bad spy movie."

"Kind of, but the system works and is still being used to some extent today. Computer generated voices speak the numbers and the broadcasting equipment is portable, so you can move it around. Plus, it could even be outside the US."

"So, what are you saying, JR?"

"Shortwave radio is not line of sight. If the conditions are right, you can broadcast a shortwave signal around the world. Which is perfect for communicating with someone who lives in the backwoods of the Rocky Mountains or in some of the more isolated areas of Wyoming, Montana or Idaho. Or for that matter, anywhere in the US." He paused. "I believe they are using the website to communicate the key to the numbers stations."

"But internet would be spotty at best in some locations."

"Yes, but if the numbers repeat for a while and then suddenly change, members would know to go to a Wi-Fi spot and get the key."

"So that means you can break the code, right?"

JR shook his head. "Like I told you, the website is very bland and mundane. I've searched it for hidden links and can't find any. They may use images to tell members where to look for the key for the number station broadcast. I just don't know."

"You're making it sound pretty sophisticated."

"It is." He took a sip of coffee. "That's why I don't think it's the work of a bunch of white nationalists."

Kruger's eyes narrowed. "Who do you think it is?"

"I can't be certain."

"Spit it out, JR. Who do you think it is?"

"Who's been interfering with our elections?"

"Depends on who you listen to and believe."

"Right, but the general consensus is the Russians, right?"

A nod was his answer.

"I don't have any proof of what I'm going to tell you but think back about Alexei Kozlov."

"Okay."

"He was a sleeper agent planted in the US during the Cold War to interfere with our financial institutions. Right?"

"Yes. But that didn't work out too well for them, did it?"

"No. My guess is they learned from it." JR took a deep breath and let it out slowly. "I need to do more digging into Monk's background."

"Okay, stop right there. You're talking in circles. What do you suspect?"

With a grim smile, JR said, "There's a hole in Monk's childhood of about eight years I can't find anything about. Where was he?"

Rolling his eyes, Kruger shook his head. "Would you *please* just tell me what you're talking about?"

"Looking at his elementary records, there's no mention

of his being a math prodigy as a child. His grades were so-so."

"Lots of smart children find themselves bored in elementary school and get poor grades because of it."

"I'm aware of that. But there's something about Monk's early school records that doesn't correspond with his later success as a mathematician."

"As a rule, success in college corresponds to good performance in elementary school, but not always. What are you getting at?"

"It's like the early Monk and the college-age Monk were two separate individuals."

Kruger stopped sipping his coffee and blinked as he studied the contents of the cup. "Are you going where I think you're going?"

"Probably. The eight-year gap concerns me."

"And that's why you mentioned Alexei Kozlov. You think Dorian Monk was a Russian?"

"I think it's a possibility."

Kruger was silent for several moments. "Ted Kaczynski was born to parents of Polish decent. His mother believes his antisocial behavior grew out of a long hospital stay when he was very young. Hospital stays for young children during that era were brutal on their psyche. You've mentioned several times the eight-year gap in Monk's childhood."

JR nodded.

"Are you suggesting something happened during those eight years?"

Another nod.

"Then we'd better determine what that something was."

CHAPTER 25

Lander, Wyoming

Mark's Western Wear maintained the distinction as the top western supply store in Wyoming due to tourists visiting various dude ranches located in the surrounding county. If you wanted a custom pair of cowboy boots or cowboy hat, it was the place to go. For a town like Lander, the county seat, it served as a place for locals to buy their clothes. The store also sponsored numerous professional circuit rodeo riders. For those inclined to the sport, most Saturdays would find one of these rugged individuals signing autographs or putting on demonstrations for the kids.

The proprietor was a congenial man in his mid-fifties, prone to telling tall tales to anyone who would listen and then laugh with gusto. He possessed an oval face, thick dark brown hair displaying an ever-increasing number of gray strands and thick bushy eyebrows that danced as he communicated his stories. His chocolate-colored eyes peered through rimless glasses and rested on a long slender nose. His normal uniform, during business hours, featured clothing from his store's weekly circular.

Though he was known to his friends and customers as Kevin Marks, the name on his birth certificate appeared as Kreso Markovic, a name more fitting his Eastern Slavic ancestry. With his westernized name and cowboy-influenced wardrobe, he fit the description of a typical American entrepreneur not a flame-throwing leader of the Sovereign Citizen Movement. The reality was he held a profound suspicion of any form of government, especially the one in Washington, DC. Because of this distrust, he secretly plotted to undermine the confidence ordinary people held in their so-called-leaders in Washington.

The store opened at 10 a.m. every day except Sunday, when it opened at noon to allow the good people of Lander to attend church services. His morning duties included welcoming customers as he roamed the aisles of his store. At precisely 11:30, Marks was assisting an elderly customer pick-out a pair of jeans for her grandson's birthday when he noticed the short, stocky middle-aged man walk past him carrying three pairs of jeans to a particular fitting room.

"Ms. Carlson, I have a conference call in a few minutes. I'll get Linda to assist you further."

"Thank you, Kevin. I would appreciate it."

With one of his assistants heading to Ms. Carlson's location, Marks entered his office and locked the door. He immediately went to a bookshelf standing against the wall separating his office from the showroom floor and released a latch hidden behind the books on the third shelf. The unit swung open like a door and the short, stocky man entered his office.

The man, whose broad shoulders tapered to a thin waist, giving him the appearance of a Y, frowned as he entered the room. "Where the hell did you find that cowboy from Montana?"

Marks folded his arms. "Montana, why do you ask?"

"Because he was incredibly stupid and didn't check to see if Monk was being watched. His other dumbass move was trying to take Monk out in broad daylight. Now Monk's disappeared, the cowboy's dead and the FBI's swarming all over Monk's apartment."

"Monk's no longer a problem."

The shorter man blinked several times. "What do you mean Monk's no longer a problem? He's been acting squirrely ever since he showed up at his cabin two-and-a-half months ago."

Marks walked over to a Mr. Coffee unit he kept in his office and poured himself a cup. "We don't have to worry about Professor Monk anymore."

The shorter man folded his arms. "Really. Since when?"

"Since an associate of ours followed him to his cabin."

"Interesting."

"There's also a gaggle of federal agents at the place right now."

"How do you know?"

"The Fremont County Sheriff told me. He also told me they don't have a clue what happened."

"Good. Can they trace the cowboy back to us?"

With a shake of his head, Marks smiled. "I don't see how."

"You sure?"

"Positive."

"Okay. What's next?"

"I think we need to find out how the FBI became interested in Monk. He did it for five years without raising suspicions. Then all of a sudden he draws all of this attention."

"Maybe he got careless."

"Maybe." He looked at the stocky man. "But I doubt it. Monk may have been weird, but he was meticulous in his planning."

"I'm told there were four FBI agents at the apartment."

"Yes, all of them will be dealt with in time, but I want to know which agent started suspecting Monk."

"What do you want done about him?"

"Tell everyone to stay low and quiet until this all blows over. Then we'll deal with the FBI agent. Remember, patience is a virtue. A virtue that has served us well so far."

A smile appeared on the man who was shaped like a Y as he headed back to the hidden door. After it closed, Marks locked it and returned to his desk. He sat and turned to a large flat screen monitor that displayed nine views from various security cameras dispersed around the sales floor. The top right image showed the visitor taking a pair of jeans to one of the cash registers at the front.

Yes, it was time to find out how the FBI had learned of Monk and his activities. Using his cell phone, he dialed a number.

When the call was answered, he said, "We need to talk."

***

Sheriff Roger Blake watched as Marks approached his table. He was sitting in a small cafe across from the sheriff's office in downtown Landers.

When the western wear shop owner sat, Blake said, "How long is this going to take, Kevin? I have a meeting in twenty minutes."

"Need I remind you of who was your largest donor in the last election, Sheriff?"

"You remind me of it constantly. What did you want to talk about?"

"Spare me the attitude, Roger." He paused. "We may have a slight problem."

Blake took a deep breath and let it out slowly. "Concerning?"

"The FBI's sudden interest in Dorian Monk."

"You've never been a law enforcement officer, have

you?"

"No, and I don't intend to be."

"Then you don't understand what happens when a fellow officer falls in the line of duty."

"No, but I bet you're going to tell me."

Ignoring the comment, Blake continued, "Monk made a mistake shooting the Deputy Director of the FBI. A huge mistake."

"He was a black man in a position of authority. We both know that isn't good for this country."

"No, it isn't. But killing the man brought the entire resources of the FBI into the picture. Before that, your group's activities weren't even on the radar."

"Should I remind you that you too are part of the group, Roger? Besides, Monk's not a problem anymore."

"That's the part you don't get, do you? I'm going to have more FBI agents snooping around now that Monk is dead. They'll want to know who killed him and why. You should have just let him stay in the woods, out of sight, out of mind."

"That wasn't possible."

Blake shut his eyes and shook his head. "Why did he go to Laramie?"

"We don't know. Monk seldom mentioned his plans to me."

"I suggest you find out, because I have a Special Agent in Charge from Denver on the way to oversee the investigation."

Marks was quiet for several moments. "When?"

"Later today. He's taking over. I also suspect he will bring in agents we don't know."

"Why do you say that?"

"Because the two agents assigned to this county were suddenly transferred to the east coast two days ago."

"What about the ones in Laramie?"

"Also transferred."

"So, we don't have any eyes and ears left?"

"Correct."

"What are you doing about that, Sheriff?"

Blake chuckled. "For now, nothing. I'm going to sit back and let them investigate. If Monk did as he was told, it will be a dead end."

"Monk seldom did as he was told."

"Then you are correct, you may have a problem."

"I believe you mean *we* have a problem."

"We'll see."

"Who was the FBI agent who found Monk?"

"He wasn't with the FBI. He was with Homeland Security."

One of Marks' eyebrows rose. "He wasn't an FBI agent?"

"No. Like I said, his badge indicated he was with Homeland Security."

"What was his name?"

"I don't remember."

"First name?"

"Don or John, something like that."

"You're supposed to remember those types of details, Sheriff."

"I just heard him referred to as agent. I saw his ID once and was surprised it said Homeland Security. He put it away before I could see his name."

"You're no help."

"One more issue you need to know about."

"What?"

"The FBI hauled at least thirty bank storage boxes out of Monk's cabin."

Marks grew quiet, then said, "Did you get a look at them?"

"No. I asked but was told it was evidence in a Federal crime. When I protested, I was told to file a complaint."

"Did they say what was in the boxes?"

"Only that they were Monk's class notes."

"We need to know what was in those boxes."

"Good luck with that. Now, if you don't mind, I need to get ready for this new FBI SAC that's coming to town." The sheriff stood and walked out of the little shop.

Marks sipped the coffee he'd purchased before sitting down. The news about Homeland Security, while surprising, offered an opportunity to get ahead of this possible crisis. He left the cafe for his Ford pickup to make a phone call.

CHAPTER 26

Springfield, MO

The team once again commandeered JR's conference room on the second floor. The files beneath the false bottom of the banker's box Gibbs had found were spread over the large table. Four additional boxes with false bottoms were discovered and transported from the remote cabin to this room. While Monk's avocation of mathematics was a structured discipline, his filing system could best be described as chaotic and haphazard.

Ninety percent of the files were class notes and mathematical proofs. Those files were transferred to the FBI forensic lab at Quantico, Virginia. The remaining ten percent were now being sorted and categorized by Kruger. As someone who would never delegate a task he wouldn't do himself, he carefully read each piece of paper. He suspected somewhere in this stack of random papers might be a clue as to why Alan Seltzer had been gunned down in cold blood.

JR entered the room and watched his friend skim a page

and place it in a stack to his right. "How long do you think this is going to take?"

Looking up, Kruger shrugged. "Not sure. I let everyone else go home. Too much overtime. Since I'm not on the FBI's clock anymore," he smiled, "I get to do it. Besides, this way I don't have anyone breathing over my shoulder expecting me to hurry."

"Are you finding anything useful?"

With a slight nod, Kruger skimmed another page. As he laid it on a stack in the center of the table, he pointed to a pile next to it. "Those are bank records. Currently, they aren't in any chronological or financial institute order, so it's hard to confirm what I'm suspecting. The guy has way too much cash for someone who was a part-time college professor. I've noticed he receives a large deposit of cash at random times during the year. Once I get the pages in chronological order, they might give us a better idea of where the money came from."

"Can I look?"

"Help yourself."

JR remained quiet as he glanced through the stack of papers. He picked out several and then returned the remaining ones to their place on the table. With the pages in hand, he returned to his cubicle and started typing away on the keyboard.

Kruger ignored his friend as he concentrated on his own task.

Ten minutes later, JR appeared in the conference room door again. "Take a break. I've got something to show you."

Kruger removed his reading glasses and rubbed his weary eyes. "What'd you find?"

JR pointed to the middle of the three monitors. "That may be the source of Monk's cash."

Putting his reading glasses back on, Kruger leaned over and stared at the screen. He straightened and turned toward his friend. "How about that."

***

Stephanie Kruger sat on the corner of their bed as she watched her husband pack an overnight bag. "How long do you think you'll be gone this time?"

"One night, no more."

"Good."

The corner of his lip rose in a half smile. "This will be my last official trip to FBI headquarters. Dorian Monk's death changed everything. I'll turn everything we found over to the bureau and they can figure it out."

"Can you do that, Sean?"

He folded a pair of jeans and concentrated on fitting them into the bag. After taking a deep breath and letting it out slowly, he nodded. "I won't miss the travel."

"Mia told me Sandy and Jimmie are thinking about quitting."

Kruger nodded. "More than thinking about it, they are. However, there is a reason. They've decided to form a business and become private defense contractors."

She frowned. "You're kidding."

"Nope. They asked me to join them."

The frown intensified. "Are you?"

"At this point..." He hesitated and gave her a grim smile. "Probably not."

"Probably not?"

He stopped packing and looked at her. "I'm done, Steph. The government says I'm too old to carry a gun and do the job. I have to accept that. Besides, I'm looking forward to being a full-time husband and father."

She chuckled and shook her head. "No, you're not."

"What do you mean?"

"I know you, Sean Kruger. You will not be happy staying at home while the world collapses around us. You are too young to simply retire and fade into the background."

He straightened and stared at her but remained quiet.

She continued, "You need to find something to do. If you retire, it will kill you, literally. Not at first, but eventually. I didn't marry you for that to happen. You need to be around to walk Kristin down the aisle on her wedding day. So, find something useful to do."

A small smile creased his lips as he returned to his packing.

***

Sitting at the departure gate for his flight to Washington, DC, Kruger cupped his chin in his hand, an elbow on the arm rest of the seat. This was one of the many aspects of traveling he would not miss, waiting for a flight whose current status showed *delayed* on the departure board. As the minutes ticked down, the possibility of missing his connecting flight in Chicago loomed.

How many hours of his life, over the course of his career, had been wasted sitting in an airport waiting on a flight? If he knew the truth, he was sure his depression would intensify.

He reached into his sport coat pocket and retrieved his cell phone. The number he dialed was answered on the third ring.

"Let me guess, your flight's delayed."

"How'd you guess, Joseph?"

"Have you left yet?"

"No, that's why I'm calling. It appears I will miss my connecting flight in Chicago."

"Why do you say that?"

"Because if the plane left now, I'd have fifteen minutes to make my connection at O'Hare. We both know that won't happen. Plus, as this airport is fond of saying, the equipment hasn't arrived yet."

"No plane?"

"Nope."

Kruger heard a chuckle and then, "Let me make a call."

Fifteen minutes later his phone vibrated. Looking at the Caller ID, he smiled and answered.

Joseph said, "How fast can you get over to the private aviation FBO?"

"About thirty minutes, why?"

"There's a pilot there who owns a HA-420 HondaJet. He's currently in a meeting, but can get you to Washington, DC by afternoon."

"What's his name?"

"Stewart Barnett."

"I'm heading his way."

***

As they shook hands, Kruger studied the young pilot. He wore a Nike ballcap over close-cropped dark brown hair and his three-day-old beard showed no signs of gray. With a slender build and cocky attitude he radiated self-confidence. The faded blue jeans, scuffed brown loafers, and untucked white oxford shirt with rolled-up sleeves reminded Kruger of several fighter pilots he had known over the years. "Nice to meet you, Stewart."

The pilot tilted his head and gave Kruger a knowing smile. "Good to meet you, too. Have we met before?"

"I don't think so, why?"

"You look familiar, that's all."

"How do you know Joseph?"

"I used to work for him, before he joined the ruling elite."

Nodding, Kruger said, "I've known him a long time. Maybe our paths crossed at some time."

"Maybe. He said you need to be in Washington, DC."

"Yes. I have a meeting with him this afternoon."

"I have to be there myself this afternoon. Glad I was going your way." Barnett pointed to a small business jet sitting on the tarmac outside the hanger containing the FBO. "That's mine."

Kruger asked, "What is it?"

"HondaJet HA-420."

Kruger studied the small jet as they approached. The white paint on the fuselage contrasted with the red surrounding the cockpit area and the red tip on the vertical stabilizer gave it a sports car appearance. "It looks fast."

"She can make 422 knots at 30,000 feet and climb at 3,990 feet per minute."

"Is that good?"

Barnett smiled. "I saw you drive a Mustang."

Kruger nodded.

"My guess is you drive it because it's a little more fun to drive than an SUV."

Another nod.

"Well, that's why I fly a HondaJet. It's a little more fun to fly than a Gulfstream."

As they climbed the airstair leading to the interior of the Jet, Kruger said, "Joseph told me you were in a meeting. Hope I didn't interrupt it."

Barnett shook his head. "No, we were finished. I was meeting with a couple of friends of yours."

"Really."

"Yeah, Sandy Knoll and Jimmie Gibbs."

Kruger smiled. "Hope it was a good meeting."

"Oh, yeah. A very good meeting." He paused. "I'll be landing at Dulles."

"That's fine. That's where I was originally scheduled to land. I have a car reserved."

"Great." He glanced at his watch. "When were you scheduled to get there?"

"Two-thirty."

Barnett laughed. "You'll beat your original flight."

With a huge smile, Kruger replied, "Where've you been all my life?"

CHAPTER 27

Washington, DC

Though it was originally planned for the White House, Kruger's meeting with Joseph occurred elsewhere. Directed by a text message received upon his arrival at Dulles, he drove his rental car to an attorney's office located close to Tysons Square.

The law firm's lobby screamed high-dollar legal advice and well-heeled clients. Two receptionists sat behind a long waist-high front desk composed of white polished marble on the top and front side. One of the two concentrated on a computer monitor as she spoke into a telephone headset and the other smiled when he entered the lobby.

The smiling receptionist appeared to be in her mid-thirties and wore professionally styled business attire. When he arrived at the desk, she said, "Welcome to Kelly, Flowers and Newman. You must be Sean Kruger."

A little surprised at the welcome, he replied, "Yes. Apparently, I'm expected."

She stood. "Everyone is already in the conference room.

Please follow me."

He followed and noticed an open office concept with numerous small conference areas for private legal consultations. Halfway down the hall, she opened a door, smiled again and walked back toward the front desk.

The conference room held a large round table with high-back leather office chairs. Three individuals were already seated, one being Joseph. The other two individuals Kruger did not recognize.

Joseph stood and offered his hand. "Good to see you, Sean. Let me introduce you." He gestured toward the woman. "This is Sharon Newman. She is the managing partner here at Kelly, Flowers and Newman."

"It is nice to finally meet you, Agent Kruger. Some of our associates have represented individuals you apprehended. They found the evidence you gathered against their clients rather daunting to defend against."

Kruger blinked several times as he tried to think of something witty and intelligent to say but couldn't. He simply smiled and said, "It's nice to meet you too, Ms. Newman."

The man offered his hand. Joseph said, "Sean, this is David Wu."

The two shook and Wu said, "I want to thank you for identifying the individual who murdered my sister."

With a smile, Kruger replied, "I have a good team."

Wu bowed slightly.

"Let's all take a seat and David can explain why we requested this meeting." Joseph returned to his seat and gave his attention to Wu.

"I'm sure you are wondering what the heck this is all about, Agent Kruger."

"Yes, but I'll assume you are going to explain, Mr. Wu."

"Please call me, David."

A nod came from Kruger.

"You saved the life of a dear friend of mine some years

back. And now, you identified the individual who took my sister from me and ended this madman's crimes. For those two events, I can never repay you."

Kruger started to say something, but he noticed Joseph shaking his head slightly, so he remained quiet.

Continuing, Wu said, "I understand because of some antiquated ruling you are now retired from the FBI."

"That is correct."

"Our country is less safe because of our politician's short-sightedness."

Glancing at Joseph, Kruger again remained silent.

"I want to remedy that situation."

"With all due respect, David…"

With a smile and a raised palm, Wu continued, "Let me explain. The dear friend you saved from an assassin's bullet some years ago was my roommate in college. We are still very close. He explained the situation you find yourself in and agrees with me. You need to carry on your life's work, as they say, catching bad-guys."

Kruger chuckled but did not respond.

Joseph spoke next. "Sean, what did you find in Monk's cabin?"

Looking at Joseph and then at Newman and Wu, Kruger answered, "Evidence of a larger conspiracy against our government by currently unknown individuals."

The National Security Adviser tilted his head. "How bad?"

"I can't say a lot more. We're still sifting through the information we gathered." He turned to Wu. "David, your sister's murder was not random. Neither was Alan Seltzer's."

"Which reinforces my decision and the reason you are here." Wu motioned for the file sitting in front of Sharon Newman. She handed it to him, and he placed the document inside in front of the retired FBI agent. Wu said, "After consulting with the President of the United States and his National Security Advisor, I asked Sharon to draw up a contract I would like for you to review and consider."

"What's in it?"

"A proposal."

"Want to be more specific?"

Wu shook his head. "You have a conference with Paul Stumpf tomorrow morning. Study the contract tonight, talk with Paul tomorrow, and then meet me at Dulles. I am returning to San Francisco in the afternoon and I would be honored if you would allow me to take you home. We can discuss the proposal on our flight."

With a raised eyebrow, Kruger started to ask a question, but Joseph answered before Kruger could say anything. "He has a private jet, Sean."

***

"Did you enjoy your dinner with Joseph and Mary last night?"

Kruger sat in front of Paul Stumpf's desk, fresh coffee mug in hand and nodded. "Yes, although I talked to Mary more than Joseph. His phone wouldn't stop ringing."

Stumpf chuckled. "Comes with the territory. Did you know Joseph's decided to stay with the president if he wins the election this fall?"

"That's what Mary told me. So much for the one year he originally agreed to."

"Yes, funny how things work out."

"Okay, Paul, what's this meeting about? I'm retired, remember?"

"That's what I wanted to talk to you about."

Taking a sip of coffee, Kruger remained silent.

"As you know, I haven't replaced Alan yet. The job of Deputy Director is still open."

More silence.

"I want you to take the job."

Closing his eyes, Kruger chuckled. "You're joking? Right?"

"Dead serious."

"Paul, I'm flattered, but if you remember correctly, I am retired."

"You're retired as an agent. Management status is different."

"No."

"You haven't thought about it."

"I don't have to. I'm not moving."

"You can commute."

"*No.*"

With a chuckle, Stumpf placed his arms on his desk and leaned forward. "That's what I thought you would say, but I wanted to make the offer."

"Thank you. I'm honored, but no."

"Did you read the contract David Wu drew up?"

"Yes."

"And?"

With a deep breath and a sigh, Kruger said, "I don't know yet. I'll have to discuss it with Stephanie before I make a decision."

"It keeps you in the game, Sean. Something we need right now."

"That's all well and good, but where does the authority for the proposal come from?"

"The president."

"What if he loses the election?"

"He won't. He's too popular. A rare situation these days."

"So, if he wins, the proposal could go another four years?"

"More likely eight."

"Didn't think he could serve more than two terms."

"He can't, but his first two years were after the death of Bryant. He can be elected twice on his own. There is a strong possibility the United States will have an effective president for ten years."

"Your term will be up by then."

Stumpf grinned. "Isn't it wonderful?"

Kruger responded with a sad smile.

"Now that you are retired, what is JR going to do?"

"He has zero chance of being bored. The recent outbreak of ransomware attacks has his company swamped. His original plan was to step back a little—those plans were interrupted."

The director handed Kruger a piece of paper. "I received this memo just before you got here."

"About?"

"Agents Benedict Knoll and James Gibbs turned in their resignations. Were you aware they were going to do that?"

"Yes."

"Do you know why?"

"Jimmie just built a house for his family near Stockton Lake in Missouri. During his tenure with the Navy, he bounced around without a real home for years. Same thing happened after he left the service. He told me he received notice he would be transferred to the Phoenix Field Office at the end of the month. That didn't go over too well with him."

"Okay, I get that. What about Knoll?"

"Same issue. Sandy and his wife, Linda, were in the service for twenty years. They just sold their house in Dallas and are looking for a place close to Jimmie and Alexia. They, too, are tired of moving. Sandy and Linda consider Jimmie to be their third son."

"I forgot about the moving an agent has to expect during their early career."

"It can be hard on families."

Stumpf looked over his glasses. "Case in point?"

With a nod, Kruger said, "I was lucky. If my mom and dad hadn't been able to move in with Brian and me when they did, I would have done the same thing. Resign."

"What are Sandy and Jimmie going to do?"

"You'll have to ask them."

"But you suspect something."

A shrug was Kruger's answer.

"If you don't take Wu's offer, what are you going to do?"

"Stephanie and I have been discussing the fact we haven't taken a real vacation together since Kristin and Mikey arrived. She suggested we visit my old college roommate in South Dakota. Since neither one of us have been to that part of the United States, we thought it would be fun to show the kids Mount Rushmore and some of the other historical spots while we're there."

"What about Wu's offer?"

"I'm going to think about it."

***

David Wu's private plane turned out to be a Learjet 75 with seating for seven. Kruger and Wu were the only passengers. As the plane streaked down the runway at Dulles and climbed into the sky, Wu turned to Kruger and asked, "Have you had a chance to read my proposal?"

Kruger nodded.

"What do you think?"

"I haven't had a chance to discuss it with my wife yet."

With a nod, Wu turned silent for several moments. "But you're interested."

"Yes."

"Good."

"Mr. Wu…"

"Please call me, David."

"David, I just completed a career with the FBI that lasted over twenty-five years. During that time, I can count on one hand the number of long vacations I've taken.

Actually, I can count them on two fingers. My wife and I have a trip planned and I would like to take that time to thoroughly discuss it with her."

"That's a fair request." Wu smiled mischievously. "Did I tell you I'm going to offer two friends of yours financial backing for a new endeavor they are starting?"

"Really? That's very generous of you."

"Joseph told me you made the suggestion to him during dinner last night."

"Urban legend."

Wu tilted his head and studied Kruger for a few moments. "You don't like taking credit for your accomplishments, do you?"

"The end results are what matters, not who gets the credit."

"I'll have to remember that. Do you mind if I use that in my next board meeting?"

With a shrug, Kruger said, "It's the truth, you can use it however you see fit."

With a chuckle, Wu said, "I now see why Roy Griffin likes you so well."

PART THREE

DOWN THE RABBIT HOLE

Mount Rushmore, South Dakota

Kristin Kruger looked up at her father and said, "Daddy, can we do something more fun tomorrow?"

Kruger looked down at his daughter, who held her mother's hand as they walked toward the parking lot away from the observation deck. He carried her younger brother Mikey, who had fallen asleep during their time looking at the mountain.

"I'm sorry you didn't enjoy our trip to Mount Rushmore, Kristin."

"I did enjoy it, but there's not a lot to do here except stare at a mountain with faces on it."

"That's the point, Kristin. Think of all the work it took to carve those images into a mountainside."

She blinked a few times as she looked up. "Wouldn't it

have been easier to just take a picture of those men with a cell phone and look at those?"

Suppressing a smile, Stephanie said, "I can see your point. What do you think, Sean?"

He shot her a quick glance and saw the smirk on her face and knew she was baiting him to answer.

"Well, Kristin, it would have been. But, when those images were carved into the mountain, cameras weren't on cell phones. In fact, cell phones didn't exist at that time."

"Why?"

Looking at his daughter, Kruger smiled. "Because they hadn't been invented yet."

"Okay, but why not take those men's picture with a regular camera?"

With a sigh, Kruger said, "Their images were carved into the mountain to honor their service to the United States."

"Why isn't your picture up there, Daddy? You've served the United States as an FBI agent."

Hearing his wife stifle a chuckle, Kruger looked at his daughter again. "My service was different than those men on the mountainside. All of them were very important presidents. Each one of them helped shape the path of this country."

"Oh." She paused for a few seconds. "Can we get something to drink? I'm thirsty."

Stephanie pointed to their left and said, "There's a café over there. We can get some ice cream and something to drink."

Kristin bounced up and down. "Yeah—ice cream."

***

Failed college student Peter Greer parked his dirty ten-year old Toyota Corolla in the back half of the parking lot at the Mount Rushmore National Memorial. Tourists were coming and going, which would assist his ability to get where he wanted to go unnoticed. He looked toward the mountain and could just see the top of the four dead presidents' heads above the facility's structures. He took a deep breath and looked at the shirt lying on the passenger seat next to him. After putting it on he stepped out. As he stood beside the car, he tucked the shirt into his navy-blue Dickies work pants. He then reached into the backseat to retrieve his backpack and slung it over his shoulder. The pack was heavy with the tools he needed to carry out his plan.

His last task before walking toward the Memorial was to place the Smokey the Bear hat on top of his head. He glanced at his image in the car's window and nodded slightly. With this completed, he started his trek toward the Memorial's entrance.

***

After consuming ice cream and a bottle of water, Mikey, now fully awake, joined his sister in complaining about wanting to go. As they approached the parking lot, Kruger noticed a man pass them on their left. The hairs on the back of his neck tingled when he saw the face.

He stopped, turned and watched the man walk toward the Memorial grounds. When he looked back at Stephanie and the kids, they were five feet in front of him. "Hey, Steph, I left something at the café. Take the kids to the car. I'll be right back."

She turned. "What did you forget?"

Kruger did not respond as he walked rapidly after the man with the backpack over his shoulder.

With a shrug, Stephanie said to the kids, "Let's go to the car. Your father's getting forgetful in his old age."

As Kruger approached the concrete bollards used to prevent vehicles from gaining access to the Memorial grounds, he noticed a park ranger sitting in a golf cart. As he approached, he removed his FBI credentials from his rear jean pocket. Since his retirement had been less than two months ago, he had not received the one with the word *retired* on it yet. He showed his ID to the park ranger sitting in the golf cart. "Sean Kruger, FBI. Who's in charge of your detail today?"

"Me. Why?"

"You may have a serious problem"—he glanced at the name tag—"Sergeant Miller."

Miller titled his head, "What kind of problem?"

"What color of pants does your team wear?"

With a frown, the man said, "Black, why?"

"I believe you have an active shooter situation about to erupt."

The sergeant's eyes grew wide. "How can you tell?"

Kruger pointed toward the man with the backpack. "The man with the backpack is dressed like a park ranger, but his pants are navy blue and he's nervous."

Miller immediately spoke into his shoulder microphone and said, "All units, we have a possible 10-32, ranger shirt and hat, navy pants with a backpack over his shoulder heading northeast toward the observation deck. Approach with caution." He turned to Kruger. "You staying here?"

With a shake of his head, Kruger said, "No, I'm with you."

"Let's go."

At a hurried pace, they followed the man and were only thirty feet behind him when he passed through the arches where the gift shop and café were located. The man kept looking around and stopped when he noticed two park rangers approaching rapidly from the observation deck. When he looked back and saw Kruger and the park ranger, his eyes grew wide.

Kruger said, "Uh, oh."

Miller turned. "What…"

The retired FBI agent did not hear Miller. With practiced efficiency, Kruger drew his Glock 19 from inside the pant holster hidden by his untucked polo shirt. He crouched and moved to his left looking for an angle between himself and the man, making sure tourists would not be in his line of fire behind the suspect.

***

Greer noticed the two park rangers walking rapidly toward him from the direction of the mountain. The tightness in his stomach increased and sweat broke out on his forehead. He stopped and looked around him. Nothing on the sides, but behind him, he saw a park ranger and a tall man wearing jeans and a blue polo shirt.

Feeling his opportunity slipping away, he unslung the backpack and withdrew the Mac 10 9mm machine pistol. With a laugh and a wild grin on his face he raised it toward the man in the blue polo shirt, who was yelling, and pulled the trigger.

***

Kruger saw the man's hand slip into his backpack and recognized the weapon being withdrawn. The suspect went from being worried to manic in a split second. Stopping his forward movement, Kruger stood twenty-five feet from the man when he raised his Glock and yelled, "FBI, drop the weapon."

The man hesitated and then laughed. All three park rangers now had their weapons drawn and aimed at the imposter.

As Kruger dropped to a crouch, the Mac 10 fired in his direction. Without hesitation, he pulled the Glock's trigger, sending five bullets into the assailant.

The whole incident was over in less than ten seconds.

The after-incident report would reveal the shooter fired ten rounds in Kruger's direction, all striking pine trees on the side of the walkway. All five of Kruger's bullet hit their mark, as did the shots fired by the park rangers.

The man collapsed in the middle of the walkway and bled profusely as Sergeant Miller called for a medical evac unit.

Kruger approached the downed suspect and kicked the Mac 10 out of his reach. The eyes of the assailant were already glassy as they tracked Kruger's approach. Holstering his weapon, Kruger bent down and said, "What's your name, son?"

"Peter." The answer came through clenched teeth. "Am I going to die?"

"Yes, Peter, I'm afraid you are."

The man inhaled and exhaled rapidly as he turned his gaze skyward. Finally, his body convulsed, and he exhaled for the last time. Unseeing eyes now stared at the cloudless blue sky above.

***

Stephanie Kruger stood beside her husband with her hand on his shoulder as they watched the helicopter take off with the body of Peter Greer inside. She said, "When I heard the gun shots, I knew something was wrong. How did you know?"

"I'm not sure. I think it was his eyes when he walked past us."

"I didn't even notice him."

"That's the problem, Steph. I notice those things." He turned his attention to his children as they sat on the ground playing games on his and Stephanie's cell phones.

"What's next?"

"Lots of questions from all kinds of federal agencies. I talked to Paul Stumpf a few minutes ago and he said not to worry about it. He'd have someone handle it on his end. We'll be free to go in an hour or so."

"What about the media?"

"Park rangers will get the credit."

"Why? You noticed him and stopped him."

Kruger shrugged. "That's not the point. No one got hurt except the gunman."

She smiled grimly and closed her eyes momentarily. "That's just like you." Her expression softened. "I'm proud of you, even though you lied to me about forgetting something."

"I couldn't let you three be in danger."

She was quiet for a few minutes. "You can't retire, can you?"

He shook his head. "Nope. It's not in me yet."

"Oh, Sean."

He looked at her. Stephanie's expression was not of anger, but of understanding.

She said, "You need to take the offer from David Wu."

He nodded. "Yeah, that's kind of what I was thinking."

CHAPTER 29

Springfield, MO

JR walked through the front door of his home after checking on Sean and Stephanie's house across the street. As he entered, he heard Mia calling for him.

"JR, hurry, you have to see this."

He hurried toward the family room located in the rear of the home and saw Mia, one hand covering her mouth as she stared at their big screen TV. She looked at him and lowered her hand. "Did you know about this?"

"Know about what?" Moving beside her, he saw a reporter standing in front of the Mount Rushmore Memorial entrance reading from notes on a cell phone.

"A park ranger spokesperson just released a statement that at 2:46 Mountain Time, a lone gunman entered the Memorial grounds. Alert members of the on-site park ranger team determined the man posed a threat to tourists and followed him. When the man was confronted, he withdrew a weapon from his backpack and shots were exchanged with park security. We have several cell phone recordings of the incident. Keep in mind, parts of this video can be disturbing to watch."

With a mumble, JR said, "Why do they say that?"

"Shh…"

As a shaky video played, JR leaned forward and saw a tall man in a blue polo shirt withdraw his gun from a holster and move to his left. "Oh, shit—that's Sean."

"I know. There are several other videos where you can see him clearer."

"Let me guess. He noticed the guy and told the park rangers. Now they get the credit."

She smiled and looked at her husband. "Sounds familiar, doesn't it."

JR straightened and crossed his arms. "Too familiar. Have you heard from them?"

Mia nodded. "Stephanie called an hour ago and said they were coming home early. When I asked why, she completely changed the subject."

"Now we know. Did the reporter mention anything about casualties?"

"According to what I've been hearing, no one was hurt except the gunman. He's dead."

The talking head at the studio came back on camera. "The United States Park Ranger service told CNN the quick action by their team at the Memorial saved thirty or more lives. A Girl Scout troop was on the observation deck at the time of the incident. The gunman's direction indicated this may have been his objective. The tall man in the blue polo shirt has not been identified at this time. Our reporter on scene has learned he is a federal law enforcement official who was at the Memorial as a visitor and assisted."

JR tilted his head. "Wonder how this will affect Sean's attitude about retiring?"

With a chuckle, Mia said, "Wanna make a bet?"

"About?"

"Whether Sean takes David Wu's offer or not."

"I'm not going to bet against it. I'd lose."

***

With dusk turning to night, Kruger sat on his back deck and watched the sky darken as more stars made their evening appearance. JR sat in a chair beside him. Both sipped on bottles of Boulevard Pale Ale. Neither man spoke, lost in their own thoughts.

Finally, Kruger said, "Thanks for bringing pizza over tonight."

"You're welcome. We figured you two would be tired. Plus, Joey missed Kristin and Mikey and was anxious to see them."

Kruger nodded still staring at the now-black sky. "Still overwhelmed with ransomware complaints?"

"Yeah." JR chuckled. "I was able to trace one of my client's attackers to a server in eastern Belarus."

"Really?"

With a nod, JR continued, "Yeah, two can play that game. Their server suddenly got hacked and all of its files converted to an ending file format of dot FU."

Kruger chuckled and looked at his friend. "I can only guess what that meant."

"Use your imagination."

"How much ransom did you demand?"

"I didn't. The program I slipped into their system waited until they were doing backup and corrupted all their files. They're dead in the water and out of business for the moment. Serves them right."

Gazing at the stars visible above his house and another sip of beer, Kruger asked, "Exactly where in Belarus?"

"A town called Horki."

Kruger thumbed something into his cell phone and stared at the screen. "That's less than twenty miles from the

Russian border."

"Yeah, so?"

"I thought you suspected the virus came from Russia."

"We do, but computers make it easy to be anywhere…" He stopped and turned his attention to Kruger. "What are you suggesting?"

"I'm not suggesting anything. I just find it curious one of the locations you found for the hackers is close to Russia."

"Huh."

"How much money do these hackers demand once they compromise a company's files?"

"It depends. Sometimes the amount is small and other times fairly high. There are a lot of statistics floating around the industry, but I saw a report the other day that the FBI believes ransomware payouts are approaching one billion dollars per year."

"Really."

With a nod, JR continued, "The ransomware demands are just the tip of the iceberg. The real cost to small businesses is the lost productivity. That cost is estimated to be seventy-five billion per year."

"Why small businesses?"

"Think about it for a second. They have fewer IT resources. If they do have any, it's because they've contracted with a company like mine."

"How many pay the ransom?"

"About forty-one percent, at least that's the statistic I saw. Why are you so curious?"

"No particular reason."

"BS. What are you thinking?"

Kruger stared at the sky again. "I was just curious about how much money I could make if I started hacking computers."

JR chuckled. "Okay, if you're not ready to discuss it, that's fine with me."

The two men fell into silence again, sipping beer and watching the sky. Finally, JR turned to his friend. "We saw you on TV and your name was never mentioned."

"Paul Stumpf took care of that."

"You saved a lot of lives, Sean."

He shrugged.

"How'd you know?"

"I'm really not sure. The guy walked past me as we were returning to the parking lot and I noticed his eyes. Also, he was dressed like a Park Ranger, except the shirt and pants were the wrong color. Alarm bells went off. I didn't even think about it. I sent Steph and the kids to the car and followed him."

"What about his eyes?"

"Hard to explain. To me he looked like he was staring into the future and didn't like what he saw."

"Glad you noticed it."

Kruger's only response was to take a sip of his beer.

"What did Stephanie say afterwards?"

"She wasn't happy, but okay with how things worked out."

With a nod, JR asked, "So, what about David Wu's offer?"

"There's something I didn't tell you the other day."

"Oh?"

"Wu made the decision to be the financial backer of Sandy and Jimmie's new company."

"You told me that."

"What I didn't tell you is they asked me to join them."

"And you said?"

"I told him no. I wasn't interested at the time."

"Uh-oh, now you are?"

Kruger nodded. "In a different way. Steph and I talked about it on the flight home. If I accept Wu's offer and hire Sandy and Jimmie's company, it gives them instant legitimacy."

JR frowned. "How does that work?"

In the dim light from the kitchen, JR could see a grin on Kruger's lips. "President Griffin issued an Executive Order authorizing the formation of a group under Homeland Security to investigate and prevent domestic terrorist attacks. The group is separate from the FBI, DEA, US Marshal Service and all the other law enforcement agencies. He thinks he can get the Senate to sign off on it because it will be privately funded for the first year."

"He thinks?"

"There's still one individual he has to get on board."

"Who's that?"

"A senator named Quinn."

"Okay. When this Quinn okays it, what happens after the first year?"

"If it works, Congress will consider funding it permanently."

"Let me guess. You'll be the director."

Kruger shook his head. "No, my title will be Special Agent in Charge. They are still working it out who I will report to, but it won't be Paul Stumpf. Although I will be working closely with the FBI."

"What about..." JR paused and chuckled. "So, that's where Sandy and Jimmie's company comes in."

"Yup. I will have carte blanche the first year to hire whoever I want."

"Huh, sounds like you'll have the old team together."

"Not yet." He paused and looked at JR in the dim light. "Want a job?"

***

Two Days Later

David Wu shook Kruger's hand as they met in the new office of KKG Solutions, LLC. Located at the back corner of a hanger on the private aviation side of the Springfield

National Airport, the space had served many purposes over time, the most recent being a storage area. Now newly remodeled with secondhand desks and furniture, the room still held the distinct odor of aviation lubricants.

Wu said, "I'm pleased you decided to accept my offer, Sean."

"I apologize for taking so long to make the decision."

"Nonsense. I respect someone who is deliberate in their decision-making process."

Kruger just nodded.

Looking around the room, Wu said, "Humble beginnings for our friends Sandy and Jimmie. I understand they signed a contract to work with you."

"Yes, sir. We've operated well together in the past and I see no reason to break us up."

"Good."

"What's my budget for the year?"

"As far as I'm concerned, you don't have a limit this first year. I've allocated a hundred million dollars and can put more into the coffer if needed. I want this endeavor to be successful."

Kruger's eyes widened. "I—don't believe we will need that much."

Placing a hand on Kruger's shoulder, Wu smiled. "Regardless, it's there when you need it."

"Thank you."

Joseph Kincaid walked into the conference room and said, "Sorry, I'm late."

After the three men sat around a small round table, the details of Kruger's new responsibilities began to take shape. An hour later all were in agreement.

Joseph read from his notes and started the summary. "David, President Griffin agrees with your assessment that Sean and his team need to be independent of the federal bureaucracy. Therefore, they will report directly to the president through his representative—me."

Wu and Kruger nodded.

Continuing, Joseph pushed his reading glasses up his nose. "Their autonomy will be ensured by private funding through the Wu Foundation."

More nods.

"Authority to investigate, arrest, and detain suspects is granted under the auspices of Homeland Security, although, they will not directly engage with this agency. While Secretary Watson is aware of the existence of this new department, she's been informed she has no jurisdiction over its mission."

The two other men said in unison, "Agreed."

Additional details of the new department were discussed and notes taken. When they were through, Joseph smiled and said, "Gentlemen, we have a good plan here. I will have it typed up and then review it with the president. Once he signs it, you'll be in business."

Wu turned to Kruger. "Where are you going to start?"

"I received an email this morning summarizing the agency's investigation of Peter Greer, the Mount Rushmore Memorial shooter. They had a hard time identifying him at first. He wasn't on anybody's radar and didn't have a social media presence." Kruger took a sip from a bottle of water sitting in front of him. "They know he was a sophomore at the University of Wyoming in Laramie up until last semester. His cumulative GPA was only 1.6 and there is no record of him registering for the fall semester. So far their investigation raises more questions than answers."

Joseph frowned. "In what way?"

"While nothing is conclusive, when they searched his apartment, they found references to a group mentioned in several of the documents found in Dorian Monk's cabin. Plus, Laramie, Wyoming was where we first found Monk. I don't believe in coincidences gentlemen, only connections. We'll start there."

CHAPTER 30

Lander, Wyoming

The cell phone recording acquired by CNN showed a man in a blue polo shirt withdrawing his gun and moving toward his left. The video, now on YouTube with over a hundred thousand views, played on a sixty-five-inch large flat-screen TV in Kevin Marks' office. He hit the reverse button on the remote and returned to the point where the video started. He pressed the play button and watched it again. Pausing the forward motion, he stared at the frozen image of the man and cursed under his breath.

"Dammit, it is him."

He clenched his fists as he watched the video again. "Something has to be done about this bothersome FBI agent."

He stopped the video and switched the input on the TV to his local cable company and Fox News. He punched in a number and made a call. It was answered on the fourth ring.

"Blake."

"We need to talk."

"So, talk."

"Not on the phone."

There was a sigh and a long pause. "Where?"

"Wanda's Diner, thirty minutes."

"You're buying lunch."

After ending the call, Marks muttered, "Probably not."

***

Wanda's Diner resembled an old fashion greasy spoon common in the 1950s, mainly because it had been built in the fifties and received little remodeling since its original opening. Booths lined the wall near the front entrance with four top tables in the middle of the room. A counter with stools for single diners faced the kitchen.

Kevin Marks sat in the farthest booth from the front door as Fremont County Sheriff Roger Blake entered. Blake waved at the café owner and sauntered toward the booth. He stopped every once in a while, taking his time to speak to many of the café's patrons. Eventually, he sat across from Marks. "So, talk."

"I need to know the name of the FBI agent who stopped the kid at Mount Rushmore."

"Why?"

"I have my reasons."

"How do you know he was an FBI agent?"

"Because it's the same guy who chased Monk out of Laramie."

Blake stared at Marks and remained quiet while a waitress placed a white ceramic mug in front of him.

After she poured coffee from a glass decanter, she said, "Anything else for ya, hon?"

He looked up. "Not right now, Linda. Give me a few minutes."

She took the decanter and walked to another customer.

"That agent was with Homeland Security."

Marks shook his head. "Have you looked at the video yet?"

"Several times. I didn't recognize him."

"It's him. CNN identified the man as a federal law enforcement agent. To me, that means FBI. I need to know his name and where he lives."

"I'll get you his name, but where he lives is up to you. I'll only do so much."

"And I'll remember that next election day."

Blake sipped his coffee. "Be careful, Kevin. The next sheriff might not be as forgiving as I am to your extra-curricular activities."

Marks stood and said, "Get me his name." He stared at the sheriff for several seconds and then walked toward the café's front door.

The sheriff continued to sip coffee while he contemplated not running for the position again. His loathing of Marks grew every day.

After finishing his coffee, he threw three dollars on the table and headed back to his office to start making phone calls.

***

Late afternoon found Marks working in his office at the store. His cell phone sounded with an incoming call. After glancing at the caller ID, he answered, "What'd you find?"

"The agent's name is Sean Kruger. There's a problem, though."

"What?"

"He's retired."

Marks fell silent at this news. "Retired? Since when?"

"My source wouldn't say. But he is no longer an active agent."

"Did you find out where he lives?"

"I told you that was up to you. I did what you asked me to do. I found his name."

"How's the name spelled?"

Blake told him.

Marks ended the call without further comment and went to the computer on his desk. An hour later, he'd found fifteen Sean Krugers across the country, none of which were the right age or identified as working for the FBI. He tried LinkedIn, Facebook and several other websites dedicated to locating individuals. None gave him the address or even the city where the agent lived. He found zero references to siblings, a spouse or children. His frustration grew by the second.

His next search used Google and the results were the same. Nothing.

He would need to figure it out another way.

***

JR Diminski observed the pop-up alert at the bottom right corner of the middle monitor on his workstation. He clicked on the icon and read the message. With a frown, he reached for his cell phone.

"Kruger."

"Who do you know in Wyoming?"

"Beg your pardon?"

"Someone in Lander, Wyoming is burning up the internet searching for you."

"Huh."

"Know anybody there?"

Kruger grew quiet for a few moments. "Lander is the county seat for Fremont County. The county where Monk's cabin is located."

"Uh-oh."

"Yeah, uh-oh."

"Did you piss someone off while you were there?"

"Probably. Thinking back on it, the sheriff was way too interested in the boxes Jimmie found."

"What do you mean, too interested?"

"He got in my face and demanded the boxes be transferred to his office for investigation."

JR chuckled. "I'm sure that went well for him."

"Not really."

"Do you think it might be him?"

"Don't know. Maybe." He paused. "Keep an eye on it, JR."

"Always." He paused. "Hey, Sean."

"Yeah."

"Are we official yet?"

"Should be sometime tomorrow. Joseph sent a text message to let me know the president would be signing the Executive Order around noon."

"Then what?"

"We get busy."

JR smiled.

CHAPTER 31

Fremont County, Wyoming

Tom Shark stood with his hands on his hips staring at the small cabin. With this his first major investigation as a Special Agent in Charge, he felt a little overwhelmed and intimidated. Five agents, all in blue windbreakers with FBI in bold letters on the back, busied themselves in and around the structure.

One mental exercise that had served him well over the past decade came to mind. The question: What would Sean Kruger do?

Earlier in his career, he never hesitated to call his mentor and ask for advice. Now with Kruger retired, Shark felt a bit lost.

As he gazed around the area, the answer came almost as if Kruger had whispered it in his ear. *"Look outside the box."*

Dressed in jeans, hiking boots and his own navy windbreaker, Shark set out to search a larger area around the cabin. Their original search area comprised an area with the cabin in the center and a radius of only fifty feet.

An hour later he noticed a patch of ground one hundred yards north of the small building which seemed to have been recently disturbed. Few leaves littered the area and the grass looked new. He retrieved a long probe from the back of the forensic team's SUV and pushed the tip gently into the soil of the disturbed area. After several attempts he struck something hard only four inches beneath the soil's surface. Continuing to utilize the probe he determined the object was relatively flat, hard and square.

An hour later, after taking numerous pictures of the site and carefully removing the soil, two of the forensic techs lifted the box out of the ground.

Shark said, "Looks like a fireproof file box."

Lisa Sural, a twenty-something blue-eyed forensic tech from Denver, replied, "My guess is the key we found hanging on a nail in the kitchen area will fit it."

After placing the box on the only table in the cabin, they took more photographs and cleared the excess dirt away. Sural said, "We need to get this to a lab and see if we can raise any latent fingerprints."

With a nod, Shark said, "See if the key works, then we can photograph the contents and ship it back to Denver."

The key did work and contents of the box—a stack of paper roughly three quarters of an inch thick—were removed. Over two hundred pages were then photographed one by one and kept in the original order. During this process, Shark skimmed several of the pages and grew more excited with each one. Turning back to Sural, he asked her to join him outside.

When they were out of earshot of the other techs, he asked, "Can you get those pictures of the documents to the cloud so we can have someone at Quantico start examining them?"

She nodded. "I can with my satellite phone, if that's what you're asking."

"It is."

"Sure. As soon as we finish, I'll transfer the file."

"Good. I'll make the call and let them know they're coming."

Thirty minutes later she told him the pictures were in the bureau's cloud-based file system and gave him the name of the file.

"Thanks, Lisa."

When she returned to the cabin, Shark dialed a number on his satellite phone and waited.

***

Three men dressed in forest-camo fatigues watched the FBI activity surrounding the cabin. One was short and stocky with broad shoulders and narrow hips. As he watched the activity through binoculars, he said in a low voice, "Once they have everything loaded in the SUVs and prepare to leave, we'll take them out."

The other two men nodded in agreement.

***

Shark's call went straight to the cell phone of the head of the forensic lab at Quantico, who answered on the fourth ring.

"Forensics. This is Charlie Craft."

"Charlie, Tom Shark. How are you?"

With a smile, Craft said, "Great, Tom. It's been a while."

"Yes, it has. I've been assigned to Denver as the new SAC."

"Congratulations. I guess you heard Sean Kruger retired."

"Yeah, I know. Have you spoken to him?"

"Not yet. I'm kind of afraid to call him."

"Don't be, he'd love to hear from you. I spoke to him just the other day."

"Good, I will. Why the call?"

"We found a buried fireproof and waterproof file box on Dorian Monk's property. I didn't read all of the documents, but on the few pages I looked at, Alan Seltzer's name appears several times."

"How fast can you get them here?"

"That's why I'm calling. We've uploaded photos of the documents to our cloud storage and wanted to give you the file name."

"Great. I'm ready when you are."

Shark gave him the information and then said, "We're getting everything we found of value loaded right now for the trip back to Denver. We're planning on testing the file box to see if we can raise…"

Automatic weapons fire could be heard in the background of the phone call. When Shark did not finish his statement, Charlie checked to make sure the call was still active. It was. Unintelligible shouts could be heard along with the sound of small weapons fire. More shouts and the sound of automatic weapons returned. Finally, there was only silence. The call ended suddenly, and Craft reached for his desk phone.

***

The first rounds of gunfire struck the SUV in the engine compartment sparking a fire in the gas line. Coolant leaked on the ground as the fire spread. Ducking behind the big vehicle away from the gunfire, Shark drew his weapon and fired in the direction of the sound. Lisa Sural took several bullets in the chest as she loaded evidence boxes into the back of the SUV. She collapsed next to where Shark stood.

More gunfire came from his left. These rounds struck Shark in the head and upper torso—he was dead before he hit the ground. The other four FBI agents went down one by one as they defended themselves. With only handguns against AR-15 style rifles, it was an unfair fight.

The firefight lasted less than thirty seconds and quiet returned to the wooded landscape surrounding the late-Dorian Monk's property. The ever-present sound of wildlife in the background remained still, giving the scene a surrealistic feel. Three men dressed in forest camo outfits approached from three different directions, training their weapons on the prone and still FBI agents. As fire consumed the FBI vehicle, they checked each agent to make sure none survived.

The short stocky man with the wide shoulders checked the last agent near the cabin. The wounded man stared up at his assailant with a defiant expression and blinked once. His reward for surviving the initial attack was an AR-15 pointed at his head and one bullet fired.

When the SUV fire burned itself out and the background noise of birds and small animals scurrying about returned, the three assailants were gone along with all the evidence gathered by the now dead FBI team.

Another three hours would pass before first responders arrived at the scene.

CHAPTER 32

Washington, DC

Charlie Craft listened as details of the massacre in the forest of Fremont County, Wyoming became clear. The phone call came from the individual he'd contacted about the interrupted call and the gunfire he'd heard in the background. The fact he might have been on the phone with Tom as the FBI agent died intensified the numbness he felt.

He asked, "Did they recover any of the evidence Tom told me about?"

Executive Assistant Director for Science and Technology Denise Perkins hesitated before she answered. "No. From what I was told, one of the SUVs they arrived in was burned. There appeared to be boxes of paper in the back."

"Okay, so the file they uploaded might be the only evidence we have left?"

"It would appear so. Have you looked at it?"

"Just a cursory glance. Why?"

"The director's ordered a full court press on this. He's assigned over a hundred agents to the investigation. My suggestion would be for you to get your team started on the file right away."

"Yes, ma'am."

"Charlie…"

"Yes."

"I know you and Tom were close. Let's get these bastards for his sake."

"Yes, ma'am."

The call ended and the emptiness inside Charlie Craft intensified. He glanced at the clock on his desk—it would be just past six p.m. in the Central Time Zone. He took his cell phone out, found the number he needed and pressed the send icon.

**

"Kruger."

"Sean, it's Charlie Craft."

Kruger smiled. "Charlie, it's been a while. How are you?"

"Sean, I don't have good news."

A frown replaced the smile. "Oh—what's happened?"

"Have you heard about a team of FBI agents being ambushed in Wyoming?"

"No. Again, what happened?"

"Five agents were at Dorian Monk's cabin when they were shot and killed by unknown assailants."

"Dear God."

"Thomas Shark was among those agents."

Kruger went silent, unable to respond right away. It took several moments for him to trust his voice not to break. "When did this occur?"

"Earlier today."

Taking a deep breath, Kruger felt a pang of guilt about

his status as a retired agent. "Who's in charge of the investigation?"

"Don't know yet. I was just told about it and thought I should let you know before you heard it on the news."

"I appreciate that, Charlie. I really do."

"There's one more thing you need to know."

"What's that?"

"Tom called me just before the attack and told me they found a buried file box about one hundred yards from the cabin. They took photographs of the pages and uploaded them to the bureau's cloud-based server."

Kruger straightened.

Charlie continued, "My department has been ordered to start going through those files immediately."

"Okay, sounds reasonable."

"Uh…"

"What is it, Charlie?"

"Uh—I—uh…"

"Spit it out."

"I know you're retired and all that, but if you had access to the file, do you think you and JR could go over it? You know, second set of eyes, so to speak."

Realizing Charlie was violating every rule in the FBI handbook and jeopardizing his career with the bureau, Kruger said, "Send it, Charlie. I won't tell a soul."

"I can't send it to you, but I can tell JR how to access it."

"Even better."

***

Sitting next to JR at his cubicle, Kruger watched the computer wizard's fingers dance over the keyboard as he stared at the left monitor. Turning to his friend, JR pointed toward the screen. "I've got the file downloaded and saved to my server. I've covered my tracks so no one at the bureau will know it's been accessed."

"Good."

"Now what, Sean?"

"Thomas Shark and five other agents died getting these files." He paused as he took a breath. "Whatever's in those pages must be pretty damning evidence." He glanced at JR. "Let's make sure we don't miss anything."

"You know I hate printing files."

Kruger nodded.

"But I was thinking, if it's printed, we can categorize it better."

Kruger gave his friend a smile. "Good idea."

JR pointed his mouse cursor to an icon and pressed the left button. On the other side of the cubicle wall, Kruger heard a laser printer spool up and hum as it spat out paper.

As the file printed, JR asked, "So, what's the status of this new group you've talked me into joining?"

"Typical government bureaucracy. President Griffin is supposed to sign the Executive Order anytime now. David Wu has already transferred the money to the account we will use. But once the president puts his signature on it, Homeland Security has to sign off as well."

With a frown, JR asked, "Why?"

His answer was a chuckle. "The Secretary of Homeland Security told the president they could not issue IDs for us until a background check was conducted on each one of us."

"You're kidding, a background check? I bet that didn't go over too well with Griffin."

"Nope, it didn't. Joseph told me the discussion between the two occurred behind closed doors and—uh—got heated."

"Does she still have her job?"

"Probably, Roy isn't like that."

"So, what about the IDs?"

"Once we have them, we can be operational."

"When will that be?"

Kruger shrugged. "When we get them."

JR rolled his eyes and stood to go to the printer. He took the stack into the conference room and placed it on the long table. "Didn't know it was going to be half a ream of paper."

After taking the first fifty pages from the stack, Kruger glanced through them. "It appears a lot of the pages are handwritten notes. I was told Thomas felt it important enough to have the information sent immediately to Quantico. So, he had them photograph every page and saved it to the cloud. Otherwise, we wouldn't have it."

"Monk wasn't much of a file clerk, was he?"

"No, we saw that with the files he hid in the bank boxes."

The two men were silent as they looked through the stack of papers. Kruger stopped skimming and read one carefully. He held it in one hand while grabbing a page he had already returned to the table. "Oh, boy."

"What?"

"Dorian Monk wasn't the horrible file clerk we've been accusing him of."

"I'm not following you."

"These pages are out of order for a reason. It appears to be a way of hiding the information from prying eyes."

"Still not following you."

"Monk was a mathematician, right?"

JR nodded.

"These pages were photographed in the order they were found, right?"

"Don't know, I wasn't there."

"Trust me, they were."

"Okay."

"Note the handwritten number in the left bottom corner."

"Yeah."

"Now, look at this page and then this one."

JR studied each piece of paper and handed it back to Kruger. "The first page is continued on the second."

"Correct. Now look at the number on the bottom."

"They aren't in sequence."

Kruger shook his head. "No, they aren't. We need to find more examples. Once we have a few examples, we might be able to break Monk's filing code."

The pattern eluded them. The two men worked until eight p.m. when Kruger went home to spend a few moments with his kids. JR stayed another hour staring at the pages on the conference table.

At six a.m. the next morning, armed with freshly poured coffee, they studied the pages.

Kruger said, "I can't see a pattern."

JR nodded. "I can't either. Now what?"

Taking a sip of coffee, Kruger shrugged. "Not sure. Without identifying the pattern of the sequence, it will take forever to pair the correct pages together."

They were interrupted by Alexia Gibbs, who knocked on the conference room door frame.

JR looked up. "Good morning, Alexia. You're here early."

"Morning, JR." She smiled and went to Kruger for her customary hug from the man she considered a substitute dad. "Morning, Sean."

Kruger gave her a fatherly hug and said, "How are you this morning, Alexia?"

"Good." She stared at the pages on the table. "What's that?"

After taking a sip of his coffee, JR told her and said, "We think Monk has hidden information within the pages. We figured out the first few, but after that, we can't see the pattern."

Alexia studied the pages in the sequences as they appeared on the table. She smiled. "It's a Fibonacci

Sequence."

Kruger frowned and JR gave her a small grin. He quickly did the math in his head and went to the next sequential page number. "That's it, Alexia." He looked at Kruger, who stared blankly at the pages on the table. "Do you know what a Fibonacci Sequence is?"

"I'm a psychologist, not a mathematician."

With a giggle, Alexia said, "To create the sequence, you add the first two numbers in the sequence together to generate the following number. For instance, if you add three and four together, the next number would be seven. Four and seven equal eleven; seven and eleven would produce eighteen and so forth."

While she explained, Kruger started sorting and identified the next ten pages in the narrative. He looked up and said, "My guess is the pages in between are nonsense and have no purpose, other than to confuse the person looking at the file."

Twenty minutes later, they had the chronicle in order. JR looked over his glasses at Kruger. "Aren't you glad I hired her?"

With a nod, Kruger said, "Very." He paused and read a few of the now in order pages. "I wonder if Charlie's team found this pattern?"

JR chuckled. "What are the odds?"

"Hush, Charlie's good at his job."

"No argument there, but do you wanna bet?"

"No."

"Chicken."

Kruger paused for a second. "No, not really. I just don't have that much confidence in other members of his team."

"My point exactly."

"Shhh…" He punched in the number for Charlie's cell phone.

"Hey, Sean. What'd you find?"

"Did you guys find a pattern in the order of the

documents?"

"No. It all seems to be miscellaneous nonsense."

"It isn't. There's an order to his filing system. Here's the key." He told Charlie about the Fibonacci sequence.

"We didn't see that."

"Like you said, sometimes it just takes another set of eyes."

"What does it say?"

"It's a manifesto."

"A manifesto?"

"Yes, similar to the one Ted Kaczynski wrote, which was published by the Washington Post in 1995. Only this one is much darker."

"They were both mathematicians, Sean."

"True, but Monk only retreated to his cabin during the summers and he didn't send bombs through the United States Postal System. He used a gun and managed to kill twenty-one innocent souls. Unfortunately, there is also mention of a group of like-minded individuals."

"The director has over a hundred agents assigned to the investigation of Thomas Shark's ambush. What are they going to find?"

"Not a thing. Whoever these people are, they have gone to great lengths to keep their identities secret."

"I'd better get this bumped upstairs."

"Remember, Charlie, your team found it."

"Yeah. I'd better go."

The call ended and Kruger stared at JR. "They didn't find it."

"Told ya."

"That's not the point, JR. We have a group of white nationalist plotting against the US Government and no one seems to have a clue."

"Then we have an advantage."

Shaking his head, Kruger said, "What's that supposed to mean?"

JR raised his eyebrows and smiled. "They don't know we know."

Kruger smiled too.

CHAPTER 33

Christian County, MO

Due to Joseph's position within the Griffin administration, an invitation to gather at his secluded Christian County home seldom occurred. When one did come, few if any of the invitees felt the desire to turn it down. Rather, they relished the opportunity to gather as an extended family and enjoy each other's company socially.

With the growing number of children within the group, separate SUVs were required for each family.

Sean, Stephanie, Kristin and Mikey Kruger arrived first and parked Stephanie's new Ford Explorer behind Joseph's gun metal gray Range Rover.

Joseph greeted them on the wraparound porch of his rustic log-cabin style home. After giving Stephanie and the kids a hug, he suggested they go on inside to join Mary.

When they disappeared into the house, he turned to Kruger. "When'd you get the Explorer?"

"Right after the Cherokee was totaled."

"Ah, forgot about that."

"I haven't. The Explorer's bigger, which will help with the kids as they grow. The dealer ordered it specifically for us. Since I was with the FBI at the time, he was able to order it with the same engine and suspension as a Police Interceptor. It's basically a police vehicle without the special wiring while retaining the comforts of a passenger one." He gave Joseph a brief smile. "I think Stephanie feels safer with the kids in it."

Joseph nodded thoughtfully. "I'm sure she does."

"Okay, you didn't keep me out here to discuss cars. What's going on?"

"We've run into a bit of bureaucratic red-tape with getting official IDs for your new organization."

Kruger's eyebrows rose. "Oh—such as?"

"Senator Jordan Quinn is the Chairman of the Senate Committee on Homeland Security and Government Affairs. He's been meeting on a regular basis behind closed doors with Joan Watson. Now, Secretary Watson is protesting the new department not being under her jurisdiction and Quinn put a squelch on finalizing it until it is."

"Disloyalty within the Griffin Administration?"

With a nod, Joseph continued, "I'm afraid so."

"Is Ms. Watson still the Secretary of Homeland Security?"

"Uh—no. She met with the president earlier today and after a brief discussion decided it was in her best interest to spend more time with her family."

With a chuckle, Kruger said, "Let me guess, something in her past might have been mentioned."

Joseph displayed a sly grin. "It seems she hired someone to take the LSAT for her to gain admission to law school." He paused. "She went to Yale, by the way."

"Oh, dear, what a naughty girl. Did this information just get discovered?"

"Kind of."

"You wouldn't have had anything to do with it, would

you?"

"Me? Of course not. I don't work for the CIA anymore, remember?"

"Oh, yeah, I forgot." After a thoughtful pause, Kruger asked, "What about Quinn?"

"He agrees we need the department but expressed his disappointment with how the president handled the sudden departure of Joan Watson."

After a few moments of silence, Kruger said, "So, where does that leave us?"

"For the moment, dead in the water. The president is working on something with Paul Stumpf, but nothing is going to happen anytime soon."

Kruger grew quiet as he returned his attention to the Explorer in the driveway.

"The matter's being addressed, Sean. That's all I can tell you at the moment."

Kruger pressed his lips together, shook his head with frustration and started to say something. He hesitated for a few seconds, thought better about his words and said, "I appreciate everyone's efforts, Joseph." With a grim smile, he continued, "There's been a development with the papers found buried on Monk's property."

"I heard."

"No, you heard about the manifesto. Last night Alexia and JR found another document hidden within the pages. A document we haven't told anyone about yet."

Joseph stared at his friend.

"It seems Monk had a simmering hatred for anyone who did not look like him, act like him, or believe the same things he did."

"Kind of what you thought, wasn't it?"

"Yes, but we didn't know the extent of it. JR and I can't prove any of what I am going to tell you, the only source we have is from Monk's papers."

"I'm listening."

Taking a deep breath, Kruger stared out over the front property. "Most of the recent mass shootings are being encouraged by the group Monk was associated with."

"You say *most*."

With a nod, Kruger continued, "Some are wannabe shooters or copycats. Those are the ones the police usually identify, stop, and the public never hears about it. The majority of the successful ones are being committed by individuals this group encourages."

"How?"

"Very easy—social media. They've taken a page out of the ISIS handbook about spreading jihad over the internet. However, this group is spreading hate here in the US. They target individuals on the fringe of society who already carry a grudge."

"Did this document mention their purpose?"

"Yeah, it's a little farfetched, but so was the purpose of ISIS. They want to establish a Caucasian-only society. They believe if they encourage enough of these mass shootings against ethnic groups, it will scare them into leaving the country."

"That won't happen."

"You and I both know that, but…" He paused. "That's their plan."

Joseph stared at his friend. "How do we stop them?"

"That's a good question. Right now, I don't have an answer." He paused for second. "There's something else."

"This just keeps getting better."

"There's reference to a source of money the group uses to buy influence."

Now frowning, Joseph asked, "What kind of influence?"

"Political."

The frown on Joseph's face intensified.

Kruger continued. "Monk's writing doesn't specify the source of the funds or who the beneficiaries are."

"But you suspect something."

"Yeah, I do."

"Care to share?"

"While this new document does mention it, we know Monk was running a bank scam that produced a lot of cash. Apparently, it didn't generate the amount they needed. There is mention, within the second document, of another source creating the bulk of the group's revenue."

"I take it this source is not identified."

"No, but JR and I have a theory. We think it has something to do with the Russians."

Joseph closed his eyes and slowly shook his head. "Oh, boy. How?"

"JR's company's been busy with a rash of ransomware attacks on current and new clients." When Joseph did not respond, Kruger continued, "The night Steph and I got back from South Dakota, JR and I were on my back deck talking about these attacks. He mentioned he traced one back to a town in eastern Belarus, near the border with Russia."

"Is this going where I think it's going?"

"Probably. He also told me how much money the FBI believes is being paid in ransoms to get the encryption keys. I checked with a source at the bureau this morning. The amount is huge."

"How much?"

"Over a billion dollars."

"You think this group Monk was associated with is involved?"

Kruger nodded.

"And?"

"I really hope I'm wrong, but I think the Russians are orchestrating the ransomware attacks and funneling some of the money to the group Monk was involved with. Those funds are now being used to buy influence in our government."

***

By six p.m., all the guests were present at Joseph's home. The large back deck found, as usual, Jimmie Gibbs and Sandy Knoll tending the competition-size charcoal grill while the growing number of children played in the yard. Enjoying his first time at one of these gatherings, Bobby Knoll was home on leave from the Navy Seals. He stood next to Jimmie and the two were catching up on each other's activities.

Bobby Knoll possessed broad shoulders and a trim waist, although his muscles did not stretch the fabric of the polo shirt like his father's did. Like his mother, his hair was dark brown and his eyes were hazel. Also like his mother, the eyes betrayed an innate wisdom for a person his age.

He watched Jimmie flipping burgers and said, "I want to thank you for talking Mom and Dad into moving to the Stockton Lake area."

Jimmie smiled. "Alexia and I are pleased they are. Sandy told me they found a piece of land and made an offer on it this past week."

"Yeah, I saw it today. It's east of the lake. There's a small house already on the property. Dad said they would live there until one could be built. Then he'll turn it into a guest house for when Peter or I visit."

"How's Peter?"

"He's good. He asked me to tell you he'd be here sometime in September and wanted to see you."

"Looking forward to it."

"Jimmie?"

Gibbs looked at the younger Seal. "Yeah."

Bobby Knoll's expression turned serious. "Is this venture you and my dad are starting gonna fly?"

The older ex-Seal offered a sly smile. "Don't know, but with your dad's and my contacts, we've already had a number of inquiries. Why?"

"I enjoy being a Seal, but…"

"I understand. What happens next, right?"

A nod was his answer.

"All I can tell you, Bobby, is you'll know when the time is right to move on to the next adventure. If our little experiment goes well, and it will, you can join your dad and me anytime you want."

"Thanks, Jimmie. I appreciate it."

Sandy Knoll, having gone inside to grab fresh trout and a few steaks, returned to the grill. "You two look like you're plotting something."

Gibbs shook his head. "Nope, just learning more of your family's secrets."

Knoll smiled and threw three New York Strips onto the grill. "More likely you two are plotting against his mother and me."

***

Kruger leaned against the deck railing and stared off into the woods behind Joseph's home. Stephanie walked up to him and handed him a beer.

"You look lost. What's going on?"

He took the beer. "Thanks." He returned his gaze back toward the woods. "Just thinking about my encounter with Randolph Bishop."

"Not one of our more memorable moments here."

"No—not really."

"Did your conversation with Joseph go well?"

He shook his head, opened the beer and took a sip.

She frowned and crossed her arms. "Okay, Mr. Kruger, feeling sorry for yourself doesn't suit you. Besides, everyone else is having a good time. You're the only one sulking and ignoring your friends."

Giving her a half smile, he said, "Apparently, getting credentials for myself and the others is creating a problem in Washington for Roy. That's not what I had in mind."

"He's a big boy, he'll figure it out. You, on the other hand, need to face the fact you might actually have to walk away from it. Can you do that?"

Blinking several times, he did not respond immediately. Finally, he turned to her. "Trust me, the longer the delay, the more likely that will be the outcome. And, yes, I can walk away from it."

Her stern look softened and she placed her hand on his arm. "Your actions at Mount Rushmore saved a lot of innocent lives."

He shrugged.

"Well, they did. Maybe instead of working with Sandy and Jimmie, you talk to your friend at the Highway Patrol. He's been after you, for what, five years to come work for him."

"Seven, actually."

"Then maybe it's time to do that instead."

"What about the information we found about Monk and this group he was associated with?"

She chuckled. "Sean, you are not the only FBI agent in the world. As I told you a few days ago, there are over fourteen thousand other special agents. I bet more than one of them is competent enough to figure this Monk business out."

Kruger tried not to grin or smile but failed. He turned to her, chuckled under his breath and gave her a hug. "Thank you."

"For what, telling you the truth?"

"Yes, and for being a little voice in my head telling me I'm being silly and stupid."

"You're not stupid. Silly and stubborn yes, but not stupid."

He laughed and took hold of her hand. "Let's go join the party."

CHAPTER 34

Washington, DC
Two Days Later

President of the United States Roy Griffin seldom displayed anger or annoyance, but this morning was an exception. Joseph stood in front of the Resolute desk and watched as Griffin paced behind it.

"Joseph, this stalemate with the Senate and the status of our new venture is intolerable."

"Yes, sir."

"There has to be a way for us to make a new department under Homeland Security without members of Congress getting up in arms about it."

"There is, sir."

Griffin stopped pacing and stared at his National Security Advisor. "Well, what is it?"

"It's called the Presidential Reorganization Authority."

"I'm listening."

"It gives the president the authority to divide,

consolidate, abolish, or create agencies of the United States federal government by presidential directive. However, it is subject to limited legislative oversight and can be overturned by Congress."

"Why have I never heard of this?"

"It's fairly obscure and last used successfully by Richard Nixon to create the Environmental Protection Agency. Reagan tried to use it, but Congress failed to act on his proposal in a timely fashion."

Griffin blinked. "It hasn't been used since?"

With a shake of his head, Joseph said, "No, sir."

"Why?"

"Don't know. My guess would be because Congress has to allocate funding for any changes."

"What if the changes are minor and they don't cost the taxpayers a dime?"

"Can't say, sir. Congress still has to approve it." He paused for a minute. "Sir, why do you want this new department to be under Homeland Security?"

"Personally, Joseph, I couldn't care less what department it's under. I just know we need it."

"No arguments from me, sir." He cleared his throat. "May I suggest putting it under the Department of Justice? The Attorney General might be easier to deal with. Joan Watson had her own agenda. The AG doesn't. Besides, he doesn't like talking to members of Congress."

"If we make it a separate department, don't we have to appoint a director?"

Joseph shook his head. "Not if you stick it under the jurisdiction of the FBI."

Griffin displayed a small smile as he stared at Joseph. "In other words, Sean Kruger is all of a sudden back under the FBI umbrella."

"Why didn't we think of this sooner?"

With a shrug, Joseph said, "Because we were concentrating too hard on getting it under Homeland

Security."

"What will Paul Stumpf say?"

"It was his idea."

"Are you two making plans behind my back?"

"Wouldn't dream of it, sir."

"Well, keep doing it. If this works, we can turn Sean loose, can't we?"

"Yes, sir." He paused. "There's also been a development you need to be aware of."

Griffin raised an eyebrow. "What's that?"

Joseph told him about the other document JR and Alexia found.

***

His cell phone vibrated as he started his cool down walk from an afternoon run. Kruger glanced at the caller ID and accepted the call. "Good afternoon, Paul."

"Yes, it is a good afternoon, Sean."

A little surprised, Kruger stopped walking and rubbed the sweat from his eyes with the back of his hand. "How so?"

"Do you still have your FBI badge and ID?"

"Yes, sir. I've never been asked to return it."

"Good, it's official again. A new one will be issued in the next week or so with your new title."

Without knowing how to respond, he was silent for a second. "Beg your pardon."

"The president issued a Presidential Directive today reorganizing the FBI and creating a new department. Since the funding for this department is from a private source, the Speaker of the House and the Senate Majority Leader told him they would not override it. You are now officially an assistant director and not subject to the mandatory retirement requirements."

"I'm not moving to Washington, Paul."

"Not necessary."

"Then I'm on board."

"Glad we worked it out."

"What about my team?"

"It's your budget—you can hire who you want. There is a sub-clause in the department structure that allows the hiring of qualified sub-contractors with the needed skills. Those you choose will be provided with the appropriate identification."

Kruger smiled. "What's the name of the department?"

"Right now, we're calling it the Domestic Terrorist Division, but that may change."

"Who do I report to?"

"Straight line to me."

"Even better."

"Sean."

"Yes, sir."

"Joseph told me about the second document you found in Monk's buried papers. Do you believe what's in it?"

"I don't think we have the luxury of not believing it."

The call went silent for a few moments. "We have a very intense investigation going on right now into the ambush of Thomas Shark's team. I'll let the SAC know you will be involved."

"Thank you, Paul."

"Let's get these guys, Sean."

"Yes, sir."

***

Early the next morning, Kruger sat at the end of the table in JR's second floor conference room. Associates of JR's company were used to strangers meeting in the room and normally paid little attention to the goings on within those walls. Today was a different story.

The big man with bulging biceps and a weathered face

had not been to the room for a long time. Neither had the slender athletic man who followed him.

Another man, whom the associates had never seen before, appeared at the top of the stairs and wound his way around the peripheral of the second floor. As he entered the conference room the man shook everyone's hand like they were old friends.

JR was the last to enter the conference room and after the door was shut, the associates went back to their duties. The inhabitants of the conference room were quickly forgotten.

Sandy Knoll and Jimmie Gibbs were noticeably anxious to hear what Kruger would say. The summons to meet had them hopeful with the anticipation of good news. The appearance of Ryan Clark brought smiles as everyone sat at the table.

Kruger started the meeting. "As you all know from previous conversations, getting this new group together has been challenging, to say the least. I can now report that the Homeland Security route has been discarded."

Frowns were displayed by everyone, except Kruger. "However," he continued, "a better solution was found."

The frowns disappeared.

He took out his FBI badge and ID and placed them on the table. "I'm not sure how it transpired, but this little group is now part of a new department within the FBI. The Domestic Terrorist Division."

Gibbs said, "Did Sandy and I resign too quickly?"

Shaking his head, Kruger replied, "No, you did the right thing. You and Sandy would have been transferred to new assignments somewhere else in the country. Your new company will be an independent sub-contractor for this new group."

Clark tilted his head. "What's our structure?"

"Lean. I'm classified as an assistant director, which negates the mandatory retirement age clause for active special agents." He gave the team a sly smile. "Because we are so lean, I'll be in the field instead of behind a desk. At this point, Ryan and I will be the only employees on the FBI payroll within this division. That might change over time, but for now that's it. The rest will be sub-contractors. This gives us more options about who we need as we get involved with investigations. To avoid the red tape of the bureau, Sandy and Jimmie's company has been vetted and will be the primary supplier of these individuals."

Knoll chuckled. "Sounds like we just hit a trifecta."

With a nod, Kruger said, "We did. Ryan's title is now Special Agent in Charge. It comes with a nice salary bump and a new line on his resume."

With a grin, Clark said, "Thank you, Sean."

"You're welcome, you deserve it." He paused. "Because our budget is—uh—substantial, we won't be flying commercial." He nodded at Sandy. "Your company will be in charge of providing transportation to and from any location the team needs to travel to and arranging vehicles while the team is on site. For now, we won't have to rely on commercial air travel or FBI pool vehicles."

Knoll made a note and nodded. "We already have a pilot who comes with his own plane."

"I believe I met him."

"You did."

"Finally, I will pass this out." Kruger extracted five sets of papers stapled together and passed one set to each person. "This is a second manifesto JR and Alexia found within the pages of the pages Thomas Shark found on Monk's property. It's a disturbing summary of the activities of an, until recently, unknown organization."

The room was quiet as the pages were read. Jimmie looked up first. "I was wondering when another group might start using the ISIS model for recruitment. It was extremely effective."

The newly installed assistant director said, "Our first

task is to identify the leaders."

"I thought there was a vigorous investigation effort underway right now looking into the ambush." Clark continued to stare at the document in his hands.

"There is, but they are looking for the individuals who committed the attack. We won't be a part of it. Our task is broader. Find the individuals who are organizing this group and quietly shut it down."

Jimmie asked, "Where do we start?"

Kruger pointed at JR. "He already has."

CHAPTER 35

Lander, Wyoming

Kevin Marks took a long pull from a bottle of beer as he waited for his dinner companions to arrive. The table where he sat occupied a small alcove near the back of the brew pub. Since he ate there often, the owner reserved it for him most evenings. The fact he owned twenty-five percent of the establishment didn't hurt either.

Sheriff Roger Blake sat down across from Marks and frowned. "Do you know how many FBI agents we have in this county?"

With a shake of his head, Marks took a sip of beer.

"We have at least twenty and probably more I'm not aware of."

"Why are you not aware of them?"

"Because my department has been told, in no uncertain terms, we aren't involved with their investigation."

"Sounds like you didn't use your charm."

Blake leaned forward and said in a low whisper, "I hope those three goons you hired are in another state right now."

"Extended fishing trip in Manitoba."

"Keep them there."

Marks just nodded.

Gordon Lyon, Chairman of the Fremont County Board of Commissioners, joined them. He sat next to Marks and stared at Blake. "What are you doing about all the FBI agents running around here?"

"Not a damn thing."

Lyon puffed his chest out and started to say something when Marks touched his arm. "Gordon…"

"Sorry, but the phones in our office have been ringing off the walls with complaints."

"About?"

"How rude they are."

With a chuckle, Marks nodded. "Perfect representatives of this country's out-of-control federal government." He drained his beer and handed the empty to a young waitress who had just deposited a new one in front of him. "We will have to endure this for a few more days, gentlemen. When they don't find anything, they'll lose interest."

After ordering their dinner, the two newcomers contemplated their beers. Blake scowled as he twisted the bottle clockwise and then counter clockwise. Lyon nervously peeled the wet label from the bottle. Marks looked at each one and, in a low voice, said, "You two knew what you were doing when you signed up for this. We all agreed on how to move forward."

Lyon's face reddened as he shot Marks an angry glare. "Didn't agree to an ambush of six FBI agents."

"Sure, you did." Marks returned the glare. "You agreed to it when you took my money to get elected Commissioner."

"I did no such…" He stopped and raised the beer bottle to his lips.

"What's next, Kevin?" Blake had not taken his eyes off the richest man in Fremont County for several minutes.

"You don't seem to be worried about the FBI."

His eyes narrowed. "Who's going to talk to them? I'm not and I know you two are too scared to say anything. So, who?"

Lyon just shook his head and peeled more label off the bottle.

The sheriff stopped twisting his bottle. "They have ways of finding things out, Kevin."

Marks slammed his palm down on the table and leaned forward. "Not if you and Gordon keep your damn mouths shut. There is nothing written down about our activities." He touched his temple. "Everything is supposed to be up here and if you don't say anything, it can't be found."

Blake took a deep breath. "What if Monk had notes?"

"What do you mean? Notes."

"During the initial search of his property, my deputies saw them hauling off all those bank boxes."

"Class notes."

"Maybe. What if there was something else hidden in the class notes."

Marks grinned. "There was, but those three goons you mentioned found it when they took care of the FBI agents at Monk's cabin."

Lyon gasped. "Where's the information now?'

"Ashes, buried in the Canadian back country."

"What about the papers they hauled off?"

"What about them? If there was anything there, we would know by now. Besides, Monk didn't know about you two, and he definitely didn't know the full story. He was a tool, gentlemen, nothing more. A tool we used for five years."

"Well, he wasn't a very effective tool. We've made no progress in those five years." Blake's eyes were narrow as he glared at Marks.

Marks shook his head. "I disagree. He set the stage for the next phase."

Lyon sat up straighter. "What do you mean?"

"The fact that the FBI is crawling all over this area tells me they are concerned and our long-term plan is working. Why do you think there are so many incidents right now with someone walking into a soft-target and opening up with an AR-15?"

The other two men remained quiet.

"Because Monk sowed the seeds. We have a group watering those seeds as we speak."

For the first time this evening, Sheriff Blake chuckled. "You mean those nerds you've got in Montana playing with Facebook?"

With a nod, Marks said, "Those nerds as you describe them, are the ones who are spreading the word over the internet about Monk. They are calling him a martyr who died trying to save this great country from…" He hesitated. "Being overrun by immigrants."

Neither man spoke as they stared at Marks. He continued, "Very soon, the internet will explode with information about what Monk was really doing. When that occurs," he took a sip of beer," all of those seeds we've been sowing will start sprouting and producing results."

Lyon smiled for the first time.

While they ate, Marks decided to tell them about the next step. "While the FBI is running around our county like chickens with their heads cut off, the real activity is taking place in Iowa and Kansas."

Blake held a napkin to his lips to cover his full mouth. "What are you talking about?"

"What happens in Kansas and Iowa?"

With a snort, Lyons said, "Not much."

"Farming, gentlemen, farming."

"So?" This from Blake.

"What do farmers need to grow a good crop?"

A small smile appeared on Blake's face. "Fertilizer?"

Marks nodded. "Exactly." There was a pause as he

popped a piece of steak into his mouth. The two other men stared at him while he chewed. After swallowing, he said, "We've been doing it for two years now. Our associates have been slowly collecting bags of ammonium nitrate, one at a time and storing them carefully in four different locations."

"How the heck can you do that? Ammonium nitrate is highly regulated."

"Yes, but if you have an individual sympathetic to our cause buying small amounts of it on a regular basis for their farm, you can get around the regulation. Then, once a month, one of our people drives around and collects those bags from our sympathetic farmers and takes them to a storage site. We're buying other chemicals, but that is the main one we need."

"Why are we just now hearing about this?" Lyon had not taken a bite since this part of the conversation started.

"There was no need to discuss it. We were simply gathering and accumulating. A need to know was kept to a minimum number of individuals."

Blake frowned. "What if one of these sympathetic farmers gets a guilty conscience?"

"We've had a few of them, it is unfortunate, but several met with a freak accident on their farms. So, they are no longer in a position to discuss their guilty consciences. And remember, gentlemen, none of these farmers knows the others exist. They are in different counties all over the two states."

"How much do you have stored?"

Marks smiled and said, "Enough."

"What do you mean enough?"

"Enough that we aren't collecting anymore."

Lyon frowned. "Why?"

"Because we have our targets identified."

"What are they?"

"It's best neither of you know. Plausible deniability and

all that. What I can tell you is one site will be on the east coast and another on the west coast."

Blake smiled just before he took a bite of mashed potatoes. "I like that."

"One will target Washington DC and the other will affect all those bleeding-heart liberals in San Francisco."

"Those are also the areas with the larger concentration of the population."

Marks nodded. "Exactly."

CHAPTER 36

Springfield, MO
The Next Day

"What did the labs find on Monk's and Peter Greer's laptop?" JR sipped coffee as he sat down in his cubicle.

Kruger leaned against the credenza behind the cubicle, studying the brownish black liquid in his mug. "Not much."

"Who looked at them?"

"Charlie's group."

"And they didn't find anything?'

"Nothing useful. Why?"

"What if Alexia and I look at them?"

"I'm actually ahead of you on that request."

Looking up at his friend, JR tilted his head. "And that means?"

"Both computers will be here sometime today via FedEx." He looked up. "It's amazing what a newly ordained assistant director can get accomplished."

JR chuckled. "Don't let it go to your head."

With a sheepish grin, Kruger said, "That's what Stephanie told me." He paused for a second. "What do you think you'll find on them?"

"That's the question I've been asking myself. We know they followed the same Facebook pages, right?"

A nod was his answer.

"All but one of those pages has been deleted."

"Really."

"Yeah, they disappeared right after the attack on Thomas's team. Whoever took them down knew exactly what to do—they're gone without a trace."

"What was the content, JR?"

"Mundane stuff, mostly. However, Alexia looked at them before they disappeared and thought she saw code words within the posts."

Sipping his now-cold coffee, Kruger remained quiet.

"Uh—she said it reminded her of the ways the Russians communicated with her when she was in Mexico."

Kruger frowned. "Do you remember a conversation we had a few weeks ago where you mentioned something about shortwave radio stations that only broadcast numbers?"

"Yeah." He paused as his eyes grew wide. "Oh, shit." JR turned to the computer and his fingers danced on the keyboard. It was several minutes before he sat back in his chair and pointed at the left screen. "That's the only remaining page that both Monk and Greer followed."

Leaning over, Kruger put his half-readers on and stared. "It's a gun enthusiast page."

"Yeah." JR cupped his chin with his right hand and leaned forward. "What if the numbers stations are telling followers how to find the hidden messages on a Facebook page?"

"It'd be an almost unbreakable communication system because you'd have to know what numbers station to listen to and which Facebook page to use."

JR looked up at Sean. "I need those laptops."

***

At exactly 11:34 a.m., JR's receptionist sent him an instant message that appeared on the bottom right of his middle screen. He stood, hurried to the staircase and descended to the first floor. As he breezed by Alexia's cubicle on his way back to the conference room, he said, "Christmas came early this year."

She glanced at him, saw the FedEx box in his hands and followed.

As two of the world's foremost hackers entered the conference room, Kruger spoke into his cell phone. "The laptops are here, Charlie. Gotta go. We'll talk later."

JR placed the box down and turned to Kruger. "Did he tell you what they found on these?"

"Yeah, he said there were numerous encrypted files they never gained access to."

After extracting the laptops from their shipping enclosure, Alexia plugged one into the power strip on top of the conference table. She busied herself as JR placed the second laptop in front of him.

Turning to Kruger, JR said, "This might take a while."

"I don't mind. I'll wait."

With a nod, JR plugged the laptop he held into the power strip.

Just as he turned on the computer, Alexia said, "The encryption software is 7-Zip."

JR smiled as his fingers danced on the keyboard. "This one uses 7-Zip also. That's interesting."

With a frown, Kruger said, "What? What's interesting?"

Alexia replied as she looked up from the laptop, "7-Zip encryption software was developed by a Russian freelance programmer. His name is Igor Pavlov and he introduced it in 1999. Since then he has been updating and maintaining the software."

Kruger tilted his head. "Why is that interesting?"

She continued, "7-Zip can be used to encrypt specific files. Plus, I find it interesting that two individuals who probably didn't know each other used encryption software developed by a Russian."

JR nodded. "I agree with Alexia." He paused. "Why 7-Zip? There are other encryption programs out there—why did Monk and Greer choose one developed by a Russian?"

Kruger considered JR's statement and smiled. "Because they were told to use it."

Alexia nodded and JR started typing faster. He studied something on the screen and typed again. He mumbled, "I thought Monk was supposed to be smart." He raised his head and said to Alexia, "Key is in a text file labeled Open."

Her hands flew over the keyboard. "Got it. There's one here labeled Open It."

Kruger waited patiently as the two worked.

Five minutes later, JR looked at his friend. "Monk may have been a mathematical genius, but he was lazy when it came to securing his computer. I'm surprised Charlie's group didn't figure this out."

"It doesn't matter, JR. What'd you find?"

"A swamp filled with Russians."

***

By the time the team assembled in JR's conference room, Alexia and JR knew the secrets held by the two laptops.

Kruger started the meeting. "JR, will you and Alexia give us a summary of what you found?"

JR nodded at Alexia. She sat next to her husband and said, "Most of the files within the encrypted sections of Peter Greer's laptop were Word documents. From what JR and I can determine, there were five Facebook pages he frequented, all of which are no longer active and deleted. The code this group is using is simple yet complicated. We found a cheat-sheet chart for a specific shortwave numbers station. It transmits in the 49-meter band."

Sandy said, "That band works great at night—not so much during the daytime."

JR nodded. "That's what we learned, too. We don't think either Monk or Greer possessed a transmitter, we believe they only had receivers. From the cheat sheet we found on Greer's laptop, the number station was static and stayed on the same frequency all the time. Alexia checked. It's still broadcasting. The numbers repeat for twenty-four hours and then change. We haven't been able to listen to it long enough to determine any pattern from day-to-day. So, we're speculating here. We think the broadcasts told the listener what Facebook page to follow and the location of the real message within the page."

Clark said, "Sounds complicated."

"It might be at first. But after using it a few times, it would become familiar. To the casual viewer, there would be no way to break the code."

Kruger spoke up. "From what I gather from his writings, Greer was a relatively new recruit for the group. He'd recently been instructed by his college to find another school due to poor grades and absenteeism. His writings suggest someone angry at just about everything without a reason for his anger. I hate to stereotype someone like him, but he fits the same profile as a lot of the individuals who conduct mass shootings."

"Why wasn't he identified, Sean?"

"Good question, Jimmie. My guess would be he kept his feelings inside and didn't broadcast them to the world. Some of these individuals do, but the really dangerous ones, as a rule, don't. He fed his anger by concentrating on social media. How he came across Monk's group would be anybody's guess."

Knoll nodded. "That's exactly how ISIS recruited."

"I agree—same process. Only these guys are doing it within our borders."

Alexia spoke next. "JR and I think there's a Russian connection."

This statement made Sandy Knoll, Jimmie Gibbs and Ryan Clark sit up straight and stare at her wide eyed.

Kruger nodded. "That's an angle we're exploring. It's pure speculation at the moment, but what little evidence we have so far sure points in that direction."

Gibbs was quiet for a few seconds. "So, what's our next step, Sean?"

"We need to find the broadcast site for the numbers station and see who's programming the broadcasts."

With a nod Knoll said, "In other words, we're going into the field?"

"Yes, Sandy, we are. All of us, including JR and Alexia."

The big man smiled. "Good, I was getting bored."

Clark asked, "Are we on our own on this?"

"I believe we have to be. While Paul was correct in assigning a lot of agents to investigate the ambush, until we know exactly what we are up against, the less attention we attract, the better."

CHAPTER 37

North Central United States

The object Sandy Knoll held in his hand resembled an old fashion TV antenna, but with a smaller profile. "The process we're going to use is called fox-hunting by ham-radio operators. They do it for fun and award prizes to who finds the hidden transmitter first. It also has military applications if your enemy is communicating with shortwave radios."

The other members of the team nodded.

Dusk would soon turn to night as four members of the team stood next to Stewart Barnett's HA-420 HondaJet parked on the tarmac at the Bismarck Municipal Airport. Knoll looked at the other three men and smiled. "JR believes the numbers station we are seeking could be somewhere between here and the Canadian border or possibly inside Canada." He pointed at Clark. "Ryan and I will take JR and head west toward Dickinson, while Sean, Jimmie and Alexia go east toward Jamestown. That will give us a roughly one-hundred-and-eighty-mile base line.

We know the signal is northwest of our current location. We'll need at least three GPS locations by each team to triangulate the station's position with accuracy."

More nods from the three men.

JR and Alexia stepped off the plane with their laptops ready. Knoll continued, "Communication will be with satellite phones. We'll probably get into some isolated areas and cell phone reception could get spotty." He paused; when no one replied, he continued, "When either JR or Alexia believe they have the location triangulated, we'll head north. If everyone is ready, let's get our equipment loaded into the SUVs and we'll head out."

Before the team ventured north from Springfield, Knoll arranged with Enterprise to have two GMC Yukon Denali's positioned in Bismarck, North Dakota for their use. Stewart Barnett, who served KKG Solutions as their pilot, flew them to the Bismarck airport and remained on standby in case they needed fast transportation elsewhere.

The two SUVs traveled in opposite directions on Interstate 94, their drivers stopping every thirty miles to take a directional reading on the shortwave signal.

At 9:51 p.m., from the back seat of Knoll's SUV, JR said, "Got a fix."

Ryan Clark twisted around in his seat. "Where?"

"Northwest of Minot Airforce Base." He paused as he typed on his laptop. "It's right on the Canadian border near a town called Portal."

Knoll picked up his satellite phone and told Kruger the info and then started looking for a highway to take them north.

Four hours later, Knoll's rented Denalis sat parked along the side of a seldom-used country road. He could through night-vision binoculars what appeared to be a deserted farm house one-hundred yards from the road. "It looks vacant. Are you sure this is the correct spot, JR?"

"Yup. Do you see an antenna anywhere?"

"No, just an old wind…" He took the binoculars from his eyes. With a smile, he looked at JR. "Mill."

JR nodded. "That will be the antenna." He took his cell phone out of his pocket and checked the time. "How long before Sean gets here?"

"Should be any minute."

This far into the countryside with no city lights near, the Milky Way ribbon provided almost the same amount of illumination as the quarter moon low in the western sky. The headlight of a vehicle could be seen off in the distance heading their way. It was a few minutes before the SUV driven by Kruger parked behind Knoll's. As he stepped out and walked up to the others, he asked, "That it?"

"Yeah, but it's in Canada."

"Huh."

"The place looks deserted. So far, we haven't seen any activity."

Kruger took out his cell phone, checked his signal strength and searched for a number. Before pressing the send icon, he glanced at the time and realized it was a little before four in the morning. Probably closer to five where the person receiving his phone call lived.

"Thatcher."

"Bentley, it's Sean Kruger."

Bentley Thatcher, recently promoted to the rank of superintendent with the Royal Canadian Mounted Police and an old acquaintance of Kruger's, replied, "A bit early isn't it?"

"You're apparently up."

"True. What can I do for you, Sean?"

"We have a logistics problem near Portal, North Dakota."

He heard a chuckle. "Logistics problem. I take it you have a suspect inside Canada."

"No, nothing like that. Have you ever heard of a shortwave numbers station?"

"Not that I can recall."

Kruger explained it to him and added, "We've triangulated the station's signal to a house about one hundred yards inside your country. I really don't want to cause an international incident, but we need to check it out."

Thatcher laughed out loud. "Do you realize how often that particular spot of nowhere is patrolled?"

"Wouldn't have a clue."

"Once a week if it's lucky. I'll make sure they skip another week."

"Thanks. Bentley, I owe you."

"I heard congratulations are in order."

Kruger frowned, not knowing where this was going. "Uh—not that I'm aware."

"I understand you're an assistant director now."

"Oh, that. How'd you know?"

"Apparently, our Minister of Public Safety and your National Security Advisor met yesterday. I'm told it was a productive and cordial meeting. Both entities pledged mutual assistance with fighting domestic terrorism."

"That was well timed."

"You wouldn't have had anything to do with the meeting, would you?"

"You give me too much credit, Bentley."

"That's not what I hear. Anyway, keep me posted. If I need to be concerned about this numbers station, I would appreciate a head's up."

"You've got it. Thanks for the assistance."

After putting his cell phone in a back-jean pocket, Kruger said, "We're good to go for crossing the border." He looked at the eastern sky. The first hints of the coming new day were already visible. "It's going to be light soon. We need to find a hotel, but I haven't seen anything for miles."

Alexia, still sitting in the back of the Denali, looked up

from her laptop and said, "Closest hotels will be in Estevan in Canada. It's about thirty miles from here."

"Let's go."

***

In daylight, the structure appeared to be a typical two-story farmhouse with a wraparound porch. A barn and a smaller shed stood fifty yards behind it. Both appeared old and on the verge of collapsing. The house, having seen harsh winters and little maintenance, also appeared to have fallen into disrepair. Sandy and Jimmie were doing reconnaissance on the structure and by mid-afternoon were preparing for a closer inspection after dark.

Knoll asked, "What do you think?"

"Looks abandoned to me."

"JR did a Saskatchewan Assessment search on it and the owner is listed as an LLC in Wyoming."

Without taking his eyes away from the binoculars, Gibbs said, "Huh." He was quiet for several moments. Taking his eyes away from the lenses, he looked at Knoll. "I could slip over there and nose around a little."

"If someone is there, you'd be seen. The plan is to do it tonight."

"I don't see any signs anyone has been there for a long time, Sandy."

"Someone has to maintain the radio station."

"Not necessarily. It could be totally automated with a computer."

"It'd have to have internet." Knoll stared at the building. "I don't even see electrical lines running to it, let alone internet."

Gibbs was quiet as he once again looked through the binoculars. "Sandy, drive past and see if we can get a better angle on those outbuildings."

The big man drove the SUV past the property and

stopped a hundred yards later. "Is that good enough?"

"Yeah." Gibbs exited and walked to the rear of vehicle to survey the barn. He climbed onto the rear bumper of the Yukon to get a better view. A minute later he returned the passenger seat. "Behind the barn is an array of solar panels on the ground. They're not visible from the road. I had to stand on the bumper to see them. There's also an antenna outside the second-floor window on the east side of the house. It's the same kind you use on a recreational vehicle and doesn't have to be pointed toward a satellite."

"Pretty sophisticated set-up this far out in the boonies." Gibbs nodded.

"Think that's where the station is, on the second floor?"

"Makes sense. Couldn't be seen by anyone looking into the first-floor windows."

"Exactly. Let's get back. Tonight, will be interesting."

***

Sunset occurred at 7:31 and with the overcast sky, complete darkness made an appearance a little after eight. By then Kruger and Jimmie were on foot and approaching the house from the west. Both wore night vision goggles, black jeans, black long sleeve T-shirts and black watch caps. When they arrived at the structure, Kruger circled toward the back with Gibbs heading toward the front.

Kruger held his Glock in his right hand as he placed his back against the west wall of the home. He cautiously looked around the corner to make sure no surprises awaited them. Seeing nothing out of the ordinary, he continued his survey of the outside. A small wooden porch in the center of the north wall indicated where the door to the inside would be located. What he found at the entry reinforced his perception of the building. A house designed to look abandoned but with hidden secrets.

The steel door he found possessed a keypad for a lock.

This meant multiple individuals could gain access to the interior without the need of a key.

Jimmie appeared around the east corner and approached Kruger. "Front door is bolted shut. Only way in is to breach it. Plus, all the windows are painted over."

"I noticed that." Kruger pointed at the keypad. "Someone has this placed locked down tight. My bet is if this door is opened by any unauthorized individual, there will be an alarm sound somewhere."

Gibbs grinned. "I have an idea."

Kruger followed the ex-Seal as he jogged toward the windmill fifty yards northeast of the house. When they arrived, Gibbs explained, "This has to be the antenna for the broadcast." He bent and examined a coax cable exiting the ground and running up the inside of a windmill leg. "That's probably the antenna lead."

"What happens if the lead is broken?"

With a mischievous grin, Jimmie said, "It stops transmitting."

"If it stops transmitting, someone has to come out and service it, right?"

Jimmie reached into his utility vest and took out a pair of wire cutting pliers. He placed the tip around the coax and snipped it. "You mean like that."

"Yeah, just like that."

Both men chuckled and headed back to the SUVs.

When they arrived, JR looked up from his laptop. "Station's off the air."

"We know."

"Now what?"

Kruger smiled and looked back at the house. "We wait."

***

During the years Jimmie Gibbs spent as a Seal, one of his skills included marksmanship. He had become a highly regarded sniper during his various tours of duty. Patience and the ability to hide in plain sight within a sniper hide were two of his more endearing attributes. The prairie grass around the house, being tall and thick, provided a perfect environment for his skills. Wearing his favorite ghillie suit, Gibbs positioned himself to blend into the natural surroundings in the house's backyard. Armed with a Remington 700 and a powerful pair of binoculars, he waited for the anticipated arrival of someone to fix the now-snipped antenna wire.

Dawn came and went as the sun rose higher in the eastern sky. His patience was rewarded by the appearance of an ancient Ford Bronco twenty minutes after ten. The individual who stepped out of the vehicle appeared to be in his late twenties, clean shaven and stocky. A backpack slung over his right shoulder indicated he might be the repair person for the facility. He punched a number into the keypad, opened the back door and walked into the house.

From his position, Gibbs could see the numbers and made note of the combination. With his mission accomplished, he started to slowly back out of his hide, but not so fast as to be detected.

Fifteen minutes later and once again stationary, he watched the man exit the house and stride purposefully toward the windmill. He whispered into the microphone of the comm set on his head. "Show time. He'll see the antenna's been cut."

The man stooped over and examined the antenna lead. Gibbs could hear him swearing as he stood and swept the area with his gaze. Putting his hand on his hips, he stared in Gibbs' direction for several seconds and then continued his survey of the surrounding area. Not seeing anything that concerned him, he went back inside the house. Less than a minute later, he reappeared with his backpack over his shoulder. When he returned to the windmill, he extracted several objects and started to repair the coax cable.

A little while later, Gibbs heard Sandy over the radio, "Station's back on the air."

Gibbs clicked the transmit button twice to acknowledge.

The man kneeling next to the windmill packed his tools, stood and swept his gaze over the area again. He then walked back toward the house and stepped inside. Ten minutes later, he returned to the Bronco, turned it around and headed back to the country road just inside the United States border.

Glancing at his watch, Gibbs noted the repair job had taken just under an hour. He dialed a number on his satellite phone. "We have the combination, head on back to the house."

CHAPTER 38

United States and Canadian Border

Knoll and Ryan Clark stood next to the two Denalis parked behind the outbuildings of the isolated farmhouse. They kept their attention trained on the road which straddled the two countries' border. Knoll held a small radio to keep in touch with the four members of the team currently inside the house.

The big man pointed off to the west. "Looks like we have company coming." A cloud of dust could be seen off in the distance heading toward their location. Knoll raised his radio and spoke, "Sean, we're about to have visitors."

"Buy us five minutes."

"Got it. Send Jimmie out."

"He's on his way."

As the dust cloud grew nearer, Gibbs emerged from the house and ran to Knoll. "What've ya got?"

Knoll pointed toward the west. "Looks like two vehicles heading this way."

Gibbs shot a quick glance at Clark who stood still, his

attention on the dust cloud and his Glock in his right hand. He rushed to the back of Knoll's SUV and extracted his Remington 700 from its case. With the rifle in hand, he headed toward the interior of the barn.

Tracing Gibbs' steps, Knoll also went to the back of the GMC and retrieved a Bushmaster ACR Pistol. This he held in his right hand by his thigh as he looked toward the approaching vehicles. With the handheld radio in his left hand, he said, "Sean, we've got two pickups with unknown numbers of occupants."

"Got it. We're almost done in here."

"Too late—they're turning off the road and approaching."

Knoll clipped the radio to his belt, kept the ACR out of sight behind him and stared at the approaching vehicles. A dusty fifteen-year-old Ford F-150 4x4 stopped first. Parking right behind it came an older model Dodge Ram 1500 with large knobby tires. Four men stepped out, two from each truck, as the dust settled around them.

The driver of the Ford glared hard at Clark and Knoll. After shutting the truck door, he said, "You fellas are trespassing."

With a shrug, Knoll replied, "Got lost."

The three remaining men kept their hands resting on their holstered handguns as they spread out from the trucks.

The driver said, "Well, you need to be lost somewhere else." He shot a glance at his partners who withdrew their handguns and trained them on Clark and Knoll.

The sound of a rifle bolt being thrown in the barn could be heard by everyone. One of the men from the Ram glanced toward the loft's opening.

Knoll saw Kruger emerge from the back of the house with his Glock in hand. Knoll said, "Sorry, boys. Can't do that—we've got business here."

"Since this ain't your property, you've got no business here."

Kruger was now behind the four men and said, "Put the guns down, gentlemen. We're with the FBI."

The driver suddenly turned to see who had spoken. Knoll brought the Bushmaster up and pointed in the direction of the men. Clark moved to his right and behind the engine compartment of one of the Denalis, his Glock trained on the newcomers.

A slim man from the Ram wiped his mouth with his sleeve and lowered his pistol slightly. He looked nervously at Clark and Knoll. His attention was drawn back to the opening above the barn door. He licked his lips and pointed. "Joel, they've got a sniper in the loft."

The driver, who was apparently Joel, shot a quick glance toward the barn. His worried look changed rapidly to a sneer. "This ain't the US. We're in Canada. FBI don't have jurisdiction here."

Kruger said, "Gentlemen, I will ask you one more time and only once more to lower your weapons. This is official FBI business and you are interfering with a lawful investigation."

The standoff in the isolated farmhouse yard continued as Joel licked his lips and shot hard glances at both Gibbs in the barn loft and Kruger behind him.

The driver of the Dodge wore a well-used cowboy hat. He spat something into the dirt in front of him and said, "This is typical overreach by the United States Federal Government, Joel. They think they can go anywhere and do anything they want."

Joel remained quiet as his stare locked on Knoll. "Let's go boys. We have to give them this round. Next time, maybe not."

All four men climbed back into their trucks and spun gravel as they accelerated back to the access road.

Kruger watched them drive off as he holstered his Glock. He walked up to Knoll and said, "Nice touch having Jimmie in the loft."

"Wasn't my idea. He did it himself."

Nodding, Kruger patted Knolls shoulder. "Let's get the hell out of here. My bet is they will shut this place down by nightfall."

***

The return drive to Bismarck took four hours. During the trip, JR and Alexia sat in the back of Kruger's rental concentrating on their laptops, saying little except to each other. Jimmie sat in the front passenger seat, staring as the barren country slid past.

Kruger glanced at him. "Good idea being in the barn loft."

"I'm lucky it didn't fall in on me." He turned, checked on the two passengers in the back seat and turned his attention to Kruger. "What did you mean when you said they'd shut the place down by nightfall?"

"Exactly that. Our purpose wasn't to stop the broadcast. Quite the contrary, we need them to keep it broadcasting. They'll just move the station to another location." He glanced in the rearview mirror at JR. "Did you get what you needed, JR?"

Without looking up from the computer, the hacker replied, "Yup and more."

A grin appeared on Kruger's lips. "Our real goal at the station was to gain access to their computer network. Nothing more." He paused for a few heartbeats. "The guy who came to the house to fix the cable knew something was amiss. Coax cables just don't separate cleanly on their own. That's why we had four visitors an hour later—the repairman reported something was wrong at the house. Now with access to their computer, JR and your wife can learn more about this group's computer connections." He glanced at his young friend. "With luck, we can start learning just who the hell these people are."

***

Sitting next to JR on the plane, Kruger watched his friend working the laptop perched on his thighs. Leaning back, he closed his eyes and felt the long hours of the past few days catch up with him. Momentary doubt crept into his thoughts about his decision to return to this lifestyle. Without even thinking about it, he said, "Am I being selfish, JR?"

"About?"

"Returning to the job."

"It's who you are, Sean. How many times did you retire and return?"

"Couple."

"Exactly. Don't fight it. You can no more not be an FBI agent than I cannot be a computer hacker."

He opened his eyes and ended the self-reflection. He pointed to JR's computer. "Have you discovered anything?"

A frown appeared. JR stopped typing and looked at Kruger. "They have something big planned."

"Were you planning to enlighten me now or wait till it happened before you told me?" This was said with a mischievous grin.

Chuckling, JR closed his eyes and leaned back in his seat. "When I knew more details, yes. That's the problem Alexia and I are having. We have access to their emails. But there is nothing specific in them. Details are never mentioned—just obscure references."

"Is there someone directing the group?"

"What was the name of the county where you found Monks' cabin?"

"Fremont."

"There are a lot of references to the county seat, which is Lander. Alexia believes directions are coming from someone there."

"Tell me about the emails, JR."

"All are Gmail accounts with either random letters or numbers as the identifier. Alexia believes, and I agree with her, somewhere in all those emails is an attachment with the key to understanding the code being transmitted by the numbers station."

"How many emails are you referring to?"

"Thousands."

"What about back-tracking to a server?"

With a shake of his head, JR touched a key on his computer and the screen went blank. "I don't think they have one." He took a deep breath and let it out slowly. In a low voice he said, "We've determined one person is directing traffic and making the decisions." He shot a glance at Alexia—she sat next to Jimmie, her head on his shoulder and her eyes closed. "Alexia has the emails from this individual isolated. The pattern is always the same. One person sends an email to three individuals, who in turn forwards it to three more individuals and so on so forth. It's always the same sender and email recipients. There're at least a hundred distinct email addresses in the chain. No one communicates with the entire group."

"Huh."

With a nod, JR continued, "There's something else."

"I'm listening."

"In the short time we've been poking around in their emails, she found several from a computer located in Belarus."

Kruger did not respond.

"These emails were addressed to the individual we think is the leader."

"The ones from Belarus?"

"Yes."

"What town?"

JR gave his friend a grim smile. "Horki."

"Same place where some of the ransomware attacks originated."

"Yes."

"That's not a coincidence, JR."

"I'm beginning to believe that as well."

"So how are you going to figure this out?"

With a sly smile, JR turned to his friend. "I have to do something I haven't done in a long time."

"Should I ask what that is?"

"Hack into the NSA computer system."

CHAPTER 39

Lander, Wyoming

The short, stocky middle-aged man bumped into Kevin Marks and mumbled, "Excuse me, sorry."

The store owner watched him carry three pairs of jeans to a specific dressing room and disappear inside. Without hesitating, he headed toward his office, closed the door and locked it. The man was already waiting for Marks when he entered his office. The hidden door stood open and the stocky man with the broad shoulders said, "You didn't lock the door."

Marks glared at the man. "Why the sudden need to see me?"

"We have a problem."

Taking a deep breath, Marks moved to his desk and sat behind it. "What now?"

"The FBI found the transmitter."

As suddenly as he had sat, Marks stood, leaned over the desk with his palms flat on top and his face a deep shade of crimson. "How?"

"We don't know. It stopped transmitting, so someone was sent to check it out. Normally when this happens, it's caused by an animal chewing through a wire. Not this time. The antenna coax was cut clean. So, the repair guy fixed it, left and reported what he found. Four men went out to find who cut it and came across a heavily armed FBI contingent. Our guys were out-gunned, so they left."

"Did they confiscate the equipment?"

The shorter man shook his head. "No, but we need to move the transmitter."

"Then do it."

"It's already being done. The problem is, we didn't see any evidence they messed with anything."

Marks sat again, rested his elbows on the chair arms and made a steeple with his hands. "You think they got into the computer?"

"That would be my first assumption."

"Hmmm…"

Silence filled the room as Marks stared at a spot on the wall over the door. "How quickly can the explosives be assembled and loaded?"

"Couple of days. Why?"

"We need to move our schedule up."

A nod was his response.

"We can't be certain they've broken our code, but we have to assume they have. I'll send out a new key for the numbers station."

Another nod.

"What's today?"

"Wednesday."

"Make sure the trucks are ready to move by Saturday."

"Got it."

The broad-shouldered man turned and walked back toward the open entrance to the fitting room. Before walking through it, he turned. "It was the same FBI agent that found Monk."

After the door closed, Marks slammed his fist on the desk. "Damn." He pressed his palms against his eyes. "It's time to do something about this guy."

He picked up his desk phone and dialed a number.

***

With all of the associates gone for the day, the sole occupant of the building sat in his cubicle and stared at the right monitor. The only illumination penetrating the second-floor gloom came from the exit lights above the stairwell, a desk lamp on the credenza behind him and the flickering of the monitors. JR moved the mouse to open a file. As the data within the file displayed on the center monitor, a small smile came to his lips. Unaware and completely oblivious to the time of night, he reached for his cell phone and pressed the call icon for a frequently called number.

"Do you have any idea what time it is?" the voice mumbled.

JR glanced at the bottom right corner of the middle monitor. "Yeah, it's 11:17 p.m."

"Normal individuals are usually asleep at that time of night, JR."

"Usually I am, but a friend of mine has a problem and I believe I found something to help him solve that problem."

Kruger's alertness immediately increased. "What'd you find?"

"It's not really what I found—it's the access information that's interesting."

"Talk to me."

"As you suspected, the numbers station was off the air for a few hours and started broadcasting from a different location about an hour ago. However, they didn't change the computer that controls it."

"Which means?"

"The worm I planted is doing its job. A string of emails is flowing over their network, which is allowing the program to search backward to the originating email."

"Oh, good grief, JR. Where is it?"

"The sheriff's office in Lander, Wyoming."

Kruger remained quiet for several moments. "The sheriff?"

"Yeah. If you think about it, it explains a lot."

"Such as?"

"You mentioned how insistent he was to gain access to all the boxes the FBI pulled out of Monks cabin."

"Not unusual for a small-town sheriff. But his persistence did raise a flag."

"Also, the only person who knew Thomas Shark and his team were at the cabin was the sheriff. Can you think of anyone else who would have known?"

"Not that I'm aware of."

"Exactly."

"Shit." Kruger was quiet for a few moments. "I have to make a call. I'll get back to you afterward."

***

Sitting on the side of his bed, Kruger took a deep breath. Stephanie placed a hand on his back as he exhaled slowly.

"What is it, Sean?"

"Hopefully the first break in this Monk business. I need to make a call. It might take a while, so I'll go to my office." He stood and walked down the hall. After sitting behind his desk, he tried to stifle a yawn. Not succeeding, he picked up his desk phone and called a number.

"Paul Stumpf."

"Paul, it's Sean."

"Calling this late, I'll assume you found something."

"How many agents do you still have in Wyoming?"

"Not sure, but with the lack of progress in the

investigation into the ambush, they've had to wind it down. Why?"

"Do I know the SAC?"

"Not sure, his name is Frank Reed."

"I don't know him."

"You're stalling."

"We have reason to believe the sheriff of Fremont County, Wyoming is involved."

"That's a serious accusation."

"I'm aware of that, sir. But he needs to be placed under surveillance."

Stumpf was quiet for several moments. "Okay, I'll have Reed called in the morning and informed about this development. When can you have more details?"

"No later than noon."

***

Sleep became elusive after Kruger returned to bed. He listened to the various sounds created by a house at night. Stephanie breathing gently and rhythmically next to him. His daughter in the room next to theirs, rustling her sheets as she slept. Air being forced through the ventilation ducts creating a slight vibration in the floor registers. A distant siren could be heard approaching and then receding. He listened with his hands behind his head, eyes open, staring at the ceiling fan as it turned slowly.

After thirty minutes, he quietly left the bedroom and went to the kitchen. As he rummaged through the pantry looking for a box of herbal tea, he felt a presence behind him.

Turning, he saw Stephanie standing there, her arms folded. "What are you looking for?"

He smiled and returned to studying the contents of the pantry. "The chamomile tea you keep in here."

"You hate chamomile tea."

"I don't hate it. I just don't care for it. But if it will help me sleep, I'll drink the stuff."

"Sean."

He returned his attention to her. "Yes."

"Your sleeplessness is getting worse. Do you think you need to see a doctor about it?"

"No, I need a neighbor who doesn't call at eleven o'clock at night."

She smiled, went to him and they embraced.

He said, "No, that's not true either. I guess I still care too much about the job when maybe I should be re-examining my priorities."

She hugged him tighter, but did not respond, letting him talk.

"This last trip wasn't that long, and we accomplished a lot."

Raising her head, she looked up at him. "There's a however, isn't there?"

"It's hard to explain, because I don't understand it myself. It's like when I'm not working, I can't get my mind off the investigation. When I am working, I'm usually traveling and missing you and the kids. Exactly like when Brian grew up, I'm missing a chunk of their childhood. Those are the times when I ask myself what the heck I'm doing this for?" He paused for just a heartbeat. "I can't have it both ways, Steph. My career has been one long battle of balancing my personal life with the bureau's demands. The bureau always wins."

When she raised her head to look at him, she could see moisture pooling in the corner of his left eye.

He continued, "Sometimes I felt like Brian was someone else's son who grew up and I only saw him on occasion."

With a smile, she said, "He doesn't blame you. You two have an excellent relationship."

The moisture in his eye leaked and ran down his cheek. "I know, but most of my memories of him growing up are based on pictures my mom and dad took for me. Why does that make me feel so guilty?"

Laying her head on his chest, she said, "It shouldn't. We can't live in the past, Sean. I hate saying this because it's such a cliché but it is what it is. Don't make any decisions right now. You told me you didn't sleep much on this last trip. You're tired. Making decisions when you feel that way are never your best ones."

He placed his chin on the top of her head. "How did I survive all those years without you?"

"The same way I did before I met you—one day at a time."

CHAPTER 40

Springfield, MO

Kruger leaned against JR's credenza and tried to stifle a yawn. Failing, he blinked several times and said, "Okay, last night you didn't have many details."

"No, I didn't. But I have a few now." He turned in his chair and looked at his friend. "Last night, I discovered the emails originated in the Fremont, Wyoming county sheriff's office. They do, in fact, originate on the sheriff's desktop computer."

"That's kind of stupid on the sheriff's part."

"My thoughts exactly. So, I hacked into the sheriff's office server."

With a grin, Kruger took a sip of coffee and then said, "I can't wait to hear what you found."

"The emails are only sent when he's logged out of the office."

"Okay, someone is using his computer to misdirect anyone from tracing the real sender."

JR nodded. "But why use the sheriff's computer? Why

not have a computer you use in a coffee shop or some other Wi-Fi spot. Why the sheriff's office."

Kruger was silent for a few moments as he stared at the far wall of the second floor. "Because someone wants to implicate the sheriff."

"That's the only reason I could think of, but the sheriff would be able to deny he's the one sending the emails because he can prove he's away from the office."

"Unless they are being sent at the behest of the sheriff."

"Huh." JR looked back at his computer. "Didn't think of that."

"What are the emails about?"

"Most of the ones I've found tell the recipients when to listen to the numbers station."

"Any attachments?"

"Not on any of the ones I've found. But the emails are purged once a month with a very sophisticated software routine. One I've never seen before. Alexia is dissecting it."

"Keep watching for one. We know they shut the numbers station down. My guess would be they're likely to change the outgoing message and everyone will need a new key. I would imagine…" He stopped and his eyebrows rose. "JR."

The hacker turned. "Uh-oh. I've seen that look before."

"Doesn't this operation seem a little too sophisticated to you?"

"Yes."

"I'm not disparaging small county sheriff's offices, but this just seems too—uh—what's the word I'm looking for?"

"High-tech?"

"Close. It reminds me too much of a communication system the FBI uncovered in 2010 used by the Russian foreign intelligence service. They were using customized steganography software to place messages in images to communicate with their agents abroad."

"Huh." JR blinked several times. "Do you know how steganography works?"

"All I know is what I've read. It's hiding a message within another message."

With a nod, JR said, "Or image."

After staring at the monitors, his hands rested above the keyboard for several moments before he started typing.

Kruger remained quiet as his friend worked his magic. As he watched, an image flashed on the center monitor and dissolved into 1s and 0s.

JR pointed at the screen. "That is what the image for the shield of the Fremont County sheriff's department reveals if it's broken down into individual bits and bytes."

"Okay, looks like binary code."

"It is. But watch this." More typing as JR said, "Colors are represented in computers using 8-bit numbers. This means that a set of eight zeroes and ones is used to represent a given color. By using all the possible combinations of eight zeroes and ones, we get two hundred and fifty-six possible colors represented by binary code."

"Okay, I'm following."

"Most computer monitors display colors by varying the red, green, and blue primary colors to create the desired image. What would happen if you varied that code by a digit or two from the original color within the image?"

"Wouldn't have a clue."

"You would get a color similar to the original one with a difference the human eye couldn't see. But the computer would know."

"Now I'm really not following you."

"Okay, let's look at the Fremont County emblem." It flashed on the screen. "I took this from their website. Let's break it down into binary code." Numbers appeared on the screen as JR typed. "Now let's compare this binary representation to one from the sheriff's emails to the group." More typing and the left screen displayed numbers.

"That is the binary code for an email emblem. Can you see a difference?"

"No."

"Watch." More typing as the two screens merged. "What about now?"

"A little."

"Exactly. If you take the slight changes in the binary code for the emblem, you can relay a message using the numbers that are different and converting them to binary code."

"So, you're telling me they are hiding the messages within the sheriff's emblem on the email signature."

"Yup."

"Huh."

"That's what I said."

"Okay, so what's the message in this one?"

More typing and five words appeared. *DEPART SATURDAY FOR DESIGNATED LOCATIONS.*

"What the heck does that mean?"

"It means I have to go back as far as I can and analyze the hidden message in the emblem."

"If the messages are hidden in the image in the email signature, what does the numbers station have to do with it?"

"Not following you, Sean."

"The numbers station is sending out a code, right?"

"That was our original theory. But their use of steganography takes the level of sophistication to another level."

Kruger was silent for a few moments. "You mentioned on the plane you would need to hack into the NSA computer. Did you?"

JR nodded.

"And?"

"Not good news."

"What?"

"A thought occurred to me on the plane there might be a foreign influence on this group. Now that we know they are communicating with the change in colors like the Russians did, what I found makes more sense."

"Please, JR, just tell me."

"The sheriff's computer does not have the software to convert images. Where are they coming from?"

Scratching his chin, Kruger titled his head. "Can you tell if the computer is receiving the image from somewhere else?"

With a mischievous grin, JR said, "I didn't think about it until just now. When Alexia was going through the emails on the sheriff's computer, she found it received an inordinate amount of spam. As a rule, we ignore these because most spam is automatically transferred to a junk file in the email program. What if the converted images are being received in an email the computer recognizes as spam?"

"It would send those emails directly to the Spam file."

"Exactly."

"Can you go back and find out if that's what's going on?"

"Looks like we will have to."

"Okay. Back to the reason for the numbers station and the embedded messages—why both systems?"

JR just shook his head.

Taking a sip of coffee, Kruger made a face and went to warm it up. When he returned, he displayed a slight smile. "JR, how much computer power does it take to convert the images like you just did?"

"It's not how much computer power, it's the software. Why?"

"Is that kind of software readily available?"

"Yes, there is an abundant number of different programs available. Some are even free."

"Are they easy to use?"

He shrugged. "Depends."

"On?"

After taking a deep breath, JR let it out slowly. "You'd have to have a certain level of computer savvy to use one. Why?"

Kruger sipped his coffee. "How many recipients did you find in the email trails?"

"About ninety-nine..." He stopped and tilted his head. "What are you getting at?"

"I could be wrong, but that seems like an awful lot of individuals to train on how to use steganography and keep them isolated from each other."

"Now that you mention it."

"Their messaging system keeps all the members from knowing the other email addresses, correct?"

JR nodded.

"Which means there may only be one or two individuals in the group who know about all the members."

"Maybe a few more."

"I would agree. So how do they train everyone to use steganography and use it correctly?"

JR remained quiet.

Kruger continued, "They don't. The hidden messages are for the leaders of the group. The short-wave numbers station is for the foot soldiers. They've got two different messages going out."

"And if only a few individuals know how to convert the images, it doesn't matter if they send the converted image in all the emails."

A nod was his answer.

***

Later That Same Day

"Here's what JR and Alexia have been able to determine. There is a server in Belarus sending what appears to be basic spam about male enhancement. To the computer on the sheriff's desk in Fremont County, it's just normal spam and moved to a separate folder. However, those emails contain an image with a coded message hidden within."

Paul Stumpf said, "Like the communication system we discovered in 2010 used by the Russian foreign intelligence service?"

"Similar, but with a few refinements. This group has two trucks loaded with what we can only surmise are explosives, departing on Saturday for two different targets. We don't know where those two trucks are located but we do know they are in states with a lot of agriculture."

"Why do you say that?"

"Because JR found a formula for making a high explosive with fertilizer imbedded in one of the images. Plus, we have a few emails acknowledging the completion of the fertilizer purchase."

"Can JR trace where the emails are being sent?"

"Public Wi-Fi hotspots all over the upper Midwest."

"This is getting serious, Sean. Why do you think the trucks are leaving on Saturday?"

"Because they announced it in one of their messages."

"What are the targets?"

"Unknown at this time."

"Do we have enough evidence to arrest this sheriff of Fremont County?"

"No, but I believe we have to anyway."

"I detect a note of hesitation."

"There is. The emails are being sent from the desktop computer on his desk. But he is always shown as logged out of the building when they are sent."

"Is it a ruse?"

"We don't know. But we're running out of time. It's Thursday and we don't know where the trucks are or where they're going. Our only link to them is the sheriff and the emails."

Stumpf was quiet for a long period. Kruger let him think.

"You have evidence the emails are sending instructions to commit a terrorist act, correct?"

"Yes."

"And you can prove they came from the sheriff's desk computer?"

"Yes."

"Do you want to be there for the arrest?"

"Yes."

"When can you get there?"

"My team can be on the ground by late tonight."

"Okay, I'll notify the SAC you are coming and to keep tabs on the whereabouts of the sheriff."

"Thanks, Paul."

"Sean."

"Yes."

"You're sure about this?"

"As sure as I've ever been."

CHAPTER 41

Fremont County, Wyoming

"This is my bust, Kruger." Special Agent in Charge Frank Reed did not look at the man standing next to him. He kept his attention on a house in the northwest section of Lander, Wyoming.

Kruger stood next to him, looking through a pair of binoculars at the same house. Ignoring the statement, he said, "How long's he been in there?"

"Pulled into the driveway behind the woman who owns the house."

"Who's she?"

"Her name is Linda Fuller. Mid-forties, not very good looking, heavy set and wears too much makeup. She works at the diner where the sheriff eats breakfast every morning."

Kruger didn't care for the way the managing FBI agent described the woman. With a frown he asked. "How often is he here?"

"We've only been following him for two days and he's

been here each night until a little after midnight."

After glancing at this wristwatch, Kruger returned his eyes to the binoculars. "As far as this being your bust, Reed, it's an FBI bust. Not your personal achievement."

Reed shot Kruger a hard stare and kept it there for a while. "I've been in this backwater part of the world for two weeks and…"

Kruger turned suddenly toward the younger agent, his face red and his eyes narrowed. He said through clenched teeth, "I don't give a damn how long you've been here, Agent Reed. This is an investigation into the blatant attack and murder of six FBI agents, one of whom was a friend of mine. You will do your job, get your ego in check and keep your mouth shut. Is that clear?"

Reed's eyes widened at the outburst, but he quickly recovered. "I've heard about you, Kruger. You're a prima donna and the personal pet of the director. You do your job and I'll do mine. If you can't keep up, then get out of our way."

With a slight smile, Kruger replied, "I'll keep that in mind. Just make sure you remember why you're here." Kruger turned and walked toward Sandy Knoll, Jimmie Gibbs and Ryan Clark who waited next to a black GMC Yukon.

When he arrived, he said, "You three ready?"

Everyone nodded.

"The local SAC is worried about us getting in his way. I suggest we keep out of it and go arrest the sheriff."

Knoll smiled, Gibbs turned his FBI ballcap backward and Clark nodded.

Kruger turned to Knoll. "Where's the rest of Reed's team?"

"Two are in a car a block east, another two are west about two blocks and there's another one fifteen yards to the right of where you and the SAC were standing."

"Anyone behind the house?"

"Not that I could tell."

With a shake of his head, Kruger mumbled. "Geez, what a cluster." A quick glance at his watch told him the time was approaching eleven p.m. "We have about an hour before the sheriff leaves. Sandy, you and Ryan slip into the backyard and cover the back door. Jimmie and I will breach the front door at exactly fourteen minutes past eleven. Sync our watches and you two go through the back door at the same time. I want the sheriff rattled."

Gibbs said, "I take it we're not waiting for the others to join the party."

"Nope."

Clark chuckled. "Care to tell us why?"

"Because the SAC seems intent on just watching the house, I am choosing to speed this process up." He pulled several pieces of folded paper out of an inside pocket of his FBI windbreaker. "Besides, we have this."

With a grin, Clark asked, "What is it?"

"A No-Knock Arrest Warrant for Fremont County Sheriff Roger Blake signed by a federal judge in Cheyenne."

"Cool, let's do it."

***

Frank Reed watched as Kruger and another man crossed the street and approached the front door of the house they had under surveillance. He looked through his binoculars and mumbled, "What the heck is he doing?"

The woman standing next to him said, "Looks like they're going in, Frank."

Taking the binoculars down, Reed stared at the house. "They can't do that. Call for backup, Agent…"

He didn't finish his sentence as they heard a loud pop after which Kruger and the other man disappeared through the now-open front door.

***

Kruger and Gibbs entered the home announcing they were FBI agents. Both held their weapons two handed as they cleared the front living room. The only illumination came from a lamp on a side table next to a sofa.

Knoll and Clark entered from the kitchen area, shaking their heads as Kruger shouted, "FBI, Sheriff Blake. We have a warrant for your arrest."

Noise came from the hall to their left and the four men headed toward the sound. The only illumination in the bedroom came from a digital clock on a nightstand so Knoll used his Maglite to illuminate the dark space. The four men saw a figure struggling to get his pants on. Kruger said, "FBI, Sheriff Blake. Get your hands in plain sight."

Blake stopped and stared into the light as Kruger and Gibbs entered the room with Knoll right behind.

The Sheriff said, "What's the meaning of this?"

Still standing in the doorway, his Glock trained on the half-naked man sitting on the bed, Clark said, "FBI. Are you Roger Blake?"

Knoll and Gibbs circled around to the other side of the bedroom; their handguns trained on the other occupant of the bed—a woman who stared at them with wide eyes and the covers pulled to her chin.

Clark repeated his command. "Are you Roger Blake?"

"Yes, yes. What is the meaning of this intrusion of my privacy?"

Withdrawing the papers from his windbreaker, Kruger said, "Roger Blake, you are under arrest for criminal conspiracy, domestic terrorism and the death of six federal agents. Agent Clark, please take the suspect into custody."

As the four men escorted the now handcuffed sheriff toward the front door, Clark explained his Miranda rights. At that same moment, Frank Reed and a woman agent walked through the open front door. He stared at Kruger and said, "What the hell are you doing, Agent Kruger?"

"It's Assistant Director to you, Agent Reed, and I did what you were supposed to be doing, arresting a felon. Now get out of our way. You're slowing us down."

As Knoll drove the GMC, Gibbs sat in the passenger seat with the sheriff in the back seat between Clark and Kruger. With his hands cuffed behind him, he looked at Kruger, "What do you want?"

In the dim light from the SUV's instrument panel, Kruger could see Blake sweating. "The location of the trucks."

"What trucks?"

"Don't play stupid with me, Blake. We broke the code in the emails and the numbers station. Where are the trucks?"

Shaking his head, Blake said, "I have no idea what you're talking about."

Kruger proceeded to explain what they knew. As he concluded his narrative, the sheriff kept his head down and stared at his pants. "I want an attorney."

"You'll get one, Blake, but it won't be someone you know. You might want to remember what I said earlier, you are under arrest for domestic terrorism. We aren't taking you to your own jail—we're headed to the Joseph C. O'Mahoney Federal Building in Cheyenne. From what I was told when we had the arrest warrant signed, you are not a very popular person in Cheyenne. You've got four hours to determine how you want to play this."

"You can't prove anything."

Smiling, Kruger stared out the window as they drove southeast on US-287. "You might want to rethink that statement. We know two trucks are out there somewhere, both loaded with enough fertilizer to make the bomb used on the Alfred P. Murrah Federal Building in Oklahoma City look like a firecracker. We can tie all of the instructions about the vehicles back to the computer on your desk. If they explode, any and all casualties will be blamed on you. If I remember properly, Timothy McVeigh was arrested, convicted, sentenced to death and executed in a little over six years. Most death row inmates wait fifteen years before their execution. And I am sure, considering you're a law enforcement officer, that betrayal will be noted during your trial. Sucks for you." He glanced at his watch. "I'd say you have six years left to live, Blake."

With wide eyes, Blake stared at Kruger and then at Clark.

"I think you're the patsy in this conspiracy, Roger." Kruger paused for effect. "I want the person or persons calling the shots, and I want the locations of the trucks."

Blake closed his eyes and shook his head. "I don't know where the trucks are. The person calling the shots is Kevin Marks."

"Who's he?"

"Owns the western wear shop in Lander. There's also someone else involved."

"I'm listening."

"Gordon Lyon. He's the Chairman of the Fremont County Board of Commissioners."

Kruger took his cell phone out and started making calls.

CHAPTER 42

Lander, Wyoming

Kevin Marks glanced at the time on his cell phone and hesitated before accepting the call. Phone calls at three minutes after one in the morning meant problems. "Yes."

He heard a familiar voice. "Blake was arrested by the FBI an hour and a half ago."

Fully awake, Marks threw back the covers and sat on the side of his bed. "Where's he now?"

"Don't know. They never showed up at the courthouse. My guess is they're on their way to Cheyenne."

"Where'd they arrest him?"

"In the sack with his girlfriend."

"Shit." He paused. "Have you spoken to her?"

"No. The FBI has her in custody, too."

Marks remained quiet as his mind raced. "Okay, make yourself invisible."

"That was my plan."

The call ended and Marks went to his closet. He knelt, moved several pairs of cowboy boots and lifted the carpet in the back corner revealing a floor safe. He entered the combination into the keypad and the door popped open. He withdrew a passport, three bundles of hundred-dollar bills, a Platinum American Express Card and a Springfield Armory .45ACP 1911. These he placed on the bed. Next, he retrieved a medium-sized duffle bag from the closet and placed those objects inside. Next came under garments— several pairs of jeans, numerous pullover shirts and a pre-packed men's toiletries bag.

After getting dressed in black jeans and a black sweatshirt, he headed for the garage and his Ford F-150.

***

When Kruger and JR arrived at Marks' Western Wear the next morning, they found numerous FBI agents speaking to employees in hushed conversation throughout the store. They were escorted to the owner's office where Kruger saw Frank Reed, his arms crossed, standing in the middle of the room watching two agents searching desks and filing cabinets and one working on a laptop. He turned as they entered. "Where's the sheriff, Kruger?"

"In custody."

Red faced, Reed lowered his arms and his nostrils flared. "I'm submitting a report about your actions last night."

"Good, because I've already submitted one about your inactions. Now tell your people to get away from the computer. I have an expert who will examine it."

Reed crossed his arms again. "I don't report to you."

Kruger's mouth twitched. "I suggest you ask your team to give us some privacy."

The three agents in the room stared at Reed as he nodded. They all filed out, leaving Reed, Kruger and JR alone in the room. Reed pointed to the computer hacker. "Who's he?"

"Our computer expert."

"Thought you wanted privacy."

"He's very trustworthy." Turning to JR, Kruger nodded at the desk and JR went to the laptop sitting on it. Returning his attention to Reed, he said. "You were saying?"

Reed glared back at Kruger. His arms folded. "What's this bullshit about you being an assistant director?"

"As of five minutes ago, you report to me. Your inaction in this investigation is under review and your status as an Agent in Charge is suspended for the moment." He opened his ID wallet and displayed his new identification.

Reed's face turned white and his eyes widened. "I don't believe... I thought..."

"You thought wrong. Now, if you want to keep your job, I suggest you get rid of the attitude and start acting like an FBI agent."

Reed's shoulders slumped as he stared at Kruger. "What do you need me to do?"

"Take a few agents and get to Marks' house. See if you can determine where he is. According to what we've been told, he normally comes in before eight. It's almost nine."

With a slight nod of the head, the ex-SAC left the office.

JR looked up. "That was rude."

"Not as much as I wanted to be." He paused briefly. "What've you got?"

"We might have a problem."

Kruger's eyes narrowed. "With?"

"The trucks might have already left."

"How the hell..." He paused, closed his eyes and concentrated on his breathing. "How can you tell?"

"There was an email sent from this computer last night."

"Can you trace where the emails went?"

"Given some time, yes."

"Take all the time you need, as long as it's within the next ten minutes."

JR chuckled and started typing.

***

Ryan Clark showed his FBI credentials to the young woman behind the desk on the second floor of the County Courthouse. Jimmie Gibbs and Sandy Knoll stood behind him with two Fremont County deputy sheriffs trailing them. All five men were serious and unsmiling. She looked wide eyed at the badge as Clark said, "We need to speak to Commissioner Lyon."

"He's in a meeting with the other commissioners."

"Where?"

She pointed to a door to her left. The five men proceeded in the indicated direction and Clark opened the door.

Sitting at a large conference table were two men and a woman, Lyon removed his glasses and stood. "What's the meaning of this intrusion?"

Clark withdrew the arrest warrant from his inside suitcoat breast pocket. "Gordon Lyon?"

"Yes, I demand to know what this is…" He didn't finish his sentence as the two Fremont County deputies moved behind him.

Holding the arrest warrant in his right hand, Clark said, "I'm Special Agent Ryan Clark, FBI. Gordon Lyon, you are under arrest for conspiracy, domestic terrorism and the death of six federal agents."

One of the deputies smiled as he cuffed the man's hands. "You have the right to remain silent…"

Pointing to the laptop in front of where Lyon stood, Clark turned to Sandy. "Agent Knoll, please secure Mr. Lyon's laptop."

Less than thirty seconds later, Knoll and Gibbs were escorting Gordon Lyon from the conference room toward the elevator.

***

Kruger looked up as Gordon Lyon, his hands cuffed behind him, entered Kevin Marks' office, still escorted by Knoll and Gibbs. Clark followed them into the office and closed the door. He placed the laptop he held next to JR, who still sat behind Marks' desk.

Turning to Knoll, Kruger asked, "Has he said anything?"

Shaking his head, the big man said, "He hasn't even protested his arrest."

Studying the man, Kruger tilted his head. "Why is that, Gordon?"

The commissioner stared at the carpet next to his shoes.

"Where are the trucks?"

He looked up. "What trucks?"

Taking a deep breath, Kruger pursed his lips. "We played that game with Roger Blake last night. After I explained the consequences of those trucks exploding, he—"

"I don't know where they are. Marks never told us."

"But you do know about them?"

"Yes."

"At least you're smarter than Blake. He denied knowing anything about them all the way to Cheyenne."

Lyon's eyes grew wide. "Cheyenne?"

"We're federal agents, Gordon. You're facing federal charges. Now, I suggest you tell me what I need to know."

"I want a lawyer."

With a shake of his head, Kruger stood and walked closer to the man. "I was hoping you'd be more cooperative, but I can see you aren't going to be." He paused and pinched the bridge of his nose. "I assume you remember Timothy McVeigh."

A nod.

"Do you remember the length of time it took to arrest

him, put him on trial, convict him, sentence him to the death penalty and actually execute him?"

"No."

"Six years, Gordon. Six years. The clock starts today."

A tear flowed down the soon to be ex-County Commissioner as he took a deep breath. "What exactly do you need to know?"

***

With his cell phone pressed to his ear, Kruger paced in Kevin Mark's spacious office. JR, still at the desk, started the task of tearing into Gordon Lyon's laptop.

Kruger said, "Paul, we know the trucks are on the road now. One is heading toward the east coast and one toward the west coast. Where, we don't know."

"That's a big area to cover, Sean. Lots of roads and lots of destinations."

"We know. JR's making progress, but to be honest with you, I don't think Blake and Lyon know the details. I'm not sure what their purpose was in this little drama, other than to give Marks status in the community."

"Where are they?"

"Blake is in the federal building in Cheyenne being questioned by the agents recently assigned to this area. Where are the ones who were transferred out?"

"Not sure. HR handled that."

"May I make a suggestion?"

"Yes."

"Have them questioned."

"Why?"

"I have a hunch they knew what was going on."

"Oh, boy. What else?"

"Lyon is being escorted to Cheyenne by Agent Reed for more interrogation."

"I understand you and him got sideways."

"At first. It's amazing how a little embarrassment changed his attitude."

"He's a good agent, Sean. He doesn't have your experience, but he will someday."

"He needs to learn humility first."

"So did a young agent with a cocky attitude and a PhD in psychology."

Kruger remained quiet.

Stumpf continued, "What's your next step?"

"We have to determine—"

JR interrupted Kruger. "Sean, I found something."

"Hang on, Paul." Lowering the cell phone from his ear, he looked at JR. "What is it?"

"I know the destination of the east bound truck."

Kruger smiled slightly. He returned the phone to his ear. "I'll call you right back, we might have a break."

CHAPTER 43

Sweet Grass, Montana

US Interstate 15 terminates in Sweet Grass, Montana at the Canadian border and becomes Alberta Highway 4 in the town of Coutts, Alberta. As the busiest port of entry in Montana, it is also the state's only commercial entry port operating twenty-four hours a day. Semi-trucks on their way to and from Canada with goods and agriculture pass through their own entry gate, while cars and small trucks pass through six separate gates for inspection.

At the same time Sean Kruger held his phone conversation with Paul Stumpf, Kevin Marks pulled into the only gate open and presented a passport with the name Kevin Markovic.

The board gate attendant said, "Business or pleasure in Canada, Mr. Markovic?"

"Hunting trip."

After comparing the picture with the man presenting the passport, the attendant handed it back to Marks. "Good luck and enjoy your stay."

As he entered Canada, he glanced in the Ford's rearview mirror as a small smile appeared on his lips.

***

The spacious home owned by Kevin Marks sat on a five-acre plot southwest of Lander in the foothills of the Wyoming Range. Kruger walked through the home. The décor appeared to be professionally done without any indications of a family. As he passed from room to room, he turned to Ryan Clark, who accompanied him. "Was Marks married?"

"Married to his work, according to all of the employees at the store."

"Girlfriends?"

"Not that anyone knew."

"Kids?"

"According to the employees, he never mentioned any."

"Pretty nice house for a single guy." He smiled and glanced at Clark. "Would you agree?"

"Beats the hell out of the place I lived in when I was single."

"I understand there's a floor safe in his bedroom."

"Yeah, when the first agents got here, they found the door open and nothing inside. They're testing it to see if it contained a weapon."

Kruger nodded. "I'm sure it did." He wandered into the gourmet kitchen and stood with his head cocked. "There's nothing out of place in this house. No one lives like that." He walked closer to the marble cabinet tops and ran a finger over the surface. He lifted it and showed Clark. "Cabinet tops are dusty. This room hasn't been used for a while."

Clark walked to the Subzero refrigerator and opened it. The shelves were bare except for a six-pack carton of beer containing five bottles, two apples, four oranges, four black bananas and an unopened gallon jug of milk. He picked up the milk container and looked at the expiration date. "This is out-of-date by a week and it's never been opened."

Now at the sliding glass door next to the kitchen, Kruger looked out at the view. The rear of the house faced east and from this height in the foothills, the town of Lander could be clearly seen in the distance. "Let's see the bedroom."

Kneeling, Kruger looked at the still-open floor safe. He stood and gazed at the disorder within the closet. He turned and viewed the bedroom. The contrast of this room to the rest of the home was like night and day. He said, "Marks left in a hurry."

Clark stood next to the unmade bed. "Why do you say that?"

The senior FBI agent's hand gestured to the closet. "Hangers and clothes are on the floor, there's an empty space next to the safe where I bet a suitcase or something similar was kept, plus I see an open gap where his pants are hung."

Pointing to a spot on the bed next to the nightstand, Clark said, "Looks like someone sat on the side of the bed."

Nodding, Kruger moved away from the closet. "Just like someone sat there and answered a phone call."

A young female FBI agent entered the room. "Director Kruger, we found something in his home office."

"Lead the way, Agent Nelson."

When Kruger and Clark entered the room down the hall from the bedroom, the first thing they noticed was the cluttered desk with numerous files scattered around. "Is this how you found the room?"

A different female agent stood behind the desk holding a manila file folder. "Yes, most of these appear to have been taken out of here." She pointed to an open drawer on the right side of the desk. "There were several gaps in the contents. We also found this." She handed the folder to Kruger.

"What is it?"

"Registration and ownership paperwork for a Ford F-150."

"Okay, we know what he's driving." He looked at the contents and started flipping through the pages. He stopped on one in particular and smiled. After handing the page to Clark, he said, "Nice work, Agent Cummings."

After skimming the page, Clark looked up. "Who the hell is Kreso Markovic?"

Kruger was now looking through the scattered papers on the desk. He stopped, uncovered an eight-by-five white envelope with a return address located in New York City and picked it up. He bent the metal clasps keeping it closed, opened it and extracted the papers inside. As he read it, he frowned. "Our Kevin Marks isn't who he says he is." He showed the paper to Cummings. After she took it, he turned to Clark. "It appears our Kevin Marks is actually a naturalized citizen from Queens, New York, whose real name is Kreso Markovic."

Clark frowned. "Russian?"

"That would be my guess."

With a shake of his head, Clark replied, "I wish you'd stop finding Russians under every rock you turn over, Sean."

The corner of Kruger's mouth twitched. "Getting old—isn't it?"

***

After a call to Paul Stumpf, a team of FBI forensic technicians based in Denver was dispatched to the home of Kevin Marks in Lander, Wyoming. Ryan Clark, now acting as Special Agent in Charge, took over the investigation, with Frank Reed cooling his heels in Cheyenne babysitting Blake and Lyon.

JR, still at the Marks' house, started digitally tearing

apart the computer byte by byte. While JR worked, Kruger paced with a growing concern his team would be too late to stop the trucks.

Looking up from the computer, JR said, "You're going to wear a trench in the carpet."

Kruger stopped, glared at JR and ran a hand through his hair. "Less talk, more work. We're running out of time."

With a slight grin, JR nodded. "Yes, we are. Let me ask you a question."

"What?" His tone was harsh.

"As you say sometimes, let's chase some rabbits."

Taking a deep breath, Kruger let it out slowly. The tension in his voice eased. "Okay, what've you got?"

"The destination of the eastbound truck is a warehouse in Baltimore."

Kruger remained quiet his gaze locked on his friend.

"Exploding a fertilizer bomb in a warehouse seems like a wasted effort to me."

"Agreed. Where are you going with this, JR?"

"I found a reference in a file someone tried to delete that mentioned UPS trucks."

"I'm not following you."

"What sort of trucks blend into our surroundings to the point they're basically invisible and can stop and go at will anywhere they travel?"

"Oh, boy. A UPS or FedEx truck."

"Exactly."

"You said someone tried to delete the references. If they deleted it, how did you find it?"

"I found several in the recycle bin. When you delete a file on a PC, the operating system changes the files location index so it can be recovered if you didn't mean to delete it. I will assume Marks deleted it. What he failed to do is empty the recycle bin. The file was there to be recovered."

"What was in the file?"

"Instructions for the truck drivers. While documents I

found never actually indicate it, I believe these to be semis. Both drivers have been instructed to deliver the truck to a warehouse. Lock the doors to the cab and leave. They are then instructed to walk some distance away from the warehouse and contact Uber for a ride back to the airport."

"You mentioned UPS trucks."

"The memo told the drivers there would be UPS trucks at the location and not to worry about them."

"Uber would have a record of picking up someone in a warehouse district."

JR nodded. "Or they will."

"When are they scheduled to arrive?"

"Sometime today or tomorrow."

"Where?"

"Don't know yet. I'm still looking."

"You're onto something, JR. Can you find files that were deleted from the recycle bin?"

"Yes, with the right software. Which I have."

"Well?"

He returned his attention to the computer. "Working on it."

While JR concentrated on the computer, Gibbs and Knoll returned from Cheyenne and motioned for Kruger to follow them out to the back deck of the Marks home. When they were alone, Knoll said, "Blake wants to cut a deal."

"In exchange for?"

"He thinks he knows the location of the trucks."

"Did he get a lawyer?"

"Yes, and the US Attorney in Cheyenne is talking to her. We explained what we knew so far and he's onboard with helping us."

"Did Blake offer anything specific?"

"Not yet. Frank Reed is there and, after a lengthy discussion with his boss, has seen the error of his ways about not cooperating with you."

A nod from Kruger was his response.

"It seems Blake overheard one side of a phone conversation the other day. Apparently, Marks was talking to someone, Blake didn't know who, about where the trucks were headed."

Kruger's eyebrows rose. "Where?"

"Baltimore and San Francisco."

"Did he say why?"

"No, but from listening to him and Lyon, you can tell they're both racists."

"Figures. What else?"

"They also don't like the Federal government."

"Goes without saying." Kruger turned and looked down from the location in the foothills over the town of Lander. "We have another dilemma."

Knoll folded his arms. "I take it JR found something."

With a nod, Kruger said, "The trucks are to be delivered to a central location. While the document he found didn't specifically mention it, they may have secured delivery vans and painted them to look like UPS trucks."

"That's not good." Gibbs frowned. "They have multiple targets identified, don't they?"

"Yes, they do. And we're running out of time to determine what those multiple targets might be."

JR opened the sliding glass door and leaned out. "You three better get back in here. It just got worse."

CHAPTER 44

Warehouse District – Baltimore, MD

Tommy Cole considered himself a professional truck driver, having driven just over two million miles in his twenty-year career. This was his final trip. He would make more in this one job than he did driving hard for six months.

His current location was a deserted section of a large warehouse district in Baltimore close to the Patapsco River. A sensation of dread crept into his thoughts as he drove the big rig down the length of the long building. He did not see any cars or other trucks in the area. The chain-link fence protecting the location looked rusty in spots and missing in others.

The bay number he sought appeared above an open loading door in the middle of the structure. His instructions were to drive the semi inside, park it, lock the tractor cabin and lower the door before leaving the building. His instructions also told him to ignore anyone he saw and walk back to the main road before calling Uber for a ride to the airport. A ticket would be waiting for him at the American Airline counter.

The manifest for the contents of the trailer indicated he was hauling agricultural products. Because of the amount of money being paid for his services and the mysterious destination instructions, he doubted it. He really did not care what the truck contained. His only concern was washing his hands of the load and walking out of the warehouse. This part of his life would be in his rearview mirror and he could get on with something else.

He noticed three UPS trucks parked on the far wall of the open space. Once again, his instructions were to ignore them, which he did without question.

He parked the truck, shut the diesel engine off and started the paperwork for his journey. Paperwork he would submit for his check.

With his head down concentrating on the bookkeeping, he failed to see the mustached, barrel-chested man approach the driver's side door from the rear of the trailer. As Tommy Cole stepped down from the cab, the large man startled him. The truck driver did not see the face of the man in front of him. He only saw a short double-barrel shotgun pointed at his head.

Tommy Cole did not hear the sound of two shotgun blasts as his head dissolved in a mist of blood, bone and brain tissue.

***

Lander, Wyoming

JR pointed to a Word document displayed on the laptop screen. "This was an encrypted file residing in a rather mundane file called Store Receipts. It was the only non-Excel file there."

Kruger folded his arms. "How'd you get it open if it was encrypted?"

With a grin, JR said, "Encryption key was in a file called Keys."

Gibbs laughed. "I'll have to tell Alexia about that one."

A small laser printer on a credenza behind JR spooled up and spat out several pages. He turned back to Kruger and handed him the sheets. "I believe you need to read these immediately."

Scanning the pages, Kruger smiled as he reached for his cell phone.

His call was answered on the second ring. "What did you find?"

"Warehouse district in Baltimore." He recited the address and the bay number. "According to what we found, the truck should be there already or will be shortly. Can you get a Rapid Response team rolling?"

"I'll call you back."

Ending the call, Kruger turned to Gibbs and Knoll. "We're too late to get to Baltimore. Call Stewart and tell him we will be at the airport in an hour. The four of us need to get to San Francisco as quickly as possible."

***

As the HA-420 HondaJet climbed over the northern Rocky Mountains, Kruger read the pages JR had given him in the office for the tenth time. The computer hacker sat in a seat across the aisle from him, his eyes closed.

Kruger said, "You asleep?"

JR's eyes snapped open. "Not sure, I may have been. Why?"

"I'm concerned how easily you were able to find all of this information."

JR looked over at his friend. "Actually, I'm not."

"Why?"

"Think about where we were."

"Wyoming, what about it?"

"It's the least populated state in the union. There are less than 600,000 residents in the entire state and that number is declining. Marks or Markovic, whatever his name really is, was there for a reason."

Kruger turned to look out the window next to his seat. "A predominantly rural state with a small population of mostly white Caucasians and Native Americans."

"That would be an accurate summary. A perfect place for Marks to recruit individuals for his purpose."

Turning his attention back to JR, Kruger stared at him for a few moments. "What was his purpose?"

"Before we get into that, let me ask you a question."

"Okay."

"Alexei Kozlov, or as we knew him, Abel Plymel."

Kruger frowned. "That's not a question. What about him?"

"What was his purpose?"

"Originally, he was a Russian sleeper agent planted in this country during the Cold War to help sabotage Wall Street."

JR nodded. "Yes, but after the Berlin Wall fell and the collapse of the Soviet Union, he went rogue and made a fortune for himself."

Without responding, Kruger stared at his friend.

"What if Kevin Marks is a modern-day version of Abel Plymel, only this time he's trying to stir up the already simmering kettle of race relations in this country."

"I'm not following you, JR."

"Think about it. Dorian Monk was targeting ethnic groups exclusively. There could be other Dorian Monks out there the FBI doesn't know about."

Kruger blinked rapidly for several moments and sat up straighter. "The numbers station."

"Exactly, as we discussed, it's a play right out of the Soviet Union's Cold War espionage handbook."

"With the addition of social media, they've discovered a perfect way to recruit individuals who are mad at the system."

JR nodded.

Turning again to stare out the window next to him, Kruger tapped a finger on the armrest. Fifteen seconds later, his cell phone signaled an incoming call. "Kruger." He listened for several minutes. "How many were in the warehouse?"

More silence as the person on the other end talked.

"We're about an hour from touchdown. I'll call you when we get there." The call ended and he turned to JR. "They found the tractor-trailer rig, a dead driver, three fake UPS trucks and six men transferring the contents of the semi."

"Anybody get hurt?"

"No, the raid went down without any gunshots."

"Who were they?"

"That's the worst part. All six were of Eastern European descent and lacked any form of identification."

"That's not good."

"No, it's not." Kruger pursed his lips. "We need the address of the westbound truck's destination."

Opening his laptop, JR said, "Working on it."

Gibbs appeared between the two seats occupied by JR and Kruger. "Alexia said you didn't respond to her text message."

Looking up, JR said, "I had it turned off. Why?"

The ex-Seal handed him his phone. "She knows where the westbound truck is headed."

CHAPTER 45

San Francisco, CA

By the time Kruger and his team arrived, the SAC in charge of the San Francisco Field Office had the warehouse locked down. As Charlie Brewer shook his old friend's hand, he said, "One of the three UPS trucks experienced mechanical problems, which means the other two are already on the street. We don't know where they're going."

Kruger frowned. "Where's the driver?"

Brewer pointed to a man surrounded by FBI agents firing questions at him. "The guy in the UPS uniform."

"He's a Russian, isn't he?"

"How'd you know?"

"No ID on him either, right?"

"None. Again, how'd you know?"

"Same pattern as Baltimore." Kruger turned to Jimmie Gibbs. "How's your Russian?"

"Better than it was in Paris."

"Good. Why don't you have a chat with this guy?"

Brewer led the way as the three men approached the

suspect. The SAC said to his agents, "Has he said anything?"

A tall female agent shook her head. "He keeps repeating the same words in Russian." She asked the suspect again.

When the Russian's answer was the same, Gibbs said, "He claiming he doesn't understand what you're saying."

The four agents surrounding the man stared at Gibbs who was now looking squarely at the prisoner. He said in Russian, "What is your name?"

The man stood even with Gibbs but weighed fifty pounds more. His light brown hair appeared as a stubble on his head and face. Closer up, his uniform resembled a UPS driver only in color. Bluish, gray eyes stared back at Gibbs as the two men studied each other.

The man said, "Ivan."

Chuckling, Gibbs said in Russian. "Of course, it is. Well, Ivan, I'm going to explain something to you. You are in deep shit right now."

Still speaking his native language, the Russian replied, "I want a lawyer."

Taking a page from the many interviews Jimmie Gibbs had observed Sean Kruger conduct, he said, "Can't have one."

"I am familiar with American laws. You have to supply a lawyer for me."

"Not in your case."

"What do you mean?"

"You see you were caught with a disguised truck with explosives in the back. You are also pretending to be a UPS driver, which you are not. That tells us you are planning on committing a terrorist act. Which causes us to proclaim you an enemy combatant and not entitled to laws applying to criminals in this country. In other words, as we Americans say, Ivan, you're up the creek without a paddle. If I were to guess, your future is a dark cell, deep underground in some hell hole like ADX Florence in Colorado. That's the same place they sent El Chapo, the drug cartel guy. Or, they might send you to Guantanamo Bay in Cuba. Oh, by the way, that is where no one can hear you scream."

The bigger man only blinked rapidly.

Gibbs continued, "In my opinion you have a dim future to look forward to." He paused and smiled. "I hope you got paid in advance, because you will never see it if you didn't."

More staring and blinking as the Russian kept his stare locked on Gibbs. In accented English he said, "What do you want to know?"

***

As Kruger and Gibbs rushed back to the GMC Yukon Sandy had commandeered, Kruger said, "What the heck did you say to him?"

"I just pointed out his dim future as an enemy combatant."

"You're kidding?"

"Nope, I learned from the best."

Kruger smiled as they piled into the SUV and Knoll screeched the tires exiting the parking lot.

***

After intensive interrogation, the Russian revealed the destinations for the other two trucks. Armed with this knowledge, Charlie Brewer dispatched agents to intercept. Kruger and his team would be part of the crew looking for a truck heading toward a major historic building in San Francisco.

Founded in June of 1776, Mission Dolores continued to be the oldest building in the city and the oldest intact Mission left in California. Heavily damaged in the 1906 earthquake, the structure still stood and remained a symbol of the city's ethnic diversity.

Kruger sat in the passenger seat next to Knoll, who drove. Gibbs occupied a backseat while getting his tactical gear on with JR next to him staring at the laptop resting on his legs.

JR said, "The place is a major tourist attraction. The basilica next to it doesn't have a scheduled mass today, but the gift shop and old mission building are open for tours to the public."

"What time does it close, JR?"

"Four on weekdays. Why?"

"It's two and according to the Russian, the truck is supposed to park in front of the old mission building at three-thirty."

Gibbs said, "We've got two options. Stop him before he gets to the church or we grab him as he steps off the truck before he has time to arm the bomb."

Knoll glanced at Kruger. "I think Jimmie's second option is best. No telling what this guy will do if he's surrounded by the FBI in the middle of a busy intersection."

Staring out the passenger window, Kruger nodded. "I agree with both of you. Stop him after he parks." He turned around and looked at Gibbs. "Tell me again, what did he say about the explosives?"

"He developed a serious case of diarrhea of the mouth after I told him about ADX Florence. Apparently, they found it impossible to buy used UPS trucks. Stealing one was out of the question because every vehicle in the fleet has GPS tracking built in. Their solution was to lease three Dodge Freightliners and paint them in the UPS color scheme. Since UPS uses those types of trucks for special deliveries and not regular routes, no one would get suspicious if it didn't stop every once in a while. They were to follow the same procedures as a normal UPS delivery. The driver stops in front of the building and goes to the back of the van for the package. That's when they were to arm the explosives. After that they take a package with them as they exit the truck. Nothing out of the ordinary so far, right?"

Kruger nodded.

"He was to walk across the street and disappear. The timer would be set for three minutes and then boom."

"So, we have to stop him before he gets into the back of the truck."

"Otherwise we have a problem."

"That's an understatement, Jimmie."

JR said, "What if he gets the thing armed before we can stop him?"

With a sigh, Kruger said, "Let's try not to let that happen."

***

Five miles from the Mission, Knoll spotted a UPS van. He pointed. "Looks like we might have got lucky. Is there a way to check and see if that's the fake truck?"

With binoculars already on the truck, Kruger was quiet for a second. "JR, you have access to UPS's GPS location system, is this van legit?"

Three seconds later, JR said, "No. That's one of the fake ones."

Knoll nodded and moved up closer behind the truck. "I noticed he's driving a little slow."

Gibbs said from the back, "Sean, can you determine how the rear cargo doors open?"

Kruger remained silent as he studied the rear of the truck. Finally, he said, "Two doors—both swing out from the middle. What've you got in mind?"

"We get up close and at a stop light; I join him in the van."

Turning abruptly to stare at Gibbs in the back seat,

Kruger shook his head rapidly. "Those doors could be locked from the inside. Plus, you have all of the explosives back there. Can't let you do it."

"What about the sliding side door or the passenger door?"

"I'm not authorizing that, Jimmie. Too dangerous with too many ways for it to go sideways on us."

Gibbs gave Kruger a sly smile. "Never know till you try it…"

Knoll interrupted the conversation. "A motorcycle cop just pulled in behind him with his lights on. He's pulling him over."

Everyone's attention immediately turned toward the van six car lengths in front of them. Kruger asked, "What happened, Sandy?"

"Not sure. The cop passed him going the other way, did a quick U-turn, passed us and then turned on his lights. What now, Sean?"

Kruger remained quiet as he watched the events unfold. "Jimmie, how quick can you disable the driver?"

"Pretty quick, why?"

"I don't want this cop to get hurt and that's what's going to happen if we aren't careful. Do we know if the Russian is armed?"

"Yeah, according to his buddy at the warehouse."

"Sandy, can you pull this vehicle in front of the van and block him from moving forward?"

"I've practiced the move many times. What've you got in mind?"

"As soon as the van stops and the cop parks his motorcycle, whip around the front and Jimmie and I will jump out. Let's hope he doesn't do anything stupid."

They heard Gibbs from the back. "All right—show time."

**

Veteran San Francisco Police Officer Brad Cain wore three hash marks on the left sleeve of his uniform. With fifteen years of service, he possessed a second instinct when something felt hinky. This UPS truck fit the description perfectly. Something was off on the color and the driver looked nervous.

He did a quick U-turn to get in behind the Dodge Freightliner before turning on his emergency vehicle lights. He noticed the black Yukon with four men following fifty feet behind but did not register it as important. When the van did not respond to his light, he flipped the siren on for a few seconds and kept his bike positioned so the driver could see him in his rearview side mirror.

When the UPS driver still did not respond to his lights or siren, Cain started to position his bike alongside the van.

Before he could reach the driver door, the black Yukon sped ahead, hidden emergency lights flashing. When it was ahead of the van, it slid to a stop in front, its passenger doors facing the oncoming vehicle.

The driver slammed on the brakes and Brad Cain maneuvered his bike to get behind the UPS van.

As he parked the motorcycle and dismounted, he heard, two men yelling, "FBI! FBI! Hands where we can see them."

With a frown, the patrol officer withdrew his service weapon.

***

Adam Stepanovich stared at the two men as they exited the large SUV in front of him pointing guns and yelling for him to put his hands on the steering wheel. Momentary paralysis set in as everything suddenly changed. First the motorcycle cop and now this SUV filled with FBI agents.

He could tell his hesitation to step out of the van

irritated the two men in front of him because the volume of their warnings increased.

With a slight smile, he threw off the paralysis and decided he had no desire to spend the rest of his life in an American prison. He pressed the button on the driver door to lock the doors as he stood to enter the back of the van.

***

As soon as the green van stopped, Gibbs and Kruger were out of the Yukon with their service weapons pointed at the driver. Kruger moved to the left and the passenger side while Gibbs moved toward the driver door.

Gibbs took in his surroundings with his peripheral vision and mentally noted they were in a heavily populated part of San Francisco. Apartment buildings were on both sides of the street with a gathering crowd now watching the proceedings. With this information, he made a decision as he yelled for the driver to show his hands and get out of the van.

The driver stared at him from inside. Gibbs could tell the man was weighing his options. None of which were good.

When the man stood and started for the opening leading to the rear of the van, Gibbs reacted.

The ex-Navy Seal's training took over as he aimed at the man inside the van and pulled the trigger on his Sig Sauer P226. The slide slammed open when the last of his fifteen rounds fired.

CHAPTER 46

San Francisco, Mission District / Springfield, MO

The after-action report, to be filed at a later date, would praise Jimmie Gibbs for saving the lives of his fellow FBI agents, a San Francisco police officer and hundreds of civilian lives. The explosives inside the fake UPS van were designed to do maximum damage to surrounding buildings and any living creature within its sphere of destructive power.

As FBI forensic technicians and explosive experts swarmed over the van, a city block was cordoned off and the appropriate apartment buildings evacuated.

Gibbs sat inside Knoll's SUV and listened to Kruger talk on his cell phone. When the conversation was over, Kruger put the phone in his jean pocket and smiled at Gibbs. "Well done, Jimmie. The other van was stopped at its destination. Instead of surrendering, the driver decided to shoot it out with police and a few of Charlie's agents. The driver's dead, but unfortunately, one police officer and an FBI agent were killed during the altercation. At least the only causality here was the driver."

Looking up at Kruger, Gibbs gave him a tight smile. "What if I'd been wrong?"

"You weren't. That's all that matters."

"Now what?"

"Well, we've proven the worth of our team. Stumpf will present a recommendation to Congress for permanent funding."

"Will we stay independent?"

With a shrug, Kruger shook his head. "Don't know. I hope so. Otherwise I'll have to make a decision, a real decision this time."

"Yeah, me, too."

Knoll approached the SUV and stopped next to Kruger. "JR's been poring over the guy's phone. He found something."

Kruger straightened against the door frame. "What?"

"A text message from Kevin Marks."

Both Gibbs and Kruger followed the big man back the way he had approached. When they got to where JR sat in the front seat of an FBI technician van, the computer hacker looked up. "How fast can we get back to Springfield?"

***

High over the Rockies, the HA-420 HondaJet headed east as Kruger sat with his eyes closed. Across the aisle, JR looked up from his laptop and asked, "You asleep?"

"No."

"Sorry about what I found."

Without opening his eyes, Kruger said, "Better to know than not know."

"So now what?"

A long silence ensued until Kruger opened his eyes. "Why does every two-bit hood think he can get to me through my family? It's getting old, JR."

"Marks or Markovic, whatever his name is, might not know his men in Baltimore and San Francisco are dead or under arrest."

"He will soon. Then he'll just find some other crazies to do his bidding." Kruger stared out the window next to his seat. "Where did you say the calls from Marks' cell phone originated?"

"Vancouver."

"We can assume he fled to Canada after the arrest of Blake and Lyon."

"I believe it's more than an assumption."

"I need to talk to Clark and see what they've found in Wyoming."

"Probably a good idea."

***

Clark answered Kruger's phone call on the second ring. "I was just about to call you."

"I hope you have good news?"

"We're making progress. One of the forensic techs started looking at security video of the store Marks owned. Guess what they found?"

"Not in the mood, Ryan. Just tell me."

"There's a dressing room with a hidden door into Marks' office. She found numerous shots of the same man using that specific dressing room and staying in it for a far greater time than a normal customer trying on clothes."

"And?"

"We've identified that individual."

"Who is he?"

"He's the leader of a white nationalist group here in Wyoming with a rather lengthy criminal record."

"Huh."

"We arrested him last night."

Kruger sat up straighter. "Is he talking?"

"No, he just keeps telling us he'll only talk to you."

Shaking his head, Kruger closed his eyes. "Not that again." He paused and turned in his seat to look at Knoll, who was sitting behind JR. "Sandy, tell the pilot we need to divert to Lander, Wyoming."

With a nod, the big man stood and walked toward the front cabin.

"We're on our way, Ryan. I'll call you with an ETA."

JR said, "What about Steph and the kids?"

"They're being watched over by a team of FBI agents for now. We'll make this little detour as quick as possible."

***

Clark's assumption of the role of Special Agent in Charge meant he was using the Fremont County jail as his headquarters as more of Kevin Marks' associates were identified and arrested. When Kruger, JR, Knoll and Gibbs arrived, he led Kruger to a video monitor of the interrogation room where the thin-waisted man with broad shoulders sat.

As he studied the man shackled to the floor and table he asked, "What's his name?"

"He goes by numerous alias—Fred Rivera, Freeman Rogers, Forest Roberts, plus a few others."

"What's his real name?"

"Ah, that was more difficult to determine. His fingerprints are not on file in the FBI database. However, Department of Defense had them."

Taking his eyes off the prisoner, Kruger glanced at Clark. "And?"

"Franklin Russell."

"Which service?"

"Army. He served six years as an MP."

With his eyes back on the monitor, Kruger asked, "Which alias did he use when you arrested him?"

"Fred Rivera."

"Well, let go see what Mr. Rivera has to say."

***

The door to the interrogation room opened and two men entered. The prisoner watched as the tall man with a file folder sat down across from him. "You Kruger?"

Kruger remained quiet as he opened the file folder. Ryan Clark leaned against the now closed door.

Russell asked again. "Are you FBI Agent Sean Kruger?"

Looking up, Kruger smiled. "Maybe. Who are you?"

"Fred Rivera. Why am I under arrest?"

"Why did you ask to speak to me?"

The prisoner blinked several times and shrugged. "Heard you were in charge. Now, why am I under arrest?"

Kruger extracted two pictures from the file and turned them so the prisoner could see. The man said, "So, I'm entering a dressing room to try on jeans, I like new jeans. That's not a crime last I knew."

The next picture Kruger turned around was a shot of the man entering Kevin Marks' office through the hidden door. "You weren't trying on jeans. You were meeting with Marks. A man who has been identified as a Russian agent and provocateur."

The man identifying himself as Fred Rivera stared at the picture wide eyed. "What do you mean Russian agent? Marks ain't no…" Realizing what he had just admitted, the prisoner looked up at Kruger.

With a knowing smile, Kruger said, "Your real name is Franklin Russell. You spent six years in the army as an MP, a dishonorable discharge for assault and you have a criminal record that should be required reading by every FBI agent in the country. Care to comment?"

"I want a lawyer."

"Eventually."

"What do you mean, eventually?"

"The problem is Kevin Marks has been classified as a terrorist and enemy combatant. You are accused of aiding and abetting with him, which puts you in a dangerous situation. If you choose to cooperate with us, those charges might be amended. And I want to emphasis the word, *might*."

"What kind of cooperation are you looking for?"

"Names."

"I can provide you with lots of names. Whose names?"

"I want the names of the person or persons who ambushed six FBI agents at a cabin owned by Dorian Monk."

Russell shook his head. "Don't know what you're talking about."

Kruger's mouth twitched. "Are you sure you want to go down that path, Franklin?"

"I can't tell you what I don't know, Agent Kruger."

With a loud screeching of metal chair legs on concrete, Kruger pushed back his chair and stood. "I've arranged for your transfer to ADX Florence in Colorado, pending your trial. Make sure you appreciate being outside during the trip, Russell. It will be the last time you see the sun for a long time." He turned and opened the interrogation room door.

Just before exiting through the door, Kruger heard, "I know more than you think I do."

Turning, Kruger said, "We know quite a bit already, Franklin."

"You don't know the real story. Get me a deal and I'll tell you."

"How do I know that?"

"You have to trust me."

"Something I'm not inclined to do at the moment. Tell me something I need to know, and I'll speak with the federal prosecutor. Otherwise have a nice life in the dark hole you're headed to."

Kruger waited a few seconds while Russell contemplated his future. Finally, he heard, "Sit down. It's complicated."

***

The interview with Franklin Russell lasted four hours. Clark brought coffee in for all three men and another chair so he could take meticulous notes, despite the fact there would be a recording of the entire conversation.

As Russell was taken back to his holding cell, Kruger and Clark returned to the vacant sheriff's office the FBI agents used as their command center.

After closing the door, Clark turned to Kruger. "What do you think?"

"I think I believe about half of it. I'll make a call and have a few agents check out the fishing lodge in Manitoba. If they find anybody there matching the description of the men Russell told us about, I might believe a little more of his story."

"What about his comments on Dorian Monk?"

"That's more complicated. I don't believe for a minute Monk was acting on Kevin Marks' orders." Kruger paused and walked to the window. As he stared out, he continued, "Monk was more of a Ted Kaczynski-character than a robot. Both were math geniuses and both possessed a deep-seated hatred for their fellow man. The main difference is Monk hid his inner demons better than Kaczynski and may have been smarter, too." He turned to look at Clark. "I think there is another explanation."

"And that is?"

"I think Marks used Monk as a tool for recruiting."

"Not following you."

"Think about it for a moment. Marks has this elaborate clandestine communication system set up where he can exploit what Monk is doing and use it to draw in like-minded individuals."

"What was his purpose? He's a Russian, not a white nationalist."

"Bingo, Ryan. Marks was a Russian, but he was posing as an anarchist. An anarchist who was organizing a group of individuals in a rural, isolated part of the country to fight the Federal Government. What if the Russians are doing this all over the country in rural areas?"

"Kind of like the French Resistance in World War II."

"Yes, only they're using social media to exploit these individuals. Something the French didn't have."

"What's the end game, Sean? It seems awful complicated."

"The Russians are long-term strategists, Ryan. Unlike the United States, we demand instant results. The Russians are looking out ten, fifteen, maybe fifty years. Our country is already divided politically. What happens if more and more lone wolf attacks create a public demand for less freedoms and a more authoritarian government? One that would be more in line with the current Russian government."

Clark stared at Kruger for a few moments before responding. "We'd be conquered from within."

"Exactly."

"How do we stop it?"

"That, my friend, is a good question. One I don't have an answer for right now."

CHAPTER 47

Washington, DC

Washington Post reporter, Tracy Adkins shouted a question as a gaggle of reporters followed the senior senator from the state of Montana, Jordan Quinn. "Senator, why have you changed your support for President Griffin?"

Having ignored all other questions so far, he stopped his rush for the elevators and turned toward the reporters. "I have not changed my support for President Griffin, but I must be critical of any action I deem to be an overreach."

Adkins followed up. "Which action did you feel an overreach, Senator?"

"His sudden dismissal of Secretary of Homeland Security, Joan Watson."

Another reporter next to Tracy said, "My understanding is she resigned on her own."

"Nonsense. She was fired by the president."

The reporters started shouting questions again as Quinn's Chief of Staff leaned over and whispered in his ear.

Quinn stared at the man and blinked rapidly. Turning away from the reporters, he hustled toward a bank of elevators.

***

When the two men were alone inside, Quinn said, "Why didn't he call my cell phone?"

"He didn't say, sir. Linda took the call. She said your son said it was urgent. He gave her a number for you to call."

Quinn took the piece of paper his Chief of Staff handed him and stared at the number.

While the number did not appear in his cell phone contact list, he knew the number. It did not belong to his son. Looking up, he said, "Thank you, Tim. I'll find a nice quiet corner somewhere and call him back."

"I hope everything is okay at home, sir."

As the elevator door opened, he said, "Yes, so do I."

Jordan Quinn's four terms in the United States senate provided him with a few personal conveniences other senators did not possess. One of those amenities included a little hideaway office on the Capitol Building's third floor behind a committee room. Only a handful of individuals knew it was his space and fewer had access to it. With the door locked, he sat in one of the leather wingback chairs and stared at the slip of paper handed to him. With a deep breath, he punched in the number and touched the send icon.

"I was wondering how long it would take for you to call back."

"It wasn't convenient at the time."

"Convenient? Convenience is a luxury our relationship does not recognize, Senator."

"What do you want, Marks?"

"Are you familiar with actions the FBI is taking against

your next election?"

Quinn stared at the floor, deep lines appearing on his forehead as he pressed the cell phone to his ear. "I'm not following you. What's the FBI doing?"

"They are systematically dismantling my operation and subsequently your largest source of campaign donations."

The senator did not answer right away as his mind raced through the consequences of the FBI finding out where the majority of his campaign funds originated. "How bad?"

"Let's put it this way. Unless you stop it, there won't be enough money available for an election to city council in Butte."

Quinn stood and screamed into the phone. "How dare you threaten me, Marks. I'm a US Senator."

"It's not a threat, it's a promise. Stop the FBI investigation or certain private information about you will suddenly become public. You'll be gone as quickly as Joan Watson."

Seated again, Quinn placed his free hand over his eyes. "I'm not sure what I can do at this point."

"Get me the address of an FBI agent named Sean Kruger."

"How's that going to stop what they're doing?"

"He is the one responsible for the FBI's interest."

Silence filled the room as Quinn shut his eyes. "What are you going to do, Marks?"

"A detail you have no need to know about. Now get me the address, Senator."

***

Thirty minutes later, Quinn sat at his desk in the Hart Senate Office Building, his door locked and the handset of his desk phone pressed to his ear. The individual on the line listened as the Montana Senator presented his case. "As Chairman of the Appropriations Committee, David, I find it highly irregular for a private citizen to be funding a division of the FBI."

David Clayton, Senate Majority Leader and a staunch supporter of President Roy Griffin did not answer right away. After a sigh, he said, "Jordan, we've had this discussion before. You were there for the negotiation with President Griffin and wholeheartedly agreed this was a great idea. Besides, it's temporary until it proves its worth and then we can either fund it or not."

"Who's the director?"

"Again, Jordan, there isn't a director. It falls under Stumpf."

With his voice increasing in decibels, Quinn spat out, "That's not what I agreed to, David. We agreed this would fall under Homeland Security."

"The structure stayed the same, but the new department will stay within the confines of the FBI."

"Why wasn't I and my committee informed about this change?"

"There was no need since the new department is already funded."

"Again, David, I find that highly irregular. This increases my concern that Griffin is abusing his power."

Although Quinn could not see it, David Clayton rolled his eyes. "Oh, good grief, Jordan, you've been around this town long enough to know how these things work."

"David, there is growing concern within the Senate about Griffin's—"

"Stop right there, Senator. Just because you've had your feelings hurt about not being constantly in the know, get over it. The new department is already showing results."

"What do you mean, showing results?"

His patience wearing thin, Clayton said in a calm manner, "The appropriate committees will be informed at the proper time."

With a bit of desperation in his voice, Quinn spat out,

"For gawd sake, David, you act like you don't know what they're doing. You have to shut them down until we know."

"Why are you so concerned about something this minor, Senator?" Clayton's calm demeanor evaporated with the sudden change of tone in the conversation.

"As Chairman of the Home Security and Government Affairs committee it is my sworn duty to know these things."

"That's incorrect. We are oversight, not management. I suggest you calm down and rethink what you are asking."

"I disagree. This arrangement is unconstitutional, and I will do my best to stop it."

Before Clayton could respond, the phone call ended.

***

David Clayton replaced the handset of his desk phone and tapped his lips with an index finger. After a few minutes of staring at the phone, he picked it up and punched in a number.

"White House. This is Bob Short."

"Bob, it's David Clayton. How are you this morning?"

"Fine, Senator. How can I help you?"

"I need to see him. Could you squeeze me in today?"

Robert Short, Chief of Staff for President Roy Griffin said, "Let me check, Senator."

Clayton heard the clicking of a keyboard and then, "How much time do you need?"

"Twenty minutes."

"How about two-thirty this afternoon?"

"Thanks, Bob. I appreciate it."

"What's your topic?"

"A concern about one of his projects."

***

Roy Griffin sat in a wingback chair in the Oval Office, his elbows resting on the arms and his fingers creating a steeple that touched his lips. Joseph Kincaid sat on the sofa next to him as they listened to Senate Majority Leader David Clayton recounting his conversation with Jordan Quinn. Sitting on the edge of the sofa cushion across from them, the Senator finished his narrative.

Griffin said, "Why do you think he was so agitated?"

"I don't know, Mr. President. He was all for this experiment and now he's wanting to blow it up."

Griffin shot a glance at Joseph, who wore a neutral expression. "What do you think, Joseph?"

"Don't have enough facts to have an opinion."

The President smiled. This was Joseph's way of saying he knew something but would only share it with the president. Looking back at the senator, Griffin said, "David, I appreciate your support and bringing this to our attention. I can assure you from the initial reports I have received, our experiment is working extremely well."

"Good. I would appreciate any information you can share. I want to reassure the good senator from Montana that all is well."

"The FBI will have a summary to you by tonight."

"Thank you."

All three men stood and shook hands. When Clayton left the room, Griffin turned to Joseph. "I saw that look in your eye."

"This is what Sean was concerned about the last time I spoke to him."

"What's that?"

"Sean's team found that Monk ran a bank scam which, over time, transferred a lot of money to an account he controlled. They also found this money was being transferred somewhere else when it reached a certain level. Where the money went, they haven't been able to determine yet."

"So, these people are well-funded."

Joseph nodded. "Lots of money. His team also believes additional funds are being generated from ransomware attacks coming out of Belarus."

"How much more?"

"Quite a bit, actually."

"What are you getting at?"

"The individuals they've arrested, and the evidence gathered so far, suggests the group's reach extends to several states surrounding Wyoming. Quinn is from Montana, correct?"

"Yes."

The National Security Advisor took a deep breath. "What if Senator Jordan Quinn has been compromised?"

Griffin stared at Joseph. "How could we determine that?"

"Follow the money."

CHAPTER 48

Washington, DC
Later That Evening

Just before leaving his office in the White House for the evening, Joseph Kincaid sent a text message with one symbol—a question mark. Ten minutes later his cell phone received an incoming call. The caller ID on his dashboard screen indicated the caller was Unknown. He answered anyway. "This is Joseph."

"Good evening, Joseph. I thought you'd lost my number."

"I try not to bother you, JR."

"I always enjoy talking to you. What's up?"

"It's about this group involved with Alan Seltzer's death."

"Okay."

"Have you been able to trace any of the money?"

"Yes. We've confirmed there is a sizeable amount coming from several banks in Belarus to an account in

Zurich. From there it's going to an account in Canada. Distribution out of the Canadian account looks like a normal business account with payments going to numerous vendors. Why?"

"I need you to do me a favor."

"Sure."

"Check to see if any of those funds are going to a PAC or any accounts associated with Senator Jordan Quinn."

"Interesting request."

"Why?"

"Sean already asked me to do the same thing."

Joseph smiled. "And?"

"In a roundabout way, the answer to your original request is, yes. A lot of the money is going into various political PACs. Those are providing funds to a variety of senators and members of the House."

"How much are we talking about?"

"Let's put it this way—most of the contributions are disguised as coming from a variety of different individuals and businesses. None of the payments exceed the legal amount."

"Can you get me proof they are coming from the same fund?"

"Given time."

"JR, that's a commodity we don't have an excess amount of at the moment."

"I'll see what I can do."

***

Jordan Quinn opened the envelope handed to him by one of his staff members and unfolded the piece of paper inside. He looked up at her. "Where'd you get this?"

"It was left at the reception desk by a courier."

He looked at the front. The seal of the Department of Justice appeared at the top left corner. It was addressed to him in an elegant script. "Thanks, Shellie."

The aid walked out of his office and he opened the paper again. In the same elegant script, he saw an address for FBI Agent Sean Kruger in a town in Missouri.

He returned to his office, closed and locked the door before going to his desk. Using his cell phone, he dialed the number received in a text message the previous day. A number he knew belonged to Kevin Marks.

***

JR rubbed his eyes and glanced at the clock in the bottom right hand corner of his middle screen. Taking a deep breath and letting it out slowly, he realized his late nights at the office were becoming more frequent. Mia understood, Joey did not. Maybe someday, but at four years old, not so much.

As he started to shut his system down, he received an instant message from a tripwire program he'd installed on several websites. All thoughts of leaving vanished as he stared at the message. He immediately reached for his cell phone.

***

"At least I wasn't in bed this time, JR. What's up?"

"A large sum of money was transferred out of a Canadian bank account ten minutes ago into the account of someone named Blake Morton."

"So?"

"Blake Morton is the AKA name of an individual named Yuri Romanovich who just happens to have a rap sheet longer than your height."

"Huh."

"Yuri currently resides in Kansas City, Sean."

"Uh—oh."

"Yeah, uh—oh. Are you prepared?"

"With the help of yourself, Jimmie and Sandy, about as well as I can be. I've tried not to spook Stephanie and the kids."

"Let's hope this information amounts to nothing."

"Yeah, let's."

***

The motion detector on the east side of the garage activated an alert on Kruger's cell phone at 3:42 a.m. He nudged Stephanie. "Steph."

He heard a groggy, "Yeah."

"I need you to get the kids and yourself into our bathroom."

She bolted upright. "Why?"

"Please, just do it."

Without another word, she threw the sheets back and hurried to Kristin's room. A minute later, a sleepy little girl stumbled toward the large bathroom with her mother behind her, holding a still-sleeping younger brother.

The look on Stephanie's face conveyed concern, but confidence in her husband.

Kruger reached under his side of the bed and removed a small gun safe he kept there. He punched in the code and the lid flipped up. Inside he found his spare Glock 19 and a magazine. As the bathroom door shut, he stood, slammed the clip into the gun and charged the weapon. With his Glock in his right hand and his cell phone in his left, he left the bedroom for the main body of their home.

***

An overcast sky obscured light from the moon and stars in the normally quiet neighborhood in the southwest section of the city. Yuri Romanovich crept along the eastern side of the house. The fact he was unfamiliar with the layout of the home or the occupants did not bother him. A life of improvising and surviving gave him confidence. Wearing night vision goggles, he approached the gate of a privacy fence leading to the back yard of the home.

With a slow, careful motion, he opened the gate and slipped into the darkness of the backyard.

***

Kruger felt his cell phone vibrate with a new message. Motion detectors in the backyard indicated someone had tripped a switch. Lights suddenly illuminated the deck and the yard beyond, producing a shadow of someone standing still and casting a shadow on the closed blinds of the window overlooking the deck. Kruger stood quiet, his back against a wall in the family room, his Glock raised in a Weaver Stance.

The interior of his home remained quiet. The only sound he perceived was his own heart beating loudly enough to give away his location. A bead of sweat rolled down his forehead into his eyes. He blinked rapidly to clear his vision. The shadow moved toward the back door and he heard someone working the locks with a picking tool. When the back door swung open and the shadow entered the kitchen, the silhouette of the intruder was clear to Kruger. He yelled, "Hands where I can see them. On the ground, now!"

***

When the backyard lights flicked on, Yuri stood still, expecting the owner of the house to open the door next to where he stood. With his back against a window, his thoughts turned to abandoning his task. When the door remained closed, the decision to continue won the argument. Keeping as close as possible to the wall, he stood in front of the entrance. A quick check told him he had to conquer a deadbolt and a door lock before gaining entry.

After extracting a slim tool from his jeans pocket, he worked the two locks and defeated both in a matter of minutes. He peered inside the house. No additional lights were turned on indicating no one inside was aware of his impending entry.

As he turned the door knob, he withdrew a CZ 75 hand gun from a holster located on his hip.

As the door opened, he slid into the room. At that same moment, he heard someone yelling. His first instinct caused him to raise the CZ and start pulling the trigger.

***

Lights from every sort of emergency vehicle bathed the neighborhood in an eerie strobe light effect. JR Diminski stood beside his friend, a hand on his shoulder, while paramedics attended to the body lying on the kitchen tile. Stephanie and the two children were now safe across the street in the care of Mia Diminski.

Springfield Police Detective Sam Moody stood in front of Kruger taking notes. "When did the first indication of the intruder occur, Agent Kruger?"

"About a quarter till four."

"Why didn't you call 911?"

With a sad smile, Kruger looked up at the detective. "My first thought was to get my wife and children safe. After that it was just a matter of training. The thought of calling the police didn't actually occur to me."

The detective nodded and pointed to Kruger's left arm. "Do you need to go to the hospital with that?"

A shake of Kruger's head was his response. "No, EMT said it was only superficial."

The detective looked at JR. "How long did it take you to

arrive, Mr. Diminski?"

"I installed the security system in Sean's home. It alerts me as well."

"You already said that. How long?"

"I heard the shots as I got to the front door."

"How many did you hear?"

"Four or five. It was hard to tell."

The detective nodded. "That agrees with the number of casings we found. Three from the intruder and two from Agent Kruger's weapon." He paused and looked back as the EMTs loaded the body onto a gurney for removal. "Okay." He pointed at Kruger's arm. "I strongly suggest you have that looked at." He turned and walked toward the EMTs.

Kruger looked at his friend. "How many emergency vehicles are out there?"

With a chuckle, JR said, "Seven police cars, two fire trucks, an ambulance and three county sheriff SUVs. Why?"

Standing, Kruger said, "Neighbors are going to petition Steph and me to move after this."

"Nonsense. This just adds excitement to the area. They all like the fact you're an FBI big shot now."

With a shake of his head and his hand still holding his sore left arm, he studied his friend. "You're impossible."

"That's what Mia tells me."

***

As the sun peaked over the horizon, Jimmie and Sandy arrived at the Kruger household. Only a few emergency vehicles remained—two SPD vehicles and a sheriff's department SUV. Knoll looked at the three bullet holes in the family room wall and shook his head. "Where were you, Sean?"

Kruger pointed to the gap between the three holes. "In

between those two."

Knoll looked at him and then back at the wall. "I take it yours hit the target."

A nod was his answer.

Jimmie entered the house from the back door and held up a cell phone. "Found his car and this on the seat."

JR took the phone and started punching numbers.

Kruger tilted his head. "You tell the cops?"

"About the car..." He nodded. "Just did."

The FBI Assistant Director tilted his head. "I take it you failed to tell them about the phone."

"Ahh—that might have slipped my mind."

Raising his head, JR smiled. "I've got phone numbers here, gentlemen."

CHAPTER 49

Springfield, MO

By noon, Stephanie and the kids were safe in an extended-stay hotel suite and a contractor arrived at the house to start the process of erasing evidence of the early morning events.

Kruger yawned, sipped coffee and leaned against the credenza as he watched JR working his computer. "Find anything interesting about the cell phone numbers?"

"Yes." Silence fell over the two friends as JR sat back in his chair and looked up. "Did they confirm the guy's identity?"

"Fingerprints confirmed it was Yuri Romanovich. They told me to tell you they appreciated the tip about his identity."

"Did they ask how I knew?"

"I told them you're a consultant to an FBI Cyber Task Force. They didn't ask any more questions."

"Good."

"What about the cell phone?"

"Lots of curious calls."

"Not in the mood, JR. Be specific."

"Numerous ones between Romanovich's phone and one located in Canada starting about five p.m. last night."

"Did you check the Canadian number?"

JR rolled his eyes. "What do you think?"

"Sorry, I haven't had enough coffee yet."

"Before the calls with Romanovich, the phone in Canada received a call from a number in Washington, DC."

"Can you identify the number in Canada?"

"No, it was purchased with cash. It's a burner."

Standing, Kruger held his coffee cup in both hands. "What about the phone in Washington?"

JR smiled. "The number is assigned to a personal cell phone in a Verizon account owned by Senator Jordan Quinn."

Kruger studied the liquid in his coffee mug. "How hard would it be to get Quinn's bank records?"

With a shrug, JR said, "Hard, why?"

"What about campaign funding?"

"Same answer."

"It's not a coincidence Quinn called the number in Canada and my family gets a visit by a Russian thug less than twelve hours later."

"I would agree."

"Quinn's dirty. I just want to know how dirty."

After staring at his friend for several seconds, JR turned and started doing what he did best.

***

The Next Day - Friday

A nervous Jordan Quinn looked in his rearview mirror and saw the large SUV continue to follow his BMW M8. Second thoughts about visiting his weekend getaway condo on Tangier Sound kept creeping into his mind.

The decision to turn around and head back to his

apartment occurred at the same moment the SUV turned on flashing hidden blue lights in the grill. With no other choice, Quinn slowed and pulled his car into the parking lot of a strip mall.

Aggravation and concern were his emotions as he stared at the rearview mirror. He saw both the passenger and driver side doors of the SUV open at the same time. Two men, both in dark suits, approached his car. One toward the driver's door and the other toward the passenger side.

Quinn rolled down the window. He stared up at the man now standing by his door holding his FBI credentials for the Senator to see.

"What is the meaning of this, Agent? I'm a US Senator."

"FBI, Senator. Please step out of the car."

"Not until I'm told why you stopped me."

"Senator, please step out of the car."

"Not…" The appearance of a Glock in the FBI agent's hand gave Quinn pause.

As he reached for the door handle, the agent said, "Sir, keep both hands where I can see them."

"I'm a US Senator."

"Please step out of the car with your hands visible."

After Quinn opened the door and stepped out, he said, "Did you hear me, Agent? I'm a US Senator."

"Yes, sir, I did hear you."

As he faced the agent, the other agent from the passenger side came up behind him, grabbed his left arm and applied one side of a pair of handcuffs to his wrist. The agent facing him said, "You are under arrest for violations of the McCain-Feingold Act, bribery and conspiracy to commit murder."

Quinn felt the uncomfortable experience of having both hands cuffed behind his back.

***

The high-priced attorney sat in the interview room and reviewed the evidence against his client. "Quite frankly, Jordan, you're screwed."

"What do you mean, screwed?"

"The standard definition—fucked."

Quinn rolled his eyes and screamed, "What does that mean?"

"Oh, let's see. Bank records, phone records, testimony by your staff, how much further do you want me to go?"

"Ahh...."

"Want my recommendation?"

"Yes."

"Cooperate. We'll work out a plea deal."

"How many years if I don't."

"You don't have that many years left."

***

Having flown into Dulles International Airport late the previous day, Kruger prepared to interrogate Senator Jordan Quinn. He noticed the man already had his attorney present. While not his favorite scenario, it would help shorten the process.

Ryan Clark followed Kruger into the interview room located at the DC Central Detention Center. Both had the FBI credentials on a lanyard around their neck. As they entered, the attorney stood and said, "I must protest the inhuman way my client has been treated so far. Until his treatment is improved, he will not be making a statement."

Kruger looked over his reading glasses at the tall, middle aged lawyer and dropped the heavy file he held on the table between them. It landed with a loud thump. "Wise advice for your client, counselor. However, I'm not here to ask questions or get a statement. I'm here merely to inform."

The two men locked eyes for a dozen seconds before the

attorney nodded and sat next to the Senator.

Sitting across from Quinn, Kruger opened the file and took out a series of photographs. He arranged them side-by-side facing the two men across from him. Once he finished arranging them, he folded his arms on the table, remained quiet and stared at Quinn.

The attorney said, "What is this, agent?"

Without taking his eyes off the Senator, Kruger said, "These are the faces of men and women murdered as a result of your client's complicity with a man named Kevin Marks, also known as Kreso Markovic, a Russian national." Watching Quinn's reaction was Kruger original goal and he was not disappointed. The Senator's eyes widened as he stared at the pictures which included Alan Seltzer, Thomas Shark, the FBI agents killed at Monk's cabin in Wyoming and the other victims tied to Dorian Monk.

Kruger continued, "We can link Senator Quinn to Kevin Marks with both phone calls and financial transactions. Funds for those financial transactions can be directly linked to the individual who murdered twenty-one of these victims."

The attorney chuckled. "Agent, surely you don't expect us to be intimidated by hearsay and innuendos, do you?"

With a smile, Kruger said, "It is not my intent to intimidate, counselor. But there is one more piece of information I'll mention."

"We're listening."

Extracting two additional pieces of paper, Kruger continued, "Four days ago, Senator Quinn received an envelope via courier from a DOJ employee, who, by the way, is under arrest tonight and talking freely. This envelope contained the address of an FBI agent. That FBI agent's home was invaded less than twenty-four hours later by an intruder whose intent was to murder said FBI agent and his family. I might add, this intruder was a Russian national who was in this country illegally. The exact timeline and communication sequence of this event are spelled out on the DOJ complaint." He slid the paper across the table to the attorney. During this entire conversation, Kruger's eyes remained locked on Quinn, who sat quietly with his head down concentrating on the tabletop. "That's your copy of the complaint, counselor."

"Interesting theory, Agent, but I don't see the connection to my client."

"Look harder, Counselor. We also have in custody two county officials from Fremont County, Wyoming who are providing details about the organization ran by Kevin Marks. The extent of their testimony is providing a clearer picture into the scope of a larger conspiracy." He took his eyes off Quinn and looked at the attorney. "Your client's name is mentioned and referred to frequently within their testimony."

The attorney skimmed the two pages, looked up and said, "We want a deal, Agent."

"I'm not in a position to offer one, but I can put you in touch with someone who can."

CHAPTER 50

Springfield, MO
One Week Later

With the house repaired and everyone settled again into their normal routine, Kruger and Stephanie cleaned up the kitchen after the family's evening meal.

She said, "You've been unusually quiet this evening."

A nod was her answer.

"Care to share your thoughts, Mr. Kruger?"

Kruger finished placing plates into the dishwasher, smiled and said, "I'm struggling with a decision."

"That's obvious. Is this a new one or one we've discussed before?"

"Oh, we've discussed it."

"Your retirement?"

"Yes."

"Sean, if you're worried about how this last incident made me feel, don't. You protected your family."

"I know, but it's the frequency of them that worries me.

Randolph Bishop hiring someone to kidnap you and Kristin, Dmitri Orlov hiring the assassin who ran you off the road and now a home invasion. I can't put you through that anymore."

She did not respond.

He continued, "The other factor is this new team's a success. Now Congress is clamoring to expand it and make it a fully funded part of the FBI."

"That's wonderful."

Shaking his head, he said, "Not really. What it means is if I stay, I'll have to work out of the Hoover building. Which means we have to move. *That* is not going to happen."

Once again, she chose not to respond.

"The third issue is, Kevin Marks has disappeared. The bureau doesn't have a line on him, nor does the Royal Canadian Mounted police. Even JR can't find a trace of him. Poof, he's turned into smoke.

"Finally, Sandy and Jimmie are sitting on numerous contracts willing to pay them a lot of money. They're holding off on signing them until I make a decision."

She smiled and placed a hand on his chest. "What do you want, Sean?"

"The dark trail I've been going down these past few months has taken its toll. I've come to the realization all I've ever wanted to be is an agent with the FBI. That's not possible anymore."

"So, the problem is you can't have what you really want."

"Yes, that's the problem. I have to face the cold hard reality of it. I have to get used to the fact my career with the FBI is over."

"Can you?"

He shrugged. "I have to."

She folded her arms. "I've never seen you fail to overcome a challenge, Sean. You will this one too."

"I know. I just have one more challenge before I let Paul know I'm officially done."

"What's that?"

"Find out why Alan started looking at cold cases."

EPILOGUE

Washington, DC
One Week Later

"Thank you for meeting with me, Paul."

"I hope this isn't about the restructuring of your division, Sean."

"It is."

"I was afraid of that."

"As you and I have discussed numerous times, I'm not moving to Washington, DC."

Stumpf just nodded.

"Ryan Clark is the perfect candidate to take it over."

Another nod.

"He deserves the promotion, Paul. His law-enforcement background and the experience he's gained during his time with the FBI make him the perfect candidate. There really isn't any one I can think of with a more solid resume."

"I agree." He paused and removed his glasses. "Did you ever determine what started Alan's investigation into the cold cases?"

Kruger nodded. "Another reason I wanted this meeting."

"What'd you find?"

"First, I want to make sure everyone knows, Alan was a very happily married man and devoted to his family."

"Uh-oh."

"Not what you think."

"Okay, go on."

"One of the victims in Atlanta was his ex-wife."

Stumpf frowned and sat straighter. "Ex-wife? I never knew he had an ex-wife."

"Not too many individuals did. Last week, when I was going through his papers again, I started Googling the victims' names, hoping to find connections to Alan. One of the references identified the maiden name of a victim in Atlanta. Alarm bells went off. I had to think back to a conversation he and I had while we were roommates at the academy. We'd both consumed a few more beers than we should have one night, and he told me about the failed marriage."

"Do you know what happened?"

"A little. It occurred their senior year in college. Alan was pre-law and she pre-med. After being turned down by four medical schools, she decided it was time for a new career path so they decided to get married. Two months after their wedding, she received notification she'd been accepted to med-school at Tulane in New Orleans. Alan already knew he was going to law school at Boston College."

"Long distance marriages are challenging."

"Yes, they are. Both realized their career goals were more important to them than being together. So, after six months of marriage, they got a non-contested divorce and went their separate ways. She married again after her residency and became a very successful heart surgeon in Atlanta. I spoke to Linda about all of this and he was always open with her about his previous marriage. She knew he still cared for the woman, but she also knew he loved her. It was just something he didn't tell others about, there was no need."

"Understandable."

"Alan also knew another of the Atlanta victims."

Stumpf's eyebrows rose.

"A friend of his from law school."

"He knew two of them?"

Kruger nodded. "The man's name was Roger Johnson and the circumstances of his death were similar to Alan's ex-wife's murder. We knew about Johnson from the start, I just didn't connect the ex-wife's murder until I discovered her maiden name."

"I wish he would have consulted with me about this."

"We may never know why he didn't."

"So how did Monk know Alan was investigating all of these cold cases?"

"That's a question I can't answer. But I have my suspicions."

"I'm listening."

"You know I don't like coincidences."

With a chuckle, Stumpf said, "You've always said there are only connections. Are these?"

"Maybe, but I'm working on a theory. Within the pages of Monk's manifesto, he reveals a seething hatred of successful black people. Alan's ex-wife was a prominent heart surgeon and Johnson was a high-profile attorney with the Coca-Cola Company. We can't find evidence that Monk ever interacted with these two victims or with any of his other victims for that matter. But they were all highly successful individuals.

"Alan was promoted to deputy director while Monk was in California. If you remember, there was a tremendous amount of media coverage when it happened."

Stumpf nodded.

"We've determined Monk moved to Cincinnati several

weeks after Alan's promotion. We think it was the closest job he could find to Washington, DC. He had his sights on Alan for a number of years."

"In his mind the ultimate prize, killing a successful black FBI agent."

Kruger only nodded slightly.

"Thank you for clearing that up, Sean."

"Remember this is just a theory. I don't have any facts to back it up."

The FBI Director gave Kruger a half smile. "What about you? What are you going to do now?"

"I'm going to hang it up, Paul."

"That was what I thought you would do. Can I talk you out of it?"

"No."

Stumpf reached over his desk and offered his hand. Kruger shook it and the Director of the FBI said, "It's been a pleasure to work with you and to call you a friend, Sean."

"Thank you, Paul. The feeling is mutual."

"I have one last favor to ask before you leave the bureau."

"Sure."

"Find Kevin Marks."

ABOUT THE AUTHOR

J.C. Fields is the award-winning and bestselling author of The Sean Kruger Series. He is active in numerous writing groups and serves on the board for the Springfield Writers' Guild.

With a degree in Psychology, five years in the computer industry and a long career of dealing with individuals possessing quirky personalities, J.C. has incorporated these experiences into his writing.

The Sean Kruger Series has won numerous awards. His first six novels have been presented with the Literary Titan Gold Book Award. Plus, *The Imposter's Trail* was awarded Best Mystery/Thriller at the 2017 Ozark Indie Book Fest. Three of his books have been awarded medals in the Readers' Favorite International Book contest. *The Fugitive's Trail* won a Silver Medal in the Fiction - Suspense genre in 2018 and both The Cold Trail (Fiction – Thriller – Conspiracy genre) and The Assassin's Trail (Fiction – Suspense) won Gold Medals in 2019.

He lives with his wife, Connie in Southwest Missouri.

Made in the USA
Columbia, SC
01 March 2023

13039687R00217